LOW TREASON

ALSO BY LEONARD TOURNEY

The Players' Boy Is Dead

LOW_____
TREASON

Leonard Tourney

E. P. DUTTON, INC. | NEW YORK

A portion of this story appeared in *1980-1981 Annual of the University of Tulsa* as "The Devil Spoke English."

Published in the United States by
E. P. Dutton, Inc.,
2 Park Avenue, New York, N.Y. 10016

Library of Congress Cataloging in Publication Data
Tourney, Leonard D.
Low treason.
"A Joan Kahn book."
I. Title.
PS3570.0784L6   1983   813'.54   82-9414
ISBN 0-525-24153-1   AACR2

Copyeditor: Nancy K. MacKenzie

Designed by Nicola Mazzella

10 9 8 7 6 5 4 3 2 1

First Edition

LOW TREASON

ONE _____

Since the first light of that day Thomas Ingram had avoided the high road that ran northeast from London. He had kept to himself, secure in the bristling hedges of hawthorne and oak, in the fringe of woods green and fecund to a madness, concealing himself from the curious gaze of wayfarers, the carters with their great heavy-laden rumbling wagons, the merchants and gentlemen on horseback or in coach. Now in the cool of the evening the traffic had almost disappeared. Travelers, fearful of the dark or worse, had fled to the inns or come wearily at last to their own hearths. A few straggling herdsmen sang to their cows or sheep, and a shirtless boy danced homeward between the holes and ruts, an old yellow dog snapping at his heels. Thomas reckoned he was now no more than an hour from Whitford. Once over the bridge there, he could cut across the fields and be in Chelmsford before dark.

But he was not home yet. His bones and muscles ached, his stomach groaned. He had not eaten since early the day before, except for a loaf of brown bread and two apples he had bought from a street vendor with the last of his money. This was no fit meat for a man of sixteen, tall and sturdy of limb and on the verge of a beard. Thomas dreamed of some fleshy fowl well spiced and succulent, a

1

slice of good cheese, or fresh white bread spread with butter and honey. His feet were sore, the soles of his shoes worn through.

He tried to distract himself from his own misery and thought of his friends, but then realized there was little relief in that. It was better to think about the road, about the trees and the river ahead.

But he thought of his friends just the same. Of Ralph Harbert. His friend's face hovered before him like a spirit of the air—a pale, long face with heavy-lidded, somnolent eyes and a square chin made for honest dealings. Poor lovable Ralph, as innocent as a babe and with a heart the size of a muskmelon, overripe and ready to burst with its sweetness.

He should have brought Ralph away with him, told him all. It had been a sin to leave him behind.

Thomas moved cautiously through the tangle of trees, bushes, tall angular weeds thrusting upward like spears' heads. His shirt clung to him, sticky with a week's sweat and grime, its coarse fabric chafing his flesh. Here where he trod, in this rioting verdure, fugitive rabbits and wood mice had made their habitations—traps for the unwary. Here an ill-placed step could snap an ankle like a twig. He kept his eyes on his feet, taking a short cut across a pasture, away from the road and whoever kept watch there.

He came to the end of the pasture, climbed a stone fence, and sat down to rest, leaning back against the stone. He watched while the shadows of the day lengthened. He thought of London again, the girl.

He had said to her, *Mary, you must come with me. This place, it's . . . it's . . .* He had sought to fix in a word or phrase just what the city was. Not Sodom and Gomorrah. She would have mocked the phrase, blown away the words with a laugh that would have undermined his resolve and melted his heart with desire for her. She had said earnestly and in a tone he had found compelling: *Anything is better than home. Whatever comes.* And then, out of her pain, as though probing a still festering wound, *My father, my father. Crazy with drink. A violent man. The house we lived in was no better than a sty. He would have sooner taken his pig indoors than his child. I fled and never looked behind. Whatever comes.*

All his fears for her had been inarticulate, like an infant's fit or sick man's palsy. Dumb motion. She had laughed and looked upon him as though he were the innocent one, just come to town and all agog at some novelty he had seen at Smithfield.

2

It had been no novelty, although when he spoke to her of what he had seen, what heard, she dismissed it all as though it were a fancy, an idle dream.

Well, she knew her own mind, if not the city, not willing to forgo the dangers there for her father's farm in Sussex, secure despite the filth and the old man's violence. In his mind's eye now he saw her face, her full lips and gray eyes, the fair complexion framed in honey curls. In London how long should such beauty last? Six months? A year? And that body, the long straight limbs, the delicate childlike hands? As safe from harm in London as fine glass in a tavern brawl.

He heard the groan and rattle of wagons, the voices of the drivers, and he concealed himself in the green brake. Despite his care to go unobserved that day, he had occasionally surprised a shepherd or farmer at his work and become the object of their curiosity and perhaps fear. No one liked to meet a stranger in the woods or fields, especially one in a hurry and about no apparent business, when there was a broad straight road within a stone's throw. Honest men kept to the road, traveled in pairs for safety's sake. Nervous, unkempt Thomas Ingram looked too much what he was, a runaway, likely to turn beggar, thief, or worse, given the chance.

The wagons rumbled past each pulled by six horses tied head to tail, swinging rhythmically with their dark rounded haunches and their heads lowered as though to drink up the dust. There were three wagons. Thomas counted them. The drivers' voices grew indistinct. The wagons vanished into the dust.

From his place of concealment, Thomas watched with glazed, hopeless eyes. He was sick inside now, feeling more pain in his heart than in his aching legs and feet. He knew he was fooling himself if he thought he would ever see the girl again. The city would swallow her up, swallow her up in the great maw of its corruption.

Through the trees ahead of him the tower of the old stone church and the roofs of the scattering of cottages that was Whitford came into view. Woolly smoke curled into the dusky air, and in the distance he could hear the forlorn echo of human voices and the sad lament of the village dogs. He could smell some householder's supper, but he put the thought of food from his mind. He had no money in his pocket and no friends in Whitford. In Chelmsford he would

3

find meat enough at his brother's farm and safety, too, his brother's father-in-law being constable of the place.

He hurried across the bridge and into the village. A few dirty-faced children played in the road, pausing in their game to examine him with cold, hostile eyes as he passed. A pack of dogs lumbered around the corner of one of the houses, saw Thomas approaching them, and began to growl menacingly. Thomas looked at the dogs. They were lank and sickly creatures, living off the village scraps. He was afraid of them. They glared at him with their yellow eyes, their moist pink tongues lolling from their jaws, and then they rushed toward him, formed a circle and began to yelp and bark, lunging at his feet and leaping into the air threateningly.

Thomas stopped in his tracks and quickly glanced about him for a stick or stone to beat them off. Seeming to sense this attempt at self-defense, the dogs grew more threatening. One tore at his hose and he felt a sharp jab of pain in his leg. The scent of blood excited the others. He was about to cry for help when a harsh masculine voice called out from a darkened doorway commanding the dogs to silence. They dropped their heads and mingled about in confusion for a few moments, then Thomas watched with relief as the pack trotted off obediently, as though they had been doing nothing more than sleeping in the sun. He turned in the direction from which the voice had come to thank his preserver, only to face a closed door of a shabby cottage. There was no one else in the street.

The dog, he saw, had broken the flesh, but only slightly. There was merely a trace of blood on his hose and the pain was nothing he could not tolerate. He continued to the edge of the village, looking behind him once or twice to make sure the dogs were not following. He could see the pack in the distance. They had treed some other creature and were now busy at the foot of an oak, whining clamorously.

The trees, tall and gloomy now, grew conspiratorially together and then suddenly parted to reveal the promise of a narrow path. This he took, lengthening his stride, satisfied that his journey was nearly at an end and that a half-hour more would bring him to his brother's house, a warm supper, and a clean bed. He had not gone a furlong into the wood when he saw the men. They had stepped out suddenly from behind a tree and now blocked the path.

"You take an odd way home, lad."

The man who spoke was tall and thick with a flat, swarthy face

4

and a fringe of ragged dark hair beneath his cap. He wore a dirty jerkin and in his hirsute hands he held a cudgel. Thomas thought the man looked familiar. The other man Thomas knew well enough.

"Hello, Starkey."

"Thomas."

The person Thomas Ingram addressed as Starkey stood with his hands folded behind his back like a schoolmaster. The men didn't move; they kept their eyes fixed upon him as though they were waiting for an explanation of his presence there, as though it had been their half-acre he trod upon.

"We watched you cross the bridge, then drew back to conduct our business with you privily," said Starkey.

"What business?" asked Thomas uncertainly.

"I think you know very well," said Starkey.

Thomas took a step backward. The ground beneath him was hard and even, a well-worn path. It was so all the way to the village. In his mind's eye he saw the path by which he had come and estimated the distance that lay between him and the village and the chance of his arriving there and securing help, but he thought, too, of the closed doors, the vicious dogs, and the unfriendly stares, and his heart sank. No, there would be no help for him in Whitford.

"You're not thinking of going back to London, are you, lad?" asked Starkey in a tone of exaggerated solicitude. "It's much too late for that now, you know. You had your opportunity and a golden one it was, but you didn't appreciate it. You were ungrateful, and if ingratitude is not one of the deadly sins then it should be. Some thought you ran off to sea or Smithfield. No, said I, not Thomas Ingram. Young Thomas will go home, as sure as heaven—or hell. We had naught to do but wait at the bridge until we saw you coming."

"I've quit, Starkey," said Thomas, trying, vainly, to control the tremor in his voice.

Starkey turned to his companion, the tall, thick man with the cudgel who had spoken but once and for the last few minutes had been staring at Thomas with the dull, passive expression of an ox. Starkey spoke in a low, mellifluous voice, the voice of a tempter. "Thomas wants us to let him be," he said. "Now isn't that a fine thing, him wanting us to let him be after all I've done for him?"

The tall man smiled stupidly and began to swing his cudgel to and fro like a pendulum. Thomas eyed the cudgel and looked about

5

him hurriedly for something to use in his own defense, but his eyes could focus on nothing clearly. It had grown quite dark in the woods.

"What do you want of me?" he cried in what was more protest than question. But he waited for no answer. The words were no sooner past his lips than quicker than thought the boy whirled around and fled down the path. His movement must have surprised the men. For a moment they must have just stood there because for a dozen or so yards Thomas could hear nothing but his own breathing, the hectic patter of his feet on the path, and the breaking of the twigs and small branches that he pushed violently from before his face. But then he heard the men behind him. They were running, too, racing him to the bridge. In a fatal move, he turned his head to look behind him, glimpsed for a second the taller man in the lead, swinging the cudgel in the air, and then felt himself trip in the undergrowth. He went sprawling into a bed of moist leaves.

He was nearly to his feet again when he felt the blow, not the cudgel but the body of his assailant, hard and heavy and harder for its being propelled through the dusky air. Its impetus hurled him to the earth again, and then they were struggling in the leaves and dirt, the two of them, man and boy, their arms and legs locked in a furious embrace, the man's arms clenched about the boy's chest, the boy's hands pushing against the man's shoulders. The man, sweating and grunting, had enormous strength and the cunning of an experienced fighter. He thrust upward with his knees, aiming for the groin. Thomas kept twisting, pushing, spitting out dirt and leaves, half blind with desperation and disgust, for they were face to face and the man's breath was hot and sour. Then he did it, the boy. He suddenly ceased resisting, their bodies closed like lovers, and he bit deeply into the man's face. There was a hoarse cry of rage, the taste of blood. Thomas tried again for the face, but the man had been warned.

"Dispatch the whoreson dog, dispatch the whoreson dog!"

Even in the dark Thomas could see to whom these words were addressed. Starkey stood above them, observing the fray. He had picked up his companion's cudgel. He was laughing a low, vicious laugh and wielding the shadowy thing the cudgel had become above his head. Then Thomas heard the mortal rush of rent air. There was no time to cry out, no time to hear the thud or feel the blinding pain, or worry more about the fate of his bruised senseless body.

* * *

6

Matthew Stock stood at the open window of his shop on High Street singing a melancholy air in a bright tenor voice. He seemed quite lost in the music, a sad, plaintive thing full of dark images and poignant emotions. As he sang, his wife, Joan, sat in the chimney corner, not for warmth but from custom, for the oak settle with its embroidered cushion and sturdy footstool was her sewing and thinking place. She worked busily, her nimble fingers plying their skill as though they had a mind of their own. From time to time she glanced up to study her husband's face. He sang:

> *"Flow my tears, fall from your springs,*
> *Exiled for ever, let me mourn*
> *Where night's black bird her sad infamy sings,*
> *There let me live forlorn . . ."*

It was a wondrously sad song, a grim song, and the words sounded strange in her husband's mouth, given his jolly temper, but at the moment he was singing the words with such intense feeling that she thought surely his heart must have broken. When he paused to begin a second verse she asked him the song's name.

"'Flow My Tears,'" answered Matthew Stock, clearly pleased at Joan's having asked. "It's from Mr. Dowland's new book, *The Second Booke of Songs or Aires.*"

"Indeed," she said, remembering now, "the book William Ingram's brother sent you from London at Christmas?"

"The very same," he answered, turning again to the open window.

"You should have Henry Smythe teach you to play the lute. Then you might accompany yourself."

Matthew Stock looked at his thick, stubby fingers and laughed pleasantly. "So that I might turn minstrel and play on market day? No, my music is in my voice, not my hands."

Smiling, Joan looked down at her work, pleased to see its progress and to hear, despite the song's melancholy, that her husband was in his customary good spirits. Matthew resumed singing:

> *"No nights are dark enough for those*
> *That in despair their lost fortune deplore . . ."*

She nodded dreamily. In the dim light and cooler air of evening Matthew looked younger and, turned at an angle as he was, thinner.

As she remembered him from their youth. Her mind made the long journey back to that time, across the pleasant fields of their first love, across the shared pain of starting out, the stillborn children with their little white bloodless faces, the long struggle for security and, finally, prosperity in the town. Surely she was not *that* old, she wondered, although her figure had swollen with time and her face, she sadly feared, had lost its comeliness, however her husband might deny it with his sweet flattery. At the moment her thoroughly solid husband seemed younger than she, more robust, more blessed, and she felt the sting of envy. She could not sing, she could not find her way to his satisfaction in the vibrant current of sound. His voice had not changed and that was a miracle. What was it, she wondered, about the human voice that caused it so to preserve itself from age, as though it embodied the imperishable soul, being as the soul was, a thing of no fleshly parts but a creature of the pure and timeless air?

But then she felt the shame of her envy and put it away among the thoughts she dared not think for piety's sake. She loved her husband, loved him with a pure and growing love. She listened again while his voice filled the room.

There was little light now, but she would waste no candles to draw the tiny winged creatures into the house to cavort in the rushes with the mice, fleas, and other small deer. When she could no longer see to work her needle—as though she needed to *see* for that—she would go to bed, windows wide open in midsummer to dispel the foul odors of the house and draw the moon onto her face.

Matthew stopped singing. She could hear the voices of passersby in the street, familiar voices, a knock on the shop door, Alice hurrying down the stairs to answer, footfalls of more than one person on the sturdy oak planking of the shop, and finally at the threshold of the room where she now sat she saw the faces of her daughter, Elizabeth, and Elizabeth's young husband, William Ingram.

Joan asked first, "You've brought the baby?"

She could hardly suppress her disappointment when Elizabeth said they had not. Since Elizabeth and William had moved into their own house Joan had seen too little of her grandson.

Elizabeth, plump and dark like her parents, looked at her husband, a tall, raw-boned youth of twenty with a narrow face and thin blond hair and mustache.

"Something's amiss," Joan observed fearfully, starting from her corner and glancing uncertainly at her husband.

"No," Elizabeth assured her. "We've left the baby with Molly. He's asleep and we dared not wake him." Molly was the couple's serving girl. No more than a child herself, Molly did not inspire Joan's confidence. A tiny little creature, humpbacked and nearly toothless, she seemed to pass her days in a dream, half listening to instructions, eating like a sparrow, and playing much with Nicholas, the Ingrams' cat.

"Well then, be seated," Matthew said jovially, approaching from his window to escort Elizabeth and her husband to chairs. His dark eyes were full of curiosity.

William sat down and pulled something from inside his shirt. It was a piece of paper, and he began to unfold it carefully. He squinted in the dim light, and Joan, seeing now that frugality must be sacrificed to need, called for Alice to fetch candles straightway. Bedtime would be postponed if there was to be more than casual talk in the offing, as she now felt certain there was, but before Alice could return, William began to explain the reason for their visit to the Stocks. "It is from Mr. Castell, my brother's employer in London. He says that Thomas has run off."

They all stared at the letter hanging limply in William's hand as though it would momentarily speak for itself. Alice brought the candles.

"My brother would never have run away," William declared stonily. "Thomas wanted more than anything to go to London. His apprenticeship at the jeweler's was a great stroke of fortune, arranged by our late father at considerable cost. No one recognized that more than he. He would have never given it up, never."

Listening to her son-in-law speak, Joan recalled her own misgivings when the family had bid young Thomas Godspeed to London. The city was a different world, rife with wickedness of such sort that her imagination could not contain it all. The boy had a good heart, but was that enough—in London? She decided to hold her tongue. She would not say that Thomas's coming to misfortune in the city had been in the back of her mind since the day of his leaving.

Matthew Stock took the letter from William, who was breathing heavily with excitement, and began to examine it for himself. It was written on a fine grade of paper and in a bold, authoritative hand. "This signature is that of Mr. Castell?" Matthew asked his

9

son-in-law as the constable scrutinized the elegant flourish.

"It is," said William. "Elizabeth feels something is wrong," he continued, looking to his wife for confirmation.

"Oh, I know it is," Elizabeth said. "Were he mistreated Thomas might have fled, but never to shirk. Besides, he would have returned here—at least, first."

"That he yearned for the sea we have only Mr. Castell's word," William interjected.

"Which you are obviously not prepared to take at face value," Matthew mused, almost to himself. He refolded the letter and returned it to his son-in-law. "Why should the man lie?"

Joan looked at the faces of Elizabeth and William Ingram, sharply defined in the flickering candlelight to which now had been attracted a host of little flying things. The young couple had no reply to the constable's question.

Matthew Stock's face assumed a thoughtful cast; Joan decided to help him along.

"What say you, Matthew? The young folk have come here for your advice, I have no doubt."

Elizabeth looked at her father appealingly. She said, "William would like to go to London himself, but he's never been beyond Whitford. In the city he could do little more than ask directions. Besides, he's much needed about the farm. Him gone, our two hands will pick little else than their noses. They must be constantly looked after and . . ."

Elizabeth ended her appeal, flustered. Joan looked at her daughter and thought, She fears for him—all reason was for it. A wife of little more than a year, with an infant at her breast. How soon the specter of widowhood casts a pall on the marriage feast. Elizabeth did not want William to go traipsing off to London, no matter how much merit the cause.

"Elizabeth is right," Joan agreed. "An experienced man is what's wanted there, no novice. Matthew, now, knows London, has friends—"

"Well, a few," the constable admitted.

"Enough. To make a start, at least," his wife prodded.

"My shop. This week's custom has been heavy. Next week I expect—"

"It would be a point of gratitude."

"Gratitude?"

10

"Indeed, for the *Booke of Songs*, goose!"

"Oh, that," replied Matthew, shamefacedly, for he had not thought of the book, the gift.

"Besides," Joan persisted resolutely, "Thomas is William's brother, which makes him kin. This is family business to which trade must follow second."

Matthew agreed that this was true.

"Moreover," she continued, warming to her theme, "were William to go it would mean Elizabeth would be left alone at the farm, with the baby to care for and that foolish Molly and those two men—what be their names?—who with what thoughts in their heads, the master of the house away . . ."

Matthew was about to suggest that Elizabeth could move in with them, but then thought the better of it. His wife's reasons were strong, his own little store of objections no more than an inclination to stay home and keep Joan company. Well, he would go, for what little good it might do, but he saw no reason to disbelieve the jeweler's letter, which had seemed straightforward enough. Thomas Ingram was a young man and that was a fact. Young men wander in their courses, and London was a great promoter of novelty. Had he not once felt the urge to go to sea himself, years before in that other life of his youth, distant and almost incredible now? Whatever the boy's resolve when he left Chelmsford, there would have been nothing odd about it changing.

He looked down at the songbook in his hand. What a thoughtful gift it had been. Well, he would try his best. What else could a man do?

Thomas Ingram lay on his back, conscious of little more than a ringing in his ears and the throbbing pain at the top of his head. His hair was wet, sticky. He touched the wetness, then quickly drew the hand away, appalled at the discovery. Blood, his blood.

He couldn't see well. It was night. He was in a wretched hut, no bigger than a privy and as foul. An old man and woman with grizzled hair, wrinkled faces, long noses and chins were staring down at him wide-eyed, their toothless mouths agape. There was something about their expressions, something odd. A mixture of horror and curiosity. They were looking at him queerly, as though uncertain as to what manner of creature he might be.

He tried to speak but his speech slurred. The old folks drew

11

back, their eyes fixed on him. Then the woman reached out to touch him on the forehead. Thomas winced in pain and the woman quickly withdrew her hand. She mumbled something to her husband and then disappeared into the shadows of the hut.

Thomas heard the crackle of a fire, in the distance a yelping dog. He could smell the fire, the old couple, cattle, excrement. He shut his eyes and tried to remember, but there was nothing. Nothing but the pain and the great vacant place where his memory had been.

He fell asleep and saw great swathes of color.

When he awoke again he realized he was naked. Someone had him by the bare feet and was dragging him. Then the dragging ceased. He lay limp, unable to move, hearing heavy breathing, near him. He could feel his body being turned over on its side and then rolled into a depression in the earth.

Helplessly supine, he willed his eyes to open with a fierce effort, having heard already the dull, thudding thrust and shunt of a spade at work. He felt the shock of something gritty and damp scattered across his bare chest—and onto his face, in his hands and mouth. Choking on clayey earth, pebbles, the acrid tang of rotting leaves, he spewed them forth, thinking, *I must rise, must sit up. God help me.*

Slowly his muscles responded, his eyes opened roundly to the night. The spadework ceased. There stood the old man, his captor, looming above him in the woods darker than the night, his old face sweat-streaked and ghastly, staring down into the shallow grave with an expression both fearful and apologetic. "Jesu, we thought you were dead," he whined. "O dear Jesu, we thought you were dead."

TWO_____

Gervase Castell was a man about whom a great many people were curious that summer. A jeweler by trade, he was of middle height, fifty-five or thereabouts, with a large, square head, a black thatch of hair only beginning to gray at the ears, and a magisterial countenance a bit too jowly to be called handsome. Dressed in his velvet cap and black cloth gown faced with fur, he looked like an alderman or a lawyer. He spoke softly and well, bore himself erect, and treated those beneath him with appropriate contempt. He had appeared, seemingly out of nowhere, five years earlier and set up shop in a fashionable quarter of the City and had six apprentices and various other assistants, porters, servants, all of whom went handsomely adorned in blue-and-gold livery. His shop was a fantastic place. Its long display cases garnished with the most expensive and exotic of gems, it had become the resort of those about town who wished it to be known that they had a good deal of money. The less well-to-do merely pressed their noses against the glass of the windows, peering through the iron bars Castell had had installed to ward off thieves, and dreamed of the riches of the Americas, or far Cathay, for such dreams were cheap enough.

Although reputed to be rich, Castell lived simply and privately in a house on Barbican Street rising from a solid stone foundation to two stories crowned with as many gables and a tile roof, newly laid. He had no family, kept no women, but had a great many acquaintances, none of whom he particularly liked. His origins were obscure. The story went that his father had been a Florentine, a scholar of Latin and Greek, who had eked out a poor living in the court of King Henry VIII and who, in his later years, had married a sickly girl about the court, big with child. The woman died in childbirth and Pietro Castello, for so the scholar was named, lingered on a scant dozen years more before being laid quietly to rest himself in a London churchyard beneath a wooden cross and a niggardly few lines of undecipherable Latin as an epitaph. Somehow Gervase had survived; more mysteriously, he had prospered. Now he lived there in that solid house of timber and plaster on the Barbican, with only a single manservant and a cook for company. The servant was Denwood Roley, a young man of even more obscure origins than his employer, with a mottled complexion and melancholy airs, and his mouth always puckered as though he were whistling a tune, although no sound was ever produced. The cook—no one in the neighborhood knew her name—was a sullen, ill-tempered woman of indeterminate age, blotchy, unkempt, and taciturn, who served her master's meals, swept his floors, held the mice and spiders at bay, and had a nasty way with callers, no matter their rank or condition.

That Gervase Castell was well enough off was certainly the case, but he had for some years now given over the dream of heaping up gold, which, after all, was a petty dream, no sooner realized than scorned. No, Gervase Castell's dreams were woven of finer stuff, vague and elusive in their dimensions and for that very reason indefinable, although presently he had powerful friends engaged in that effort. In sum, he was far more than a wealthy tradesman, just as his shop was more than a well-stocked shop.

It was his habit to rise early on weekdays and walk to his place of business, through St. Paul's Church, commonly called Paul's, both to avoid passing around the churchyard and to take advantage of the commercial air of the city—the throng of gentlemen, merchants, servants, countrymen, farmers, pickpurses, whores, and beggars who circulated in the aisles of the sacred precincts and conducted their business. The Council had passed an ordinance forbidding such pollutions in the temple but had not taken the pains to enforce it, and thus Paul's remained the most popular meeting place in London, a place to close deals, exchange news, or hire servants; a resort of lovers and losels, a haunt of the respectable and the something less. The walls resounded with the hum of voices and the shuffling of boots on the stone floor.

Castell watched with a kind of admiration, for to him, who had no religion, the great church was the heart of the commonwealth. Within its walls, one stood before something greater than the majesty of the law, the glory of the court, or the grace of the Church. One stood before life—its great mystery. The atmosphere of buying and selling quickened his pulse, cleared his head. Although on his daily stroll through its precincts Castell might speak to few, he would be spoken to by many, eager for favors, desperate for money or for some vaguer connection. Here he felt strong and powerful, feared and envied—even by the wellborn whose pedigrees and more certain parentage could not, in such days as these, always fill a purse.

He walked with a limp, wearing a heavy cloak even in summer, worn to conceal the bulge of his purse from the eyes of the envious, and he was followed closely by two of his assistants, sturdy young fellows with daggers at their waists and circumspect looks. These were his bodyguards, for although he carried no jewels, it was widely thought that he did and he feared for his life in crowds. Each morning they waited to escort him to his shop, and each evening they accompanied him home again. He squinted habitually, as though there was too much light even in the shadows of the great church. But it was a device. His eyesight was abnormally acute, and thus very little missed his attention.

As he made his way through the crowd, he nodded at passersby who looked after him curiously and whispered among themselves, who made way for him with fawning respect, as though he would repay their courtesy with some Indian ruby or orient pearl. To some he spoke; but most he ignored, and except for the simple countrymen gawking at the great illuminated windows or ornate statuary, everyone knew who Gervase Castell was.

He was about to leave through the little north door when his eye caught an almost too-familiar face in the throng. He waved his protectors on out the door before him into the street to keep off the beggars, and paused to watch. It was a young man Gervase Castell stared after. Dressed like an apprentice in a plain russet jerkin and

15

apron, he seemed on his master's business, finally stopping behind a countryman dressed in a black frieze coat, a new pair of white hose, and a fine felt hat a little too large for his head and cocked at a rakish angle. Castell watched as the two men collided, as if by accident, and then the one—Thomas Perryman, Castell now recalled— stumbled over himself in apologies, patting the simple fellow about the shoulders and chest as though Perryman had taken it upon himself to put the man together again.

At the same time Perryman quietly and expertly lifted the simpleton's purse.

Castell frowned and continued to watch as Perryman plied the aisles, moving quickly toward the stairs to the choir, then returning the way he had come, as though to suggest by his gait and posture that his message had been delivered and he was homeward again, bowing and scraping before gentlefolk, the stolen purse stuffed somewhere beneath his apron. Within the next five minutes Perryman took two more purses and a gold chain, slipped off its owner's neck with such agility that the man would be lucky if he noticed its absence before nightfall.

Castell screwed up his eyes and drew farther back against the wall of the church, pretending to read some inscription beneath the window but keeping his eyes on Perryman.

Perryman drew near and saw Castell watching him. The young man smiled and Castell glared back a warning. *Speak to me, even seem to know me, Thomas Perryman, and I'll have your tongue cut out and nailed to the doorpost.*

As though the jeweler's glance conveyed a perfect image of the thought, the smile of recognition vanished at once from Perryman's face; abruptly he changed his course for the north door of the church and in a moment was lost in the press.

Matthew Stock gazed at the shop. He had had no trouble finding his way to the jeweler's, for everyone, it seemed, had heard of Gervase Castell and most were ready with directions. One simply followed one's eyes to Paul's, and from there it was not a ten-minute amble to the east. It was very busy in the street. Pedestrians, some dressed very finely, moved about Matthew as though he were a rock in a stream, hardly seeming to notice him standing there gawking. He felt very awkward and alone, as though he were from a different country, wore a strange garb, or spoke an unintelligible tongue. The

16

English sky was a different color in the city. It was gray and flat and the air, he decided, was unwholesome, full of smoke, and no birds sang, save in the gardens behind the houses. There were unpleasant odors, and the faces of the people were hard and mistrustful. And the noise! There was a constant rumble of carts and coaches, the clatter of hooves, a shouting of carters, tradesmen, laborers, apprentices, as though no music would serve unless it were a thunderous din. Here every day was market day, but there was a pervasive joylessness that depressed him, and as he stood in the street he was suddenly chilled by the fear that he might be engulfed in this city, his soul lost forever in its heartless masonry.

Yet he wanted to see Castell's shop, and not only for Thomas Ingram's sake. He yearned to look upon the treasures of which he had heard so much.

The shop was smaller and less pretentious than he had expected. There it was, a narrow front, three stories above, wedged in between two larger buildings, a tobacconist and a silversmith, with a bow window and iron bars and its ornately carved and painted sign hanging above the door.

Matthew took a good look at the sign: a huge serpent with a single glaring eye beneath which was the name of the shop's proprietor in elegant script. Beneath the sign, a porter stood solemnly watching the crowd.

When Matthew approached, the porter stared at him curiously from heavy, lusterless eyes. Matthew inquired about the proprietor. Yes, Mr. Castell was at his desk, and what might be the gentleman's desire? A German clock studded with carbuncles? A gold ring made in Spain? Seed pearls from America?

Matthew told the man he sought only information—about a former employee of the jeweler's. He gave no particulars; he did not wish to get into a prolonged discussion with the porter, who looked like a fractious fellow eager to find reason for barring him from the shop.

The porter, stout and sandy-haired, folded his arms and looked sidewise at Matthew. He shuffled his feet on the cobblestones as though he were trying to remove some filth from the soles of his boots.

Patiently Matthew drew his purse, felt about inside among the odd silver, and withdrew a penny. So in the city everything had its price—German clocks and information too. He pressed the penny into the porter's hand. The man quickly stuck the coin in his pocket, looked about him furtively, and then, taking Matthew's arm, led him indoors.

Inside, the shop was long and narrow and high-ceilinged, and against the walls were display cases on top of which were candles illuminating the plate, gems, chains, and rings below. Still, reverential faces peered into the glass. The jeweler's custom. Matthew followed the porter to the rear of the shop where a man sat writing at a desk.

The porter presented Matthew to Gervase Castell.

The jeweler looked up and rose from his chair. His desk was very neat, with papers of various sizes stacked in piles and a small gold coffer at the center.

"What town did you say?" asked Castell politely, surveying Matthew from head to toe at the same time.

"Chelmsford," Matthew replied.

"Ah, yes. Chelmsford. There was a knight of that county, a magistrate. Not a year since . . ."

"That would have been Sir Henry Saltmarsh," said Matthew.

Castell nodded and smiled grimly. "He was a customer—and a good one—before his troubles." He invited Matthew to sit down. "How may I serve you, Mr. Stock? A gift for your wife perhaps? Some bauble from Persia or India to set her eyes aglow or appease her wrath at your long sojourn in the city? Oh, I tell you, it is wondrous what miracles are wrought by gems. Why, a stone properly set would turn a slattern to a lady in the time it took for me to slip it around her neck."

Before Matthew could reply, Castell walked briskly around to Matthew's side of the desk and, linking his arm in Matthew's, conducted him down the row of display cases. Before one, Castell paused and drew a ring of keys from his belt. Smiling with satisfaction, the jeweler selected one of the keys and bent down to unlock the case. He withdrew a small gold casket. The workmanship was exquisite. The gold had a dark sheen and looked very old.

Castell opened the casket and held it under the candle. There on a purple velvet cushion was the most brilliant gem Matthew had ever seen. Round and smooth as glass, the gem caught the light and exploded in color.

"A sapphire," Castell whispered reverently. "Taken from the headpiece of a heathen idol, transported across the Arabian desert by caravan to be the wedding gift of some caliph's bride, then snatched by one whose greed was more intense than his piety and so to Rome. It is called the Eye of the Basilisk and is worth a king's ransom."

Matthew drew closer to examine the jewel. It was dark blue, transparent, and very much like an eye, though unlike any human organ he had ever seen. As Castell moved the casket, the color changed, the eye gleamed and seemed alive. Then he took the gem from its resting place and held it delicately between his thumb and middle finger, turning it admiringly. Other customers in the shop had drawn about them to look on. There were oohs and aahs of admiration. Castell seemed greatly pleased.

He smiled and replaced the gem in its casket. "A fabulous creature, the basilisk. Something like a lizard. One may read about it in Livy. But it is a most dangerous creature as well, Mr. Stock, said to have a fatal breath and glance. But see how we gaze on with impunity, eh? Well, it is as I've often said about such fables—they are but baubles to young children, but for grown men they are *ignes fatui,* fool's fires."

"I could never afford such a stone," Matthew admitted candidly.

"No matter. You see, the gem is not for sale. The Eye was my first acquisition and I keep it for fortune's sake. I got it for a pittance from a poor nobleman in Rome who knew nothing more of its value than it would buy him a new sword to replace the one he had used in some murder thereabouts, and a fast horse to the next city. He had, you see, a *pressing* need. So I pressed upon him what silver I had about me. He nearly wet himself in gratitude. Within the hour he was twenty miles for the next town and I had my purse full of the stone. I have named my shop after it."

Matthew remembered the sign of the serpent, the great glaring eye. The Basilisk. It was a strange word, a foreign-sounding word. He tried it on his tongue. No, it was not a word for English lips. There were too many syllables. He preferred the plain English *snake* or *worm*—words that could be spit out in an instant. Words that plainly said what they meant.

Castell approached another case and seemed prepared to show Matthew another of his treasures.

"I've not come for gems or plate, but to inquire about one of your apprentices."

19

Castell looked up curiously, replacing the keys in his pocket at the same time. "My apprentice? What say you of my apprentice?"

"Thomas Ingram."

"He's a relation of yours?"

"The younger brother of my daughter's husband."

"Ah, yes, young Thomas Ingram. Of course."

Castell stood erect behind the case and shook his head sadly. "An unfortunate story, Mr. Stock, a most unfortunate story. Thomas served me not more than six months before running off. He had no cause. Why, look about you here, does the labor seem hard? Do I seem a stern master? Is there not wealth enough to garner for an honest man willing to work and learn the jeweler's trade?"

Gervase Castell made a beckoning motion. Behind him, Matthew heard footfalls on the carpet and he turned to see a young man not much older than Thomas Ingram approach. The man—boy— was well favored and neatly dressed in the blue-and-gold livery of the establishment. He kept his eyes fixed on his employer.

"Roger, tell Mr. Stock, who has just come from Chelmsford seeking—what is it, your nephew?"

Matthew again explained his relationship to Thomas Ingram.

"Yes, well then, pray tell Mr. Stock about Thomas Ingram."

Roger turned to Matthew. The young man had a frank, open face. He spoke very well. "Tom Ingram was my friend, sir. We slept together above the shop here, as a watch against roisterers and hurly-burly. Tom seemed very happy. He did his work, as do I." Here Roger paused to look at his employer uncertainly. The jeweler urged him to proceed. "Until around Easter last. These months since he has talked of nothing but turning sailor. All of his conversation was of masts and rigging, great ships and southern seas, monstrous folk with their heads inverted and other fanciful wonders."

"The lure of Spanish gold, Spanish gold," Castell murmured disapprovingly.

"He was a great reader of voyagers' tales," Roger continued. "Knew Hakluyt almost by heart, and spent his holidays at Paul's, Westminster, or the Exchange hoping for a sight of Ralegh or some other great captain with whom he might set sail. One morning about two weeks ago I woke to find his bed empty. His things were gone as well. He was off, and none among us has seen him since."

Matthew thanked the apprentice for his story and looked at Castell. "It seems, then, that I have come this long way for nothing.

The boy's brother will be disappointed. Thomas was a good lad, of well-allowed and honest parents, civil and upright to his elders. I am most amazed at this discovery."

"Young saints, old devils," Castell remarked philosophically, coming around to the other side of the case and taking Matthew by the arm again. "Do not worry yourself, Mr. Stock. The boy may well be dead by now, food for fishes at the bottom of the sea or taken up with some trull and infected with the French marbles."

"The French marbles?"

"The pox. It's the fashionable term nowadays. All the gallants use it and to be truthful most of them are infected with it. It's the times, Mr. Stock, the times. *O tempora! O mores!* as Tully says."

"Well," said Matthew. "I'm sorry to hear that Thomas has broken his articles."

The jeweler smiled generously. "I willingly share in the loss for fellowship's sake. But before you go, can I not interest you in some trinket for your lady, a ring, perhaps, or a chain?"

Matthew shook his head. He felt himself growing hot and flushed under the jeweler's scrutiny, which now appeared to have as its aim the determination of the heft of his purse.

"See here, a ruby. Most exquisite. Properly mounted it might grace the finest lady in the kingdom."

Matthew looked at the jewel. He didn't bother to ask its price. Somehow he knew that Castell knew he could not afford it.

Matthew said no. There was nothing he wanted, nothing he needed. He thanked the jeweler for his trouble and left the shop. In the street, he began to walk in the general direction of Paul's. He took an irregular course; there was no need of hurrying now; he paid no attention to the scene. The lateness of the hour and the thought of the futility of his long journey had left him tired and discouraged.

Presently he found himself by the great north door of the church where booksellers had set up booths, and he thought of the travelers' tales of which Thomas Ingram had been so fond. Where might Thomas have come by such a book? Where else but here, in the very place he now stood.

He strolled from stall to stall, looking over the booksellers' wares. There was a crowd in the yard, more people than books. He paused from time to time to examine the titles. Most were religious works, sermons or treatises. The titles were often very long, as though the author had felt obliged to distill his discourse on the first page of the text. Many were in Latin. These he could not read, except for the occasional word that was like English. There were volumes of verse, and a great many penny pamphlets on a wide range of subjects. He selected one and turned the leaves. It was an exposé of cozenage by someone named Robert Greene.

"Will you buy it, sir?"

"What?"

"The pamphlet, sir, in your hand."

A stout little man of Matthew's age looked at him hopefully from the other side of the table. The man had a round flushed face, tiny eyes, and a manner of forced cheerfulness.

"All the gentleman of the city regard it as the only help against your cutpurse, coneycatcher, or common losel."

"Indeed, this pamphlet?" Matthew looked at it. *A Notable Discovery of Cozenage*. It had a paper cover, very greasy, the leaves loose and one, he noted, was torn. Obviously here was a popular work caressed, it appeared, by dozens of hands. Matthew flipped through the pages.

"It is by Robert Greene, master of arts—a great wit, sir, a university man, now dead unfortunately."

The bookseller contorted his face to suggest his regret and Matthew returned the pamphlet to him. "Have you any books about voyages?"

Matthew's question seemed much to encourage the bookseller. Full of smiles, he hastened to show Matthew a row of books, all treating the subject. Matthew examined them. He had not thought there to have been so many. What was the name of the book Thomas had read? Hakluyt, was it? He inquired of the bookseller whether any such book was to be had at this stall. Yes, there was a Hakluyt he was told, in three folio volumes, handsomely bound but very dear. Yes, very dear. The bookseller shook his head sadly, as though the price of books was quite beyond his control.

"What is the price?" asked Matthew.

Wincing, the bookseller named the sum and looked at Matthew dubiously.

Matthew thought it was a very great sum for a book. Even for one in three folio volumes. "You have no cheaper edition?"

The bookseller looked offended. "Nay, sir. It has been newly enlarged into folio size as you see and in these three volumes. I assure you, it has been most well written by Mr. Hakluyt. He is a careful author, a scholar of the subject, and I have heard it said that he once traveled two hundred miles or more to secure the true account of one of the expeditions he reports therein. Nay, sir, you shall not spend your money amiss if you buy these books. Why, the man knows every mapmaker, merchant-venturer, and great captain in the kingdom, nay in Europe."

Much impressed, Matthew picked up the first volume and turned to the title page. He read: *Principall Navigations, Voiages, and Discoveries of the English Nation*. His curiosity aroused, he began to thumb through the book. The print was large and clear and he could read it with ease. Here his eye fell upon an account of strange savages, there upon a description of a great storm. He continued to turn the pages, pausing to read about some rich islands called by their Spanish discoverer California. California, he mused. Who would have believed in Chelmsford that such an island existed? It was all very fascinating to him and soon he became quite engrossed in his reading, as though he were not standing in Paul's yard but were by his own hearth, in his own chair, with only himself and the book for company. Slowly he began to realize what a treasure he held in his hands. This work was no mere collection of tales, but a testament to the glory of England, to the courage of its sailors and the foresight of its rulers. And it required three large volumes to tell it all. His heart swelled with patriotic pride, and he had a great desire to read more.

The bookseller cleared his throat and Matthew remembered where he was. He looked up at the man who was standing now regarding him tolerantly and smiling his strained smile. The man's eyes were full of expectation.

"How much for the three volumes, again, please?"

The bookseller mentioned a somewhat lower price than before, without saying that it was lower.

Matthew stood there thoughtfully. It was still a great sum. More than he had with him in his purse. More, certainly, than Thomas Ingram could have afforded.

"I suppose, sir, for you, that is . . . given your interest in voyages, a more reasonable price . . ." The bookseller's voice trailed off. He looked as though he were calculating the new price in his head. Matthew waited. The bookseller lowered the price by sixpence. Now the books were a great bargain, declared the bookseller. Was Matthew out to ruin him? An honest man must eat.

"Many an earl and knight has not Hakluyt so well bound in his library," concluded the bookseller, lifting his eyebrow and looking at Matthew very judiciously.

Matthew's resolve began to weaken. He cared nothing about the libraries of knights and earls, but he wanted very much to own these books. Already he could see Joan and himself reading them together on a cold winter's eve, the handsome pages illuminated by candlelight.

"Perhaps another choice," persisted the bookseller, smiling more desperately now. Before Matthew could say that he would buy the Hakluyt, the little man was off to the other end of the table and rummaging furiously through a pile of volumes. He returned holding a slender brown book which he opened and thrust before Matthew. His voice fell to a whisper. "Filthy pictures, sir. Deliciously vile and curiously drawn to corrupt a saint. Aretino, the Italian. The same that is all the rage about the city."

Matthew looked at the opened page with astonishment and disgust. A naked man and woman, drawn with considerable skill, lay entwined like serpents upon a bed. The bookseller, grinning with delight, flipped the pages. There were more such pictures. What a strange book this was, thought Matthew. Why, a man who could not even read might spend his idle hours perusing it and condemn his soul to hell at the same time.

Who could not even read.

And then it came to him, that thing which had been nagging at him all afternoon like a fleabite in a boot—that snatch of casual conversation with his daughter, Elizabeth, about old Simon Ingram's sons, who despite their father's distaste for learning, had taught themselves to read. William had made himself a scholar, but Tom was not bookish. Elizabeth had said it. *Tom was not bookish.* Tom could not sit still long enough to read a page. And this was the apprentice who was alleged to have spent his meager earnings on an expensive set of books and his idle hours in perusing them?

It was unthinkable.

He returned the book to the bookseller, agreed to take the Hakluyt at the lower price quoted, and asked that the volumes be delivered to his lodgings. Then he dashed off in the direction of the jeweler's to give that smooth-faced barbermonger of an apprentice the lie.

But the shop was closed when he got there. For a while he

paced up and down, mumbling to himself what he might have said had he had the opportunity; then noticing that the tobacconist's next door was still open he decided to go inside. Perhaps someone there knew of Tom's whereabouts.

It was a small shop but very busy. Behind the counter stood the tobacconist. He was a solidly built jovial man in shirt sleeves and apron. He was holding a brass water pipe, filling the bowl with dark tobacco, and as he saw Matthew he grinned and motioned him to enter. Blue-gray smoke hung heavy in the air, a noxious mist. Matthew coughed and pressed through the tables and benches, most of which were occupied. The tobacconist offered Matthew a pipe. A penny, he cried, for a good smoke, for a head full of happiness. "Why," exclaimed the man, "it's the prince of physicians, tobacco . . . an excellent purge for the head."

There was a confused buzz of conversation in the shop. Matthew felt giddy. In the corner two gallants had a woman wedged between them trying to stuff a pipe into her mouth. She wore a rich gown and was bedecked with a quaint periwig and a ruff of the largest size. Her cheeks were dyed with surfling water. She was trying to push the pipe away and at the same time laughing until tears rolled down her cheeks, streaking the rouge. She had enormous breasts the nipples of which were just visible above her bodice, like little pink flowers.

The tobacconist thrust the pipe toward Matthew and repeated his invitation. Matthew declined, wishing that he had not entered. He tried to explain he wanted information, not a smoke, but upon his saying this the tobacconist's expression became distant and his eyes suspicious. He sold tobacco, he said indignantly, not information. What did Matthew think he was, a spy?

Undeterred, Matthew asked about Thomas Ingram. Had the tobacconist seen him? No, the man remembered no such apprentice. Besides, he said, all the jeweler's men wore blue-and-gold liveries. He could not tell one from another, a Thomas from a John. Was Matthew sure he didn't want to smoke? Only a penny.

Matthew escaped into the street and breathed deeply of the air. It was dusk and the street was growing empty. He walked to the corner where earlier he had seen a cluster of young men gathered to play at dice. They were still there. One was a short fellow with liverish complexion and quizzical eyes. He wore a filthy apron. He was not playing with the others. He was standing, watching from a distance. Some of the boys were apprentices of the jeweler's. Matthew could tell by their liveries.

"You, lad."

"Sir?"

"Know you a Thomas Ingram, apprentice to Mr. Castell at the sign of the Basilisk?"

The boy looked at Matthew blankly. "Has he done something wrong—this Thomas Ingram?"

Matthew said no. "You do know him, then?"

"I know his face, sir."

"Do you know where I can find him?"

The boy shrugged, looked about at the other boys, and then at his feet.

"He lives above the jeweler's shop," said another apprentice, who had drifted over to join the conversation. This young man was older than the first, taller, and better dressed. He was well spoken and had a frank, open countenance.

"I know that," Matthew said, "but I have heard he has run off."

"Indeed," said the young man.

"He ran off to sea," said a third apprentice, dressed in blue-and-gold. "That's true," announced a fourth. The others gave over their game and formed a circle about Matthew and the tall apprentice.

"None of you knows where I can find him, then?" said Matthew, looking from face to face.

"He has run off to sea," insisted one of Castell's apprentices. "No man has seen him for a week or more."

Matthew looked directly at the tall young man. "You have not seen him about, have you?"

The apprentice hesitated. He appeared suddenly nervous and conscious of the other apprentices around him, for the circle was very close now and Matthew and he were at its center. The young man shook his head. No, he had not seen Thomas Ingram. He knew nothing about him, nothing at all.

"I see," said Matthew, with a fresh pang of disappointment, for he had hoped that he might hear a different story. He fished in his purse and found pennies for each of the boys. "Should you hear aught of Thomas Ingram, I am Matthew Stock of Chelmsford, come to lodge for the next few days at the Blue Boar, without Aldersgate. Do you know it?"

"We do, sir," cried the apprentices, practically in unison, regarding this middle-aged countryman in his plain suit and old-fashioned hat with eyes bright with curiosity and cunning.

"Pass the word among your fellows. It's Thomas Ingram I seek. Let it be known that I will be generous to him that brings word of his whereabouts."

"But we have said he has gone to sea," protested the boy in Castell's livery who had just pressed this explanation upon Matthew. The boy had pushed himself to the front of the circle and was staring up at Matthew with a mixture of injury and contempt. Matthew's disregard for his information had clearly not sat well with him.

"So I have been told, yet do not believe it," replied Matthew, ignoring the apprentice's impudent stare.

The apprentice frowned but said nothing. Some of the others were drifting off, apparently satisfied that there was no more money to be had from this inquisitive stranger and eager to spend their pennies at some neighborhood tavern. Matthew watched them disperse and then made straight for his lodgings. It was very dark; there was but a faint glow in the west and the street was practically deserted. The houses he passed had a somber, alien look now that their color had gone, and not even their twinkling lights and the murmur of voices floating out through the open windows could give them the semblance of human habitations, crowded together as they were and made fast against the night.

The houses gradually absorbed his attention, first as objects of interest, but slowly as causes of fear, for now he no longer thought about his conversation with the apprentices or his long day of deceit but about his own safety in this strange, dark city.

He quickened his pace, and at every side street and alley he passed he was alert to who or what might be lurking in the shadows ready to snatch his purse or bludgeon him for the sheer joy of it. He did not relax his vigil until he saw the familiar outline of the Blue Boar ahead of him. By the time he reached its doors and pushed his way into its well-lighted and commodious interior he was nearly running, and puffing with labor.

He found a neighbor from Chelmsford with whom he had a good supper and long talk about home that quite drew his mind from his fears and concerns, and then he retired to his chamber, a plain but ample room with a four-poster bed, a goosedown mattress, and a window overlooking the street and away from the noise of the kitchen. He drove home the bolt to his door, placed his candle by the bed, and removed his coat, then his shoes, his netherstocks and doublet. He stood there in his shirt sniffing the air and trying to contain his dismay. Tobacco—his clothing reeked with it. He put his purse beneath his pillow along with the short dagger he wore customarily at his side when he visited the city. A serving girl had earlier brought a basin of clear water. He washed his hands, face, and neck with some strong-smelling soap, hoping that it would wash away the stench of the tobacco—his clothing would have to air itself the following day or the next. Then he dried himself vigorously and stood at the open casement.

The soft night air flooded the room, caused the buckram curtains to quicken. From the street below he could hear the occasional shout of a passerby, the cry of the watch, a few horsemen, their animals beating a methodical tattoo on the cobblestones. He could see the angular shadows of buildings, in the distance the vague massiveness of Paul's Church. Down the street someone had built a bonfire. A group of men were standing about it. He could hear their voices. He could see diffident flickers of light from lamps in the house opposite.

He parted the curtains of the bed, blew out his candle, and crawled sleepily beneath the covers, leaving the casement open. Most of his countrymen feared the night air as a carrier of pestilence but Matthew had always felt it healthful and quieting to his spirit. He prayed briefly, staring up at the canopy of the bed. He slid slowly into a dumpish melancholy, a mood to which he often fell victim when he was away from home, apart from Joan and his own bed. The house grew quiet. A wind had come up from somewhere and the walls creaked and the buckram curtains fluttered nervously. He was near sleep, his mind a welter of images of glaring eyes and city trulls in their elaborate ruff collars and half-naked breasts, when he was brought awake again by footsteps outside his door. He sat up in bed and listened. Someone tapped softly. He heard a muffled voice.

He could not make it out, the voice. He rose quietly from his bed, snatched up his dagger, and approached the door.

The tapping was repeated.

"Who's there?" he said, hoarsely.

There was no response.

28

Matthew called again, louder.

"Are you the merchant from Chelmsford, sir? He who asked about Thomas Ingram, the apprentice at the Eye?"

It was a young man's voice. Matthew had heard it before.

"I am he. What do you want of me?"

"I have news of Thomas Ingram, if you please."

"How do you know me?"

"You spoke to me this very day—in the street, not fifteen steps from the jeweler's shop. My name is John Flint, an apprentice to Mr. Milton the scrivener."

"Which boy were you?"

"Tall, sir, nigh to six foot."

Matthew remembered him. Tall, an intelligent honest face, clean hands. Yet he had been passing his time there idly. That was a mark against him. Matthew was about to unbolt the door but then hesitated. All the house was asleep. He had nearly five pounds in his wallet in gold and good white money and clothing and other gear worth another forty shillings. He would not be a fool and unbolt and end up murdered in his bed and matter for yet another tale of a countryman cozened of his purse and his life.

"Who's with you?" Matthew asked suspiciously.

"None, sir. I swear no man stands here but myself, nor woman either. If I lie, let the Devil make water on my mother's grave."

"Well, what is your news, pray, and be quick?"

"Please open the door, sir. I would speak it to you to your face. I would not wake the house."

"You'll not wake the house if you keep your voice as low as it is now. Speak and quickly, or I'll call out for the watch from the window."

There was a long pause. Matthew waited, listening.

"I knew Thomas Ingram well, better than I let on in the street. I feared to talk there."

"Why?"

"The other 'prentices. Mr. Castell's men. I was about to speak until one of them looked at me sternly. I know when to keep silent."

"Why, then, have you come to me?"

There was another long pause.

"Because of what I owe Thomas, sir. He helped me to a six-pence once when I had naught about me but my own flesh to feed upon."

"I see," Matthew replied, listening carefully now. "Speak then. I'll not open the door but I'll hear you out."

"Something *has* happened to Thomas."

"His employer says he has run off to sea."

"Never believe that, sir."

"Why should I not?"

"Why, because it is a palpable lie, sir. Thomas had no more interest in going to sea than in catching the plague. All his talk was concluding his apprenticeship and returning to Chelmsford."

"He did not study books of voyagers? This what's-his-name, Hakluyt, I think."

"Nay."

"But Mr. Castell's apprentice—Roger, I heard his name to be—said that Hakluyt and voyages were all his study."

"Roger? Tall and fair of face, with a devilish quick eye and a sugary tongue?"

"The same."

"His story's not worth a turd."

"He seemed most open and direct."

"He is a most practiced fabricator."

Matthew paused, satisfied now that John Flint had confirmed his own certain knowledge of Roger's mendacity. The lad continued:

"Where Thomas may be this instant I cannot say, but I would wage my life that there's nothing dishonest in his flight. I saw him last a fortnight Thursday, pensive he was, something thick on his mind. I asked him for the burden, but he did no more than smile and claim it was something he had eaten, something to provoke the melancholy."

"The melancholy?"

"You know, dumpishness, such as maidens are prone to, the green sickness."

"He said nothing of his plans?"

"Nary a smidgen."

"Well then," Matthew whispered impatiently, "what intelligence have you for me?"

"Only this good counsel, sir, and it has cost me no little risk to myself to bring it to you. Take heed of whom you ask about young Thomas. Something's afoot at the jeweler's, I would swear to it."

"Is this thing something that bears a name?"

"Doubtless, sir, though I know not what it may be."

30

"For your warning, then, my thanks."

"Sir?"

"Yes?"

"One thing more. Thomas had a good friend, another apprentice. Ralph, of about the same years. Ralph would have known Thomas's plans if anyone would, he and a girl Thomas had eyes for, a little thing named Mary—I know not her family name. Ralph lies in Newgate."

"The prison!" Matthew exclaimed. "For what crime?"

"Why, for purse cutting or linen filching, or some like trifle."

"Who gave evidence against him?"

"One of his fellows at Castell's, now I think upon it. The constable of the parish came, made his charge, grabs young Ralph by the wrists, and off to Newgate he was as round as a hoop."

"And the girl, this Mary, what about her?"

"She may have gone off with Thomas, sir, or dropped into the same hole he has. No one has seen her on the street for days."

"What was her business?"

"A milliner's helper. She was an honest girl."

"*Was*, you say; what's become of her?"

"I have said. She has disappeared, yet honesty is like the sun. One minute it's out, the next it's besmirched with some filthy cloud or squall. By now some pimp may have her working the streets, her face buried with her virtue beneath a foot of paint."

"I'll go to Newgate the first thing in the morning. Ralph you said his name was?"

"Ralph, sir, but I would watch where I walked. Newgate is the scurviest place this side of hell. Worse than Tyburn. They say the rats disdain it."

"I do not doubt it," said Matthew.

"I must go now, Mr. Stock. Pray remember my warning. Take good heed. Your inquiries kick up dust in someone's face."

Matthew considered the warning. So he was kicking dust in someone's face. He replied with resolve, "Then I shall watch where I step indeed, yet will I walk, though the Devil take offense at it."

Matthew told John Flint to wait, went to his bed, and withdrew his purse from beneath his pillow. He felt inside for some coins, found tuppence, and returned. He unbolted the door and peered into the passageway. John Flint was standing there looking at Matthew uncertainly. Matthew offered the tuppence but the boy refused it.

"I came for friendship's sake," he said and went on down the stairs.

Matthew shut the door and returned to bed. Somewhere in the city a clock struck a mournful succession of hours. It was midnight. He lay for a long time staring up into the canopy above him, much too excited to sleep, for there was a purpose to his being in London now, that was clear enough, and enemies about whom he must be very careful. One of these was certainly Roger, another was very likely the jeweler himself, who had seemed to encourage his apprentice in this overcurious fabrication about Hakluyt. What was behind these lies? Where was Thomas Ingram and why had he left the jeweler's employ?

Matthew pondered these questions for some time. He heard the clock strike one, but not two, for somewhere in between he prayed again, thought of Joan, and buried his face in the soft pillow that smelled of fresh grass and herbs and reminded him of his home. Sometime during that hour his reason, weary of the day's travail, lay down its burden before his imagination; there was a parade of loosely connected images—Thomas Ingram, Aretino's filthy pictures, the jeweler's shop, the Eye of the Basilisk—and finally there came sleep, profound and renewing.

THREE_____

Gervase Castell stood before the open casement, his room in darkness. He was staring out into the night and listening. It was very quiet, both in his house and in the garden. His cook lived in a hovel with her husband on a neighboring street, and Castell had sent his manservant to bed two hours before, so he had the satisfaction of knowing that it was his presence alone that filled the somber rooms of the house and competed with the glum spirits of the air for supremacy. Now a languorous tolling of a distant bell informed him it was midnight. Over the garden hung the aroma of moist earth and verdure, the sweetishness of rotting pears and quinces. The sky was a deep velvet setting for a fistful of paltry stars and a tenuous moon, canny like a courtesan's brow.

At length he heard what he had been waiting to hear, footfalls on the gravel path, then at the postern door a sharp, importunate knocking like a carpenter hammering a nail into a block.

He lit the candle and descended the stairs, pausing before the door. Again came the knocking. In good time, Flores, he thought.

"Who is it?"

There was a hoarse whisper from the other side of the door. It was the gentleman from Madrid, the friend of the Basilisk.

He unbolted the door and peered out into the night. But it was not Flores standing there. It was a taller, leaner man, wrapped up in a cloak, hat drawn down over his eyes, obscuring but the bottom half of the face.

Castell's visitor introduced himself as Miguel de Ortega—the Count of something, Castell did not catch the name. Ortega removed his hat with a gallant flourish. He looked about him impatiently, as though eager to be off again, explaining at the same time that he had had no trouble finding the jeweler's house. Flores had given him directions and they had been quite clear, every twist and turn of the alley laid out with the precision of a navigator's chart. Ortega had entered through the back gate of the garden, a small orchard of unhusbanded fruit trees, scraggly bushes, rank weeds and vines strangling what had once been a flower bed. No houses faced the alley and no constable's watch was fool enough to patrol the lonely stretch after dark. Ortega said a lousy yellow bitch had barred her fangs at him but he had slit the creature's gullet with a quick thrust and walked on.

Good, thought Castell, for whom discretion was the single moral absolute.

He led the way up the stairs and down a narrow passage to the room that served him as a parlor and bedchamber. On the way he paused to listen at the door of a small adjoining room occupied by his servant Roley. Through the door Castell heard a snore, a cough, and then a thin cry. He nodded to his satisfaction. Roley was asleep, dreaming, but dreams of what sort Castell could not begin to imagine, for his own sleep was deep and obscure and when he awoke from it he remembered nothing but having gone to bed.

He motioned to Ortega to precede him into his own room but the Spaniard hesitated. Castell smiled at the man's caution. He said, "Only a minor courtesy, sir. A custom of our nation, if you will. You are as safe here as in a church."

His guest looked at Castell skeptically. He was a stranger in a strange land, a dark house. Who knew what spies lurked in the gloom, ready to rush forth at a signal?

Castell shrugged and entered first. He invited Ortega to take a chair, struck a match and lighted the lamp, holding the long handle of the match until the little cone of red flame burned intrepidly in the wick, and then walked over to close the sashes. He untied the drapes and let them fall. The careful Spaniard would see that no assassin hid in the thick folds.

"A precaution," Castell explained. "A light from the window at this hour might arouse the curiosity of some neighbor."

"Very wise," replied Ortega, who spoke good English.

Would the gentleman take something to slake his thirst?

Yes, Ortega would drink. Castell watched while the young Spaniard removed his hat and mopped his brow with a lace handkerchief. By the glow of the lamp he saw that the man had a long serious face, a delicate nose, close-set eyes, a high forehead shining with sweat. Not more than five and twenty, Castell judged. Ortega sat down, crossed his legs confidently, and began surveying the room with an expression of amused contempt. Ah, thought the jeweler, not grand enough for you, Ortega, this plain English chamber? You miss the rich cloth of Arras, the cushions of silk and embroidered gold for your delicate buttocks, the portraits of sober-faced churchmen and counts hanging from the walls? Ortega wore black doublet and hose, a little lavender codpiece blooming over his loins like an exotic flower, a great white ruff collar and a pointed beard and mustache, well greased. He had dark eyes and a sallow complexion of the sort found among the Spanish courtiers and their English imitators. About him was the scent of decaying roses, and on the little finger of his left hand he wore a jeweled ring, a blood-red carbuncle flashing in the candlelight like the Devil's eye. Castell regarded the ring professionally and estimated its value. Flores had been an errand boy, a buffoon. This Ortega was someone to be reckoned with, his foppishness notwithstanding.

Castell went to his closet, unlocked it, and returned presently with two very handsome cups of finely wrought silver. He was very proud of these pieces. There was a story behind their acquisition, and he was tempted to tell it, but he resisted the temptation, content with Ortega's look of obvious admiration. The jeweler placed the cups on the table and then filled each with an amber-colored Madeira, very sweet. Ortega sipped. He nodded approvingly.

They exchanged toasts and small talk, Castell playing cautiously, unhurriedly. Ortega asked about the old Queen. What was the gossip around the court?

Castell smiled. Elizabeth was failing, suffering from biliousness and flatulence. It was said that she wandered about her chamber waving an old rusty sword, mourning the loss of Essex. The ache in her arm had fallen into her side. In public she stuffed many fine cloths into her mouth to fill out her cheeks. She would not last the summer.

Ortega's eyes glimmered; his lips formed into a thin smile.

And your master, Castell inquired. What of his health?

In good health, excellent health, Ortega assured him. The salubrious Spanish air, warm and dry, was excellent for the humors, prone as they were to melancholy, the worst enemy of bold enterprises.

Castell complimented Ortega on his English. Flores had slurred his consonants, squashed his vowels, fumbled like a blind man among his little store of words.

Ortega acknowledged the compliment with a stiff nod of the head, looked about him circumspectly, seemed to relax in his chair. He began to talk about himself. This was his first visit to England. The country did not please him. English weather was wet and depressing and as for the women, well . . . His father had been an ambassador to the court of Mary. Of blessed memory. Ortega made the sign of the cross, his eyes narrowed, seemed to cloud over; his brow remained smooth, shiny, and tranquil. A precocious child, Ortega had learned English from English servants, good Catholics the ambassador had taken into his service and with him upon his return to Spain when Mary died. When that *puta* Elizabeth . . . Ortega spit out the words beneath his breath, like a curse.

But Ortega restrained himself. He had not come to talk about himself or to discuss politics. He drummed his fingers on the table.

"I presume," said Castell, observing the man's impatience, "that your master has made known to you the nature of my service?"

"In part."

"Good. Then we can dispense with tiresome preliminaries."

Castell pulled his chair up close to the Spaniard's. He drew a small book from his pocket, and began turning the leaves, searching. He began: "Your master was not displeased with my last report?"

Ortega shrugged. He had not seen the report. He had replaced Flores, had been directed to come in the captain's place. Surely that said something of the esteem in which Castell was held. He urged the jeweler to proceed with his new matter.

"Sir Jeremy Parr," Castell began. "A letter to a lady. Not his wife, who waits at home in Herefordshire eating her heart out while her husband plays the virginals at court. That I have from another source, entirely trustworthy I assure you and perhaps of value at some later date."

"What says the letter?"

"Sir Jeremy is a great one with the ladies. This scrap affirms—"

"Affirms what, Mr. Castell?"

The jeweler sensed the man's impatience and smiled to himself. He looked more closely at the letter. The figures were round and clear but he wanted to make something of his ability to decipher them, as though they had been written in code and not plain English.

"Sir Jeremy declares his love, most fulsomely, I assure you." Castell began to read: "Most beloved, save for the tender mercy of your kisses and so forth . . . I would languish here. I live only until our next meeting, which if present business permit, will remain this Thursday . . . should your own circumstances require a different place, we may meet in my chambers, where I do promise—"

Castell paused, looked up. "I spare the details for brevity's sake."

"Who is the woman?"

"Alice Farnsworth. A maid about the court, not more than twenty. A lovely piece. Jeremy Parr pursued her most energetically and has bedded her at least twice this term. I have that on good authority, in addition to what is implied in this most impolitic letter. It seems he has now promised to marry her."

Ortega smirked. "How can that be if he is already married—or have the English carried their heresy so far as to permit bigamy?"

Castell smiled tolerantly. So Ortega was a zealot. How tedious. Suddenly the young don sank in his estimation. Behind that brave countenance was a conventional mind after all, a little mechanism of springs and ratchets turning to the whim of Holy Church. Castell shrugged. "Perhaps Sir Jeremy desires to emulate Abraham, Isaac, and Jacob. More likely, however, he has forgotten to mention his wife at home."

"A simple oversight," Ortega observed dryly.

"Well, let's just say an oversight. It's possible young Alice does not know the knight is married. And the two little boys—their names slip my mind just now."

"I'm surprised," Ortega said, sipping from his cup and then holding it up before him to admire the craft of the silversmith. "You seem most informed. About nearly everyone."

Castell bowed his head respectfully.

"The sons are nothing, but the wife is *everything*."

37

"How's that?"

"Her father—"

"Is?"

Castell murmured the name. A knight of Middlesex, very influential at court. A man of real power. The Spaniard's eyes shone like hard little stones.

"*Madre de Dios!*" Ortega put down his cup and regarded the jeweler intently. Castell smiled to himself and allowed the room to fill with the Spaniard's anticipation. The jeweler had a flair for the dramatic.

"The wife—Jane Parr—is the knight's only daughter and he dotes upon her. If his son-in-law therefore were to find himself in a sort of bind—"

"A bind?"

"Well, consider this. Jeremy Parr's liaison with Alice Farnsworth is discovered, bruited about. If young Alice should breed it will be all the better. As a consequence, she is disgraced and her lover is in bad odor, loses his place, and is sent packing into the country—or to the Tower, depending on the Queen's pleasure. You know how impatient she is these days with promiscuous coupling. In her dotage she has begun to take her own virginity seriously, as though she had never been niggled herself, and has become the very monarch of morality. Such a scandal must needs touch even Jane's father."

"An interesting possibility," murmured Ortega.

"Yes, indeed." Castell rose and refilled the cup. He toasted his guest's master, and then Ortega.

"Well then," Castell continued, "say Parr is made aware of the possibility of discovery. Is shown certain letters such as this which prove the affair. He would do much to prevent his adultery from becoming common knowledge, would he not? Oh, the threat of disclosure will be painful to him, but on the other hand I may at the same time offer a remedy."

"Spanish gold?"

"A pension, say. Applied to his purse as a salve for his conscience, like an indulgence."

"Do not blaspheme," Ortega warned.

"Nay, nay, sir. No offense intended. I have the most profound respect for the Holy Church."

"Of which you yourself are not a communicant, or have I been misinformed?"

38

Castell laughed genially. "You have not been misinformed. I am an *admirer,* not a follower, of His Holiness."

"A heretic, then?"

"Well, by a simple sort of logic, yes, if not to be one is to be the other. The truth is that I claim the privilege of believing as I will, and allow all men the same right."

"But such tolerance is in itself heresy."

"Perhaps." Castell responded in measured phrases. "But I build my own altar, choose my own sacrifice, and invoke whatever deity I will. Please, sir, pray let us not quarrel."

The Spaniard bent forward and looked at Castell intently.

"If you are not one of *us,* why help us?"

"Why? Because I choose to. It's a matter of business."

"It's a matter of money?"

"My dear sir, do I look as though I need money? That cup you first caressed not a minute since would put a hundred men in arms and feed their bellies for six months. It would buy twice over every house on this street, every horse in the barn, and doubtless every goodwife to whatever service I dictated."

Ortega sank back in his chair, a smile of appeasement playing about his mouth. He said, "Forgive me, Mr. Castell, if I have offended you. You must pardon my curiosity. As our acquaintance deepens, I am sure we will understand each other's motives better, yes?"

"Yes," Castell replied, regaining his composure, sorry now that he had allowed the Spaniard to cause him to lose his temper. Flores, dense and lumpish, had never inquired into Castell's motives, although the question of why the jeweler, no Catholic, should strive on behalf of a Catholic cause seemed reasonable enough. His present irritation at Ortega's probing had taken the jeweler by surprise. The sudden rupture of that smooth, inscrutable visage he wore shamed him, and he despised himself for loss of control. He returned to his report with a kind of relief.

"Say I approach Parr, inform him of what documents have fallen into my hands, being of course not too direct as to just how they have done so. Then I dilate with all rhetorical skill I can muster what great squall he is about to face when his adultery becomes public. He, answering to my helm, comes around to our direction, steers his course for Spain. We help him on his way by asking very little in return for our silence, nothing that might turn his stomach or put starch in his back. Now, then, we have him. Sometime later, say in two months, I approach his wife with this little tale of how her husband has involved himself with us. She will be appalled. What patriotism a woman may have will be inflamed—but as quickly quenched again as she learns what her husband's treason might buy for him at the block. To wit: a sudden loss of weight in the form of a head, a bleak widowhood for her, and endless disgrace for her sons. While she is savoring these dismal thoughts I put it to her that all may yet be saved—her husband, his honor, and his life—and she made the richer to boot, if she will only secure a few favors from her father."

"She becomes an accomplice in treason, then?" Ortega remarked.

"Exactly."

"All of which will do my master precisely what good?"

"This, sir," Castell replied with satisfaction. "The girl's father is at present governor of the Queen's naval ordnance. He knows every cannon, pistol, and piece of shot in Her Majesty's ships, how many man them, and in what condition."

"Such a man will not bend easily," Ortega said.

"Yet he will bend. Hold me to it."

"My master will hold you to it, Mr. Castell."

"But see, Count, we need very little more from the old man than an inch of compliance. Let him keep his inventory in his shirt for all we care. If the duke does not already have access to such information as it contains I would be very much surprised. But compliance—to any degree—becomes an entanglement of such a nature that once observed it is set down by all who do so as the very image of treason. The man would be hopelessly compromised."

"I see," said the Spaniard. "You *are* a resourceful man, Mr. Castell—though not, as you have confessed, of the faith."

"Oh, I have faith, sir—in other men's faithlessness. It is the very rock of my salvation. Empty a man's pocket or purse and you'll find his very soul down there clanking around amidst the copper and silver. All that a man has will he give for some bauble, be it a pretty jewel or a pretty eye. All religion comes down to that in the end—and a great bulk of the statecraft, which to my mind is nothing more than knavery on a grand scale. As for resourcefulness, you may lay that down to a fertile imagination."

"Sobering thoughts, Mr. Castell," said Ortega, looking at the jeweler beneath his pencil-thin brows and with a strange sort of

40

wonder. "How much will Sir Jeremy require in the way of compensation?"

"Say, two hundred pounds per annum. He will be so happy to have his adultery concealed and his father-in-law's wrath stayed that he will come to the lure more ready than a starved hawk," Castell said.

"But what of the old knight? If Parr's whoremastering is kept to him, us, and the whore, what hold may we have on the father?"

"Why, no less than what I have already said, sir. Look you now. Your question touches upon the very quintessence of my art. A trade secret. But never fear. For a paltry sum I'll have Parr and his father-in-law in our pocket in not a month's time."

"But—"

"Trust me," said Castell, smiling benignly.

Ortega shrugged. He continued. "My master trusts you, but you said you had three pieces of information."

"Item two," Castell intoned, turning to another page in his book like a preacher preparing to read the text for Sunday's sermon. "The Earl of Harvenhurst is nearly bankrupt. He has been sending desperate appeals to moneylenders throughout the City to which they, knowing of his penury and the gross unlikelihood of repayment, have turned an ear of stone."

"The Earl of Harvenhurst, you say?"

"A young fool, of your years, a very tidy dresser and great chaser of the ladies. He has pawned his estate to pay his debts and has not a barn or privy unsold."

Curious, Ortega asked: "What debts?"

"What you would expect—gambling and wenching. He does not show his face at home once a year since he came into his majority and the old earl conveniently died."

"Of natural causes?"

"So it is generally believed. The old man was swollen with gout and a dozen other vicious diseases of the flesh. Had he fallen from his horse or died in his sleep we might have made something of that. However—"

"The old earl left a large sum of money?"

"A great sum. But it was hardly enough. The young earl went through it in a year's time, then began to suck upon his friends. He has rooms at Lincoln's Inn, is much seen on the Strand and at the theaters. His former associates disdain his company like the plague, fearful he will dampen their doublets with his tears. But he has made new acquaintances."

"Could he not find some help from the Queen?"

Castell grinned in the dark and wiped his mouth on his sleeve. "Not likely," he said. "The young earl is one of your faith, sir, although his family has always been loyal to a fault. For all of that, they have found no welcome at court."

"Then how could he be useful to us?"

Castell relaxed, drank deep from his cup, then stared at the ceiling thoughtfully. "Our young friend's penury has driven him to extremes. He has become—how shall I call it?—a purveyor of sorts. You see, a desperate man has a certain odor about him. It both repels and attracts. The great ones in the City, sensing our young man's folly, have been quick to put him to use. His mind has become a bountiful purse of scandal in which we might find all manner of interesting coin—relationships, entanglements, betrayals, enormities—you know the sort of thing. Between this lord and that lady, the neither of them married—this lord and that pretty boy. Such stuff, sir, as would turn the stomach of an honest man, could such be found in London."

"And he would be willing to convey to us—"

"For a price, yes."

"But if he is as deep in debt as you say, I should hardly think we could bail him out."

"Oh, sir, a desperate man loses all sense of proportion. Though he owe a thousand pounds, yet will he grovel for a groat, thinking in his delirium that every little bit must help."

Ortega had withdrawn from his doublet his own small book. Did Mr. Castell have a pen he might use—for a few brief notes? Castell shoved ink and pen toward his guest. "Take care what you commit to paper, sir. One must have a very deep pocket in London."

Ortega wrote with nervous little strokes, holding the pen tightly in his small hand. "Never fear, Mr. Castell. I write in code. It's known but to me, my master, and but a handful of intermediaries, each of whom I would trust with my life. A curious pair of eyes would find what I write little more than gibberish."

"Your master made it clear to you, I suppose," Castell said when Ortega had finished writing and had blotted the paper, "that the strategies I use to procure such information as you now have are my own. I alone deal with Sir Jeremy and the young earl. Your agents may observe my work at a distance, but let them stand clear of me. Otherwise our enterprise may be discovered before the proper hour."

"Ah, yes, the proper hour," Ortega breathed, pushing the writing instrument across the table.

"Now, sir, one item more, which I had nearly forgotten. You will want to include some to season your notes."

Then the jeweler embarked on an interesting anecdote about a certain prominent churchman who, for the love of a choirboy, had filched silver from the chancel.

An hour later, his pockets full of papers on which he had written the intelligence Castell had delivered to him, Ortega bade the jeweler farewell and stepped out into the lesser darkness of the night. From a neighboring street, a dog whined peevishly at the moon, now but a thin ineffectual sliver of yellow about to fall off the edge of the earth. The garden through which Ortega walked was full of sounds, the incessant conversation of invisible creatures, tiny, subtle, and disgusting, concealed in the long stalks of grass or in the chaos of moist vines. At the garden gate he paused to look back at Castell's house. It was a squat, two-story structure made of timber and plaster. Like many another English house it had a solid, dignified front, an unsightly rear, and a malodorous interior that herbs and freshly mown grass strewn here and there did little to sweeten. Ortega sighed heavily, much depressed by his interview, for during the final hour of their meeting something cold had seized him about the heart—a palpable despair to which he could not give a name although he could recall a similar feeling on another occasion. Ortega had been a soldier and in one battle had seen his best friend cut down by a Dutchman's blade. His friend had lost an ear and part of the throat. The bleeding had been terrible, but worse had been his friend's expression, the eyes full of comprehension and envy, rejecting hope and the Holy Faith.

He shuddered as he thought of it. It had been an obscene death. But Ortega had disciplined himself, shaken off his horror, rushed back into battle screaming for revenge, feeling all the while that he himself had received some mortal wound.

Ortega felt he had been wounded now again. He was not sure how or why.

43

He took a final glance at the house, at the window where the jeweler was. The casement was open and although there was no light, Ortega saw the shadow of a human shape motionless there in silent vigil. He whispered a prayer to his favorite saint and crossed himself twice, then he turned on his heels and made quickly for the end of the garden and the alley beyond, almost fearing to look behind him again.

He had thought to find the jeweler a petty purveyor of gossip, someone to impress with his blood and title, with the purity of his lineage and the elegance of his manners. But Castell had not seemed to be impressed. Under normal circumstances this disregard for degree and place would have infuriated Ortega, for he was proud of his title and contemptuous of the English, whom he thought to be dogs unfit to lick his boots. It was, however, Ortega who had been impressed, awed, perhaps even appalled by his host, this bastard of an Italian father and English mother, this baublemonger who had spoken to him so familiarly and slandered the great ones of the city so casually, this heretic and, yes, atheist, too, who had shown a cunning and malice of such depth that now Ortega wondered what knot might the jeweler untie were he of a mind to do it. What reputation was so spotless that he could not make filthy like a wretched boy daubing a wall with dung to avenge some slight?

Yes, Ortega had been impressed, and as he entered the alley and quickened his step to where there were light and human voices he was not sure but that for the past two hours he had been discoursing with the Devil.

It had come as no surprise to him, however, that the Devil should have proved to be an Englishman.

No sooner had Joan's head sunk into the down-filled pillow than she fell asleep, but it was a fitful, unsatisfying sleep, with small purchase on rest. Her brain reeled with troubled images of the day, parading before her eyes in a noisome dumbshow. Unawares, she extended her hand to explore the empty side of her marriage bed. Her fingers found the indentation her husband's body had made, but the space, years in the molding, was empty and cold. Then, as though they had a mind of their own, the fingers retracted with disappointment and found a securer lodging in the folds of her nightgown.

She stirred, half awake, half remembering. Frequently that day she had thought of Tom Ingram. Strangely, she had not thought of him as having been swallowed up in London, nor as having run off to sea as Mr. Castell's letter said. That awesome expanse of monstrous creatures and dead men's bones was not the boy's fate either. She felt he was nearer than *that*, and with such force did she feel his nearness that it was almost as though any moment he would come into the room where she was and there he would be before her with his sweet, good-natured countenance just as she remembered it and him as safe and whole of limb as when he had lived in his brother's house in Chelmsford.

In such feelings as these—she called them glimmerings—Joan had great confidence, since they were nothing like dreams or visions with their motions, voices, and strange improbable plots, their impertinent mimicry of life. Unbeckoned, her glimmerings fell upon her without pictures or words, filling her with a calm and absolute certitude, with a knowledge that passed understanding. And it was for this reason she knew that Tom Ingram was not in London, nor drowned. Nor was he in France or Spain. But she knew that he was near and that things were somehow awry. He was in danger, yes, that was it. Near but in danger. Her glimmerings had not told her why.

Now she was sorry she had so strongly urged her husband to go to London. Thomas was no longer there to be found.

These were the thoughts she had in and out of sleep. But there was one final glimmering. It had to do with Matthew. It came to her that he was in danger, too, and as she passed from the world of waking to the realm of sleep she felt the premonition cold and hollow in the pit of her stomach. Momentarily her eyelids batted in a little flurry of mute hysteria, and then she went down, down, mercifully down like a leaf falling through the still air.

FOUR_____

A dung cart had broken an axle before the grim stone face of the
prison and one of the keeper's men, a beefy, ruddy-faced fellow,
had come down the stairs to see to it. The man bore his authority
with a swagger, surveyed the damage, and mumbled something vile
beneath his breath. The cart had spilled some of its load, a pile of
nightsoil garnered not an hour before from the prison privies and
middenheaps. The keeper's man and the driver of the cart were now
squared off in the middle of the street and had commenced to
quarrel. A crowd gathered about them. The driver was a puny little
man, filthily garbed as became his profession, and he spoke in a
high-pitched whine. The keeper's man stood oxlike, looming above
him, glaring and insisting that the driver clean up the mess. But the
driver refused. He was not responsible for the broken axle, he
declared. He was not responsible for the street. It was sufficient that
he should sweep the privies and fill the cart and lead the creature
that drew it. This present misfortune came under the category of an
act of God, he said, and therefore let God in heaven see to its
remedy. The driver looked at his horse accusingly. The beast was an
old mare, uncertain on her wobbly legs and her nose almost touching the cobblestones as though sensitive to her disgrace.

But it soon became apparent that God would not see to the remedy. The noxious pile steamed in the early morning chill, while the driver railed and the keeper's man glared and the crowd of spectators grew larger and larger. Finally, the keeper's man lost what little patience he had brought downstairs from his quarters and told the driver that if he did not wield his broom and do it quickly he would break his skull.

A tapster from a nearby alehouse emerged from the crowd to offer his services in the dispute. He knelt down to examine the undercarriage of the afflicted vehicle and confirmed that the axle was indeed broken. Snapped like a twig, he said, rising and making the abrupt twisting motion with his hands to illustrate. The stench from the cart and the pile was awesome. Some of the bystanders were now pushing their way to the outside of the circle of onlookers, their noses and mouths covered with handkerchiefs. So was Matthew Stock, who had been about to enter the prison, eager to see this Ralph, when the incident occurred.

Someone called for the constable and presently he and two sergeants wearing buff jerkins and bearing halberds were shoving their way through the crowd and barking out orders to disperse. It was to no avail, however. Antagonized by the roughness of the sergeants, the crowd turned unruly and from everywhere now there were curses, threats, and protests. From a side street a gang of ragged urchins assaulted the crowd with rocks and bricks filched from a nearby construction site. A dozen or so wardsmen and turnkeys from the prison rushed from the building to join the melee, their swords drawn; they charged into the crowd, pushing and shoving, brandishing their weapons in the air. Alarmed now, the crowd began to disperse in a mindless panic. There was a general rush for the side streets and alleys. Before Matthew's very eyes a blowsy red-faced woman was nearly trampled to death when she fell onto her knees in the press. Matthew himself had withdrawn earlier upwind of the cart and its malodorous burden and had situated himself under a grocer's awning where he could view the outcome in comparative safety.

Then, as suddenly as it had begun, the uproar subsided. The prison warders returned to the prison, the street cleared, and the sheriff and his men were now quietly conversing with the driver of the cart, who after the riot seemed more reconciled to the work. Then the sheriff and his confederates left and some men from the prison came down the steps and began helping the driver sweep up the fallen ordure. All this was being done under the watchful eye of the keeper's man, whose fleshy countenance twisted in a grimace of triumph. Presently another dung cart arrived, this one equipped with a solid axle, and the load was quickly transferred.

While this was being done Matthew slipped into an ordinary, drawn by the aroma of bread and bacon. He found a place to sit and enjoyed a good breakfast and then spent the best part of an hour thinking about Joan and wondering what she would advise in his present circumstances. He now understood that what information he had received from the jeweler was false, at best but half the truth. He felt that Thomas had probably had good reason for leaving the jeweler's employ but he had not an inkling of what the reason might have been, and he had no idea where to find Thomas. His present purpose, to speak to Ralph, Thomas's fellow apprentice, was his one hope, although he was afraid that Ralph might not know anything either. It was all a melancholy prospect—the long journey to London for nothing.

After breakfast, Matthew walked back to the prison. A few bricks and articles of shredded clothing lost in the fray were all that remained of the riot. Neighborhood shops had reopened to a sluggish business and their proprietors were setting out wares or conversing with customers as though nothing had happened. Across the street from Newgate a puppeteer had set up his stage and a little crowd of children had gathered. From a distance, Matthew could hear the shrill, hysterical cries of the puppets. Punch and Judy. Judy was beating Punch. Punch beat Judy. The children were laughing, and the sun was shining brightly now on the cobblestone pavement.

A gentlemen at the steps directed Matthew to the prison lodge where he understood the keeper had his office, up a flight of stone steps and then down a corridor to a broad chamber where the wardsmen and turnkeys he had seen earlier were sitting about on benches or in the rushes drinking, smoking tobacco, or playing at dice or cards. Matthew noticed that there were a few women among them, sharp-faced slatterns laughing raucously and allowing themselves to be kissed and fondled. One of the warders approached Matthew and asked him roughly what he wanted. Matthew told him he wanted to see the keeper.

"Indeed," replied the warder with a cynical snort. "So does many a one come to Newgate."

This warder had a great moon-shaped face, marred by pox, and nostrils from which sprouted coarse black hairs. Matthew explained that he was constable of Chelmsford and had come to the prison to inquire about an apprentice named Ralph. The warder took this in and then shrugged as though the purpose of Matthew's visit did not matter after all. He asked Matthew to follow him.

In a small room adjoining the larger, Matthew found the keeper seated at a desk. The room was cluttered and more like an armory than an office. Halberds, truncheons, fowling pieces, broadswords and their harnesses, odd pieces of armor much tarnished, several large iron pots, an enormous oak chest with a heavy padlock, a cupboard filled with documents, some yellowed with age and spotted by rat droppings, a corner occupied by staffs with tattered pennants attached, and an assortment of stools and chairs were the most prominent objects in view. The keeper's desk partook of the same disorder, its solid writing surface damaged by scratches and stains and littered with loose papers, a few books, and the remains of the keeper's breakfast. The keeper himself was a thickset man, somewhat younger than Matthew, with a short black beard squared like a brush, narrow eyes, and a long livid scar across his right cheek. He wore a laced green doublet and buff-colored shirt with loose flowing sleeves rolled up at the wrist and on becoming aware of Matthew's presence he looked up sharply with that quick vexed expression of one who has been interrupted while calculating a long column of figures. The keeper surveyed Matthew from head to toe, put down his pen, and dismissed the turnkey. Matthew explained again why he had come.

"Ralph," repeated the keeper, grooming his beard. "That would be his Christian name. But what of his family? Every tenth man in Newgate was given the name at birth and the rest would adopt it quickly enough if they saw it was an advantage to them."

"I don't know his surname. He is an apprentice of Gervase Castell's, the jeweler. The same who keeps shop in the City."

This information seemed to be of no help. The keeper stared at Matthew dubiously, then shuffled through the mass of papers, withdrawing at length what appeared to be a kind of roster. His eyes searched the list, then he looked up at Matthew. "What was the boy's crime?"

"Theft, I think," replied Matthew. "At least of theft he was accused. His guilt is much in question."

"His innocence you mean, sir," the keeper said, smiling grimly.

49

"As our reverend divines observe, no man's guilt is in question. It's a foregone conclusion. It's the primal curse. The great rout of our prisoners are thieves at heart, if not for fact. Why, sir, Newgate presents to the eye the largest gathering of cutpurses, priggers, praters, highwaymen, and linen-snatchers in the world. They all come here—rebels, traitors, extortioners, debtors."

The keeper grinned and stroked his beard. The thought of the diversity of crime seemed to please him. He fixed Matthew with a businesslike stare.

"Then I am out of luck unless I know Ralph's family name?" asked Matthew hopelessly.

The keeper smiled benignly on Matthew's perplexity. He was very sympathetic. But there were so many prisoners. One could hardly count them. "Well, there's yet another possibility, now I think upon it," he cried, sitting up in his chair and leaning across to Matthew as though he were about to disclose some intimacy. "Julian."

"Julian?"

"We have here among the inmates a prisoner of that name. A very marvelous fellow, I warrant you. He knows every scurvy face in the prison—from the master's chamber to the Hold. Let him have, say, sixpence of good coin and you shall find your errant apprentice in no more time than it takes to lose your purse in Paul's."

"This Julian could find Ralph?"

"Does Ralph breathe? Are his legs planted where they ought?" exclaimed the keeper as though Matthew's question was absurd. "Trust me, Julian can do it."

The keeper beamed with enthusiasm, and Matthew began to feel better.

"Clarence!"

A great, bull-necked fellow Matthew had observed loitering in the next room responded to the call. The man had been throwing dice with his friends and his countenance, craggy and jaundiced, was the very image of discontented compliance. Clarence came haltingly into the room and stood looking down at the keeper. He had just eated a plum or some other succulent fruit and the juice of it was running down his chin. He wiped his face with his sleeve and looked curiously at Matthew.

"Clarence here will convey you to Julian, sir," the keeper said. "Oh, I nearly forgot. The gratuity."

"The gratuity?"

"A custom of the prison, sir. It's a little something to feed the poor of the place."

By this Matthew understood he must pay something for the privilege of being taken to Julian. He reached into his purse and fingered some coins, waiting for the keeper to name the sum, but the keeper said nothing. After an awkward silence, Matthew asked: "How much will this gratuity be?"

The keeper appraised Matthew carefully. Matthew knew the look and waited. "A shilling," said the keeper, looking up at Clarence, who loomed above him.

Matthew handed the keeper the coin.

"It is a venerable custom of Newgate, Mr. Stock. An act of Christian charity. A single shilling shall see you to every ward in the prison, if need be. That and the leaving of that blade at your side, sir. The law permits no weapons inside the prison, save those borne by my men and me."

Matthew handed over his knife. He did it reluctantly. It was a good knife with a whalebone handle and he had carried it for years.

"This is Mr. Stock," said the keeper, addressing Clarence. "He is constable of Chelmsford."

Clarence's expression showed no sign that this information was important. The keeper's eyes had wandered over Matthew's face and form as he spoke, assessing his person. The keeper continued: "He wants to see our Julian. You know Julian, don't you, Clarence? *Julian*." The keeper emphasized the name, and Clarence brightened. Suddenly he seemed eager to do what he had been asked. He grinned at Matthew insolently, and Matthew thought it strange that this great hulk who had been on his hands and knees a minute or so before, slobbering over the dice, now seemed so tractable.

"One more thing, sir," said the keeper, rising from his chair. "I would keep my purse close about me if I were you. Though the men of the yard have lost their freedom most still practice their trade—if you get my drift."

Matthew understood all right. He thanked the keeper for his help and the warning and felt a chill of apprehension, reasoning that if the keeper and his men dwelt amid such disorder who knew what he might encounter among the inmates. He, with some misgiving, followed Clarence until they came to a spacious yard where a great throng of prisoners was taking the air. Men in various quality and stages of dress stood or walked about, with little supervision, so that

51

Matthew could hardly believe them to be prisoners. Against the walls some of the inmates had set up stalls and were carrying on business, mending shoes, peddling combs and brushes, barbering, and tailoring as though they were freemen. There were vendors of cakes and meats, a cluster of men rolling dice against the wall, while another group bowled and a third group sat at tables reading or discoursing pleasantly. It was a very strange prison, thought Matthew, for whom incarceration meant an afternoon in the stocks or a public whipping. But he had heard that Newgate was one of the sights of London and despite his distaste for what he had seen thus far he was prepared to give the rest his full attention.

Clutching his purse, Matthew followed at the heels of his guide through a doorway and down a narrow passage to some stone stairs. The stairs descended into a filthy cellar, a smoky, low-ceilinged room where some poorly dressed men were crowded around a table drinking, smoking, and playing cards. There was much noise and confusion, and although Matthew's first impression was that he had intruded on a quarrel he quickly realized that the din was the normal tenor of discourse among the prisoners.

Matthew's guide screwed up his eyes and peered through the smoke. He began to call out for Julian—in an odd, high-pitched voice, like a farmer's wife calling in the pigs.

"Julian? Julian?"

Somehow Clarence's call managed to penetrate the uproar. Suddenly the noise at the table subsided and heads twisted to stare curiously at Matthew and his companion. The men began to call out for Julian, too, but their calls were less an inquiry than an assertion.

"Julian! Julian! Julian!" the men shouted in unison.

It was all very strange, Matthew thought. Like a chant.

"Julian! Julian! Julian!" they demanded, pounding their fists on the table.

As suddenly as it had begun, the chanting ceased and the men at the table returned to their cards. The conversation again rose to a roar. No one paid any attention to Matthew now.

Confused, Matthew turned to his guide to find Clarence staring at him with a glint of amusement in his eye.

"It seems we must seek Julian elsewhere, sir," he said, his thin lips twisting in an obvious smirk. "Unless of course he is deaf. Shall I call again?"

Reddening with anger but intimidated by his guide's size, Matthew said nothing. Clarence laughed and walked away. Matthew was about to follow when someone tapped him on the shoulder.

He turned to find a thin little man with a pinched face and scraggly red beard regarding him sympathetically with watery blue eyes. "My name is Abraham," he said. "A poor Jew fallen on hard times in the City and resident of Newgate these two years. This Julian you seek doesn't exist."

Matthew stared at the little man uncomprehendingly.

"A little joke of the keeper," Abraham explained, "practiced on well-intentioned gentlemen like youself seeking friends or loved ones among the honored guests of this place. By what price were you admitted?"

Astonished, Matthew named the sum.

"You were fortunate, then. Our good keeper has been known to charge as much as a pound."

"But he said it was custom—Christian charity."

Abraham laughed scornfully. "Oh, it is custom in truth, but hardly a Christian one. The jailer also gives shelter to thieves and strumpets for fourpence a night and cheats the prisoners of their victuals. It's said his post is worth a hundred pounds or more a year. And all is custom, sir, most devilish custom. I tell you for a fact, there is more corruption in the prison lodge than in the lowest ward."

The little Jew led Matthew from the cellar into the yard. He blinked in the sunlight. "Now, then, perhaps I can help you," said Abraham. "You were told this Julian would take you to your friend for a sum?"

"Sixpence."

"Well, then, since these coins are at the ready, would you object to paying me for Julian's service?"

Matthew said he would not. He wanted nothing so much now as to see this Ralph, have of him what information he could get about Tom, and then be gone. If Abraham could help him find the boy, then Abraham could have coins for his bony bosom and Matthew's blessing besides.

Abraham wanted the money now but Matthew kept his purse safe. The little Jew would have his money, but only when his service was rendered.

Abraham agreed, reluctantly. He was dressed in an old jerkin with leather patches, a ragged shirt, and his feet were bound in

53

filthy cloth. There was a strange earthy smell about his body, as though he had been buried a long time in leaf mold. Now he scratched his bony ribs and neck with long, black fingernails and looked at Matthew apologetically.

"It's the lice," he explained. "The wee creatures run riot in the wards. Which reminds me of a riddle. How is a jailer like a louse?" Abraham looked up under shaggy red brows, his lips parted in a thin smile, and awaited Matthew's response.

But Matthew could not think of an answer. For a moment his mind struggled with these mighty contrarities of man and beast; he reckoned limbs, and looked for strange correspondences, but he could find nothing. Baffled, he looked at the little Jew for the answer.

Abraham smiled triumphantly, shaking with a dry silent laughter. "Why, the both of them feed upon the same dish. The prisoners, that is."

While this conversation was proceeding, Matthew was being led across the yard. Abraham walked with a limp and from time to time he turned to glance over his shoulder, as though to make sure Matthew was still behind him.

"This apprentice you seek—Ralph what's-his-name—he is newly arriving among us?"

"I think since two weeks," Matthew responded, looking about him in wonderment at the variety of the prisoners.

Abraham paused, stroked his chin, stared up thoughtfully at the sun, which was now high over the prison walls. Then he turned to look at Matthew.

"Yet all is not lost. Whom has he offended?"

"It's said that he stole something from the jeweler Castell, he who keeps shop at the sign of the Basilisk."

"Ah," Abraham cried, his eyes widening with comprehension. "Then I do know this Ralph of yours. A tall, strapping lad with ruddy cheeks and wide innocent eyes like a maiden come fresh to the bridal bed?"

"Yes, he could be the very one," said Matthew.

Abraham led him by the arm through another door and then down a long flight of stone steps. They descended through a hatch.

"Where are we going?" asked Matthew.

"To the Hold."

"The Hold?"

"The lowest ward. You'll tell when we come to it by the stink. It's a place of more sickness than twenty French hospitals. The boy has a strong pair of bolts on his heels and a basil of twenty-eight-pound weight."

Matthew said he thought this was very hard for a theft.

"Well, it was for something more than that, I'd say."

They had come to the lowest level of the prison. It was dark and damp and foul smelling. It was another cellar but without the amenity of tables, chairs, and gentlemen conversing over tobacco and beer. The stone floor was barely covered with a thin scattering of filthy straw and an open sewer ran down the middle. Along the walls Matthew could see the bodies of men. They were chained there, like beasts; some slept, others prayed, wept, or groaned in misery.

The ceiling was so low that Matthew, no tall man, had to bend his head for fear of scraping it against the rough smoky timber bristling with splinters and groaning, it seemed, under the weight of the several stories above. There was a smell of damp stone, earth, and ordure, something like a chicken coop long closed up and all the fowl left to die therein, a suffocating closeness.

Abraham seemed to hesitate in the midst of it all, peering around in the half-darkness—there were only two candles, puny little things—as though he was trying to remember which of the miserable creatures was Ralph. There were so many of them, lying along or against the walls.

He continued, and Matthew followed him to the end of the room. There they sat on their haunches beside one of the bodies. Of course there would be vermin in the stale, matted rushes. Other prisoners were shackled nearby but they paid no attention to the two men. Abraham reached out to touch the shoulder of the body before them.

The body moved and sat up; by the dim light a handsome youthful face wearing at the moment the confused, panicky expression of one awakened from sleep, or more precisely, from a nightmare, stared at Matthew curiously.

Abraham said some words under his breath and the boy nodded. His name was Ralph Harbert, he said. Then Matthew told the boy who he was, why he had come.

Ralph took this in slowly. He had been sleeping, he said. He was sick. He seemed almost embarrassed at having been found manacled and confined. He explained that he had been sent on an errand for his master. On his way back he had been apprehended by a sergeant who claimed to have a warrant for his arrest.

"Did he show you the warrant?" asked Matthew, who knew something of legal procedures.

Ralph looked at Matthew blankly. "I supposed it to be written in Latin," he said.

"What happened then?"

"The sergeant's men shackled me, and the next thing I knew I was being hauled before a magistrate, then bound over for the next sessions," he said. Straightway I was brought here."

"Who accused you?" asked Matthew.

Ralph hesitated, then said: "Mr. Castell—or so said the sergeant."

"For theft, was it?"

Ralph nodded. It was evident that the entire experience was painful for him to recall. "They said I stole a ring, a ring from the shop. But I swear I never did."

Matthew looked at the boy's clear eyes, the smooth guileless face. If there was ever a face modeled from its owner's honesty, Matthew gazed upon it this instant, the two weeks' ravages of the prison notwithstanding.

"The first few days I enjoyed the freedom of the yard, what enjoyment there was in it. Then came the jailer's men and dragged me down here. They said it was for charges that had not been paid."

"What charges were these?" asked Matthew.

"I don't know. Charges, they were called."

"You had no money?"

"Upon entering Newgate I did, but the warders took it all in fees, every farthing. They would have had my shirt had it not been such a pitiful thing."

Matthew said, "Tell me about Tom Ingram."

"Tom and I were friends, apprenticed not six months apart. About a month past he comes to me in a brown study, throws his arm about my neck very lubberly and says that he has been thinking to return to Chelmsford and entreats me to come with him. This surprised me, for I had no thought of his being dissatisfied. I asked him wherefore he desired to leave, to which he replied nothing to the purpose. So then, says I, it's some secret, your reason. But then he said his reason concerned some practice of the master, some practice he could not abide. Said I, what practice? Said he, nay, I cannot tell you, no, not now. Well then, said I, you be off to

Chelmsford and Godspeed to you. I said this in a way I regret now, for I thought it most uncharitable of him to keep a secret from me, his friend."

"Did you believe your master was up to no good?" asked Matthew.

Ralph hesitated and his face formed an expression suggesting that this was the first time he had considered such a thing. "Well, sir, I did believe Tom, but I believed the master, too—that is, that he was honest. He had always seemed so to me, at least until—"

"Until he pressed charges against you?"

"I cannot but believe that he has been misled. Perhaps the ring has fallen betwixt the boards. It has happened many times, I'm told."

The boy's eyes signaled their mute appeal and, keeping his doubts to himself, Matthew chose charity above the truth and nodded in agreement. What Ralph needed now was hope, no matter how slender and frail. The boy coughed from some subterranean region of the chest; his chains rattled and grew still. It had been a wrenching cough, cruel and ominous in its violence, and when the fit had passed Ralph wiped the dark frothy spittle from his nether lip with a tattered sleeve and cast upon Matthew such a piteous look of injured innocence that Matthew blushed for the tears in his eyes. Now the boy's face seemed even whiter than before, almost luminous in the half-light of the dungeon.

Matthew told Ralph about his visit to the jeweler and explained that Thomas Ingram had never come home.

"Why, an ant could crawl to Chelmsford in two weeks," Ralph said, raising himself to cough again and then falling back on his bed of filthy straw. "Whatever could have happened to him?" he asked when his new fit subsided.

Matthew shook his head sadly. But then he thought to ask: "When were you arrested?"

"Two weeks ago this Thursday," replied Ralph, lying flat upon his back now and staring up at the low ceiling.

"And this talk you had with Tom, about his running away?"

"The very morning before, I believe it was. I never saw Thomas after that."

"That's a curious coincidence, don't you think?" asked Matthew, to whom the coincidence was very curious indeed. But Ralph's eyes assumed their glazed faraway look; he continued to stare at the rafters, not at Matthew. He said he hadn't thought about it, not until now. In his mind he couldn't see how the events were connected. Tom had left the master's employ; he had been arrested. No, he could not see how the events were connected since Tom had fled willingly and he had been dragged off against his will. He insisted again, though in a weaker voice now, that he had been happy in the jeweler's employ, that he had never done anything amiss there, and that he hoped Castell would take him back into his service.

Ralph shut his eyes. His smooth forehead was like white marble, his body rigid with arms at his side like an effigy in a church.

Matthew thought he might have fallen asleep but when he asked if there were other friends of Tom's who might know of his whereabouts Ralph answered weakly yes, there was. A girl, Mary Skelton. A young milliner's helper. "Tom bought her apples of a Sunday and took walks with her on the Strand. If he opened his bosom to anyone else it was to Mary Skelton."

"Where might this Mary Skelton be found?"

"She works at a little shop without Ludgate. It has a green-and-white canopy over the front door, a sign decked with a needle and thread. Her mistress's name is Margaret Browne. You cannot miss the shop if you come through directly and keep your eyes fixed to the right."

Or was it the left? Suddenly the boy seemed confused and Matthew could offer no help. Ralph began to babble and then to cough again. There was dark blood in his spittle. The boy choked with it and Abraham, who had been sitting very quietly all the while, came to help Matthew lift Ralph into a sitting position. The fit passed; the boy's skin felt cold and clammy. They laid him back down on the straw and Matthew drew the blanket over him. But not over the face. He would not do that yet, although that was in his mind. Ralph Harbert was dying, that was clear enough. The saving grace was that he did not know of it and was too guileless to have his ignorance matter. His soul would fly heavenward as straight and true as an arrow.

Ralph turned his face to the wall and Matthew bid him goodbye in a voice full of emotion. He started to say, to promise, that he would do something for him, but the futility of the offer lodged in his throat. Ralph had fallen asleep, and it was just as well. Matthew nodded to the little Jew and the two of them made their way from the dungeon up into the light.

"I will speak to the keeper before I leave," Matthew said when they were in the yard and he had pressed the promised coin into Abraham's hand. "About Ralph, I mean. I know there's nothing can be done for him now."

"It's the fever," nodded Abraham. "It'll fetch the boy off soon enough."

"Perhaps I can see that Ralph's last hours are with friends. There must be a possibility of bail."

"Bail!" cried Abraham as though Matthew's statement had contained some subtle wit. "If he could have had bail, so it would have been done. I tell you the keeper's a hard man to do business with. Don't show him the inside of your purse unless he holds a knife to your throat or some piperly pickthank has put a snake inside it. He won't leave you a penny, I warrant."

When Matthew returned to the prison lodge he found the keeper alone and dozing in his chair. Matthew's entrance awakened him; he sat up with a start and fixed Matthew with his narrow eyes, as though he had never seen him before. The keeper asked, "You found your man?" remembering.

"Not Julian," replied Matthew dryly.

The keeper's expression did not change. He stared at Matthew.

"It's Ralph Harbert I sought and found at last," Matthew continued, deciding not to press the subject of the keeper's little joke about Julian. "I found him in what you call the Hold. It's a great wonder to me that he should be there, since he has been accused of naught but a theft."

"It's a crime to steal," replied the keeper matter-of-factly.

"I don't deny it," said Matthew. "But the Hold?" He tried to keep his voice level, but he heard it trembling and uncertain. It was always thus when he was excited about something, when his sense of injustice was aroused and raw. The inequity of Ralph's imprisonment was too palpable.

The keeper said he would look in the charge book. He rose, walked with obvious reluctance to the cupboard, and selected a heavy, leather-bound volume which he first made room for on his desk by pushing a great many loose papers aside and an empty bowl that went clattering on the floor. He turned the leaves methodically while muttering beneath his breath the names of persons Matthew took to be present and former inmates.

"Hamshaw, Hanley, Hanson."

He came to Harbert and paused. Of that name there were two, Stephen and Ralph. They were unrelated, the keeper supposed, since Stephen Harbert was of Lincolnshire and Ralph Harbert was of London.

"That's my man, Ralph Harbert, apprentice to Mr. Castell of the Basilisk's Eye."

The keeper read from the book, then he closed it and looked at Matthew. "The boy was charged with theft of a gold ring. He was to be held for the next sessions." The tone of the keeper's voice, leaden and curt, suggested that was the end of it, except of course for the hanging. That went without saying.

"He has also been labeled a dangerous man . . . prone to quarrel. I have a few enough men to help me here should riot break out in the yard, so to the Hold with him I say and there he shall abide until the sessions and good Justice John Popham send him to hell."

"All that is in your book?" Matthew asked, incredulously.

"More *is* than is written, Mr. Constable." The keeper said cryptically, tapping one stubby finger on the side of his skull, as though to indicate the precise location of his information.

Exasperated, Matthew thought to ask: "How much is the bail?"

"No bail."

"No bail?"

"No bail," the keeper repeated, leaning back in his chair and preparing himself to resume his late morning nap.

"Wherefore?" inquired Matthew, sure now that something was amiss.

"No bail. No bail," said the keeper impatiently, brandishing his arm at Matthew. "I have that on a great one's authority. Your Ralph Harbert is a malefactor of no mean order, his smooth girlish countenance notwithstanding."

"I thought you told me you didn't know Ralph Harbert!" Matthew exclaimed, his exasperation now on the verge of anger.

"Well, so I said and the truth it was," replied the keeper, beginning to redden in the face. "But now that I know of whom you speak I tell you that he must remain here in his present condition until I have other word."

"But from whom?" exclaimed Matthew in what was more a protest than a question, for he knew there would be no answer, not from the stony-faced keeper.

"That's for me to know, sir. Now if your business with us is done—"

"No, sir jailer, my business is not done," Matthew heard himself declare. "I too have friends in the City—great ones, as you call them. I hope I will have no need to call upon them for assistance in this cause. Ralph Harbert's punishment clearly exceeds his crime and that's a fact. Besides, the boy is dying."

The keeper rose slowly from his chair, his face a mask of rage. "You may call on whomever you please and be damned," he roared. "I know my duty. As for the boy, may his corpse rot for all I care."

The tone of conflict had drawn two of the keeper's men from the next room, and they came lumbering into the office like cattle heading for water. Matthew noticed they were armed with the heavy truncheons sheriffs' men sometimes carried at their sides when they patrolled the City.

Disgusted and fearful for his safety, Matthew asked if he could have his knife.

"What knife?" replied the keeper in a voice totally devoid of expression.

"The knife I left with you. You said it was the custom—like the shilling you had of me for admission."

He had been ironic without quite intending it, but the irony had no effect. The keeper stared at him stupidly, as though Matthew had just spoken in an alien tongue, and his two burly companions stood as stiff as boards and as expressionless. He realized that he represented no threat to these men now. They had him where they wanted him.

"A shilling?" said the keeper at last, looking with wonderment at his assistants. "Why, sir, charging admission to Newgate is expressly forbidden by law. Rest assured, if you had left your knife or other weapon with me before entering it would have been returned promptly and in good condition upon your departure."

"I see," said Matthew, working hard to suppress his outrage.

"Good day, sir," said the keeper brusquely, resuming his chair with a thud while his companions grinned savagely. Matthew saw that one of the men wore a knife at his belt. Matthew thought it was very like his own. The keeper's man saw where Matthew's gaze fell but rather than move to conceal the weapon he seemed actually to invite Matthew's inspection of it, as though daring Matthew to claim it.

It was Matthew's knife, he could see that. It would have his initials carved in the whalebone handle.

"I see your man has found my blade. See, now, he wears it at his side, so as not to forget to return it to me."

Matthew said this to the keeper, who now was perusing some

yellowed papers on his desk. The keeper ignored the remark and kept reading.

"You are mistaken, sir," said the keeper's man. "The knife is mine. I have had it since I was a boy."

"Indeed," said Matthew, looking very boldly at him. "Then you will explain how my initials came to be on it."

"There is nothing on the blade or handle," he said.

"Show me."

"I have said."

"Then let eyes confirm it."

The man stared at Matthew threateningly. "Are you man enough to take it from me? If you are, do so. If you are not, hold your peace and go your way."

Matthew looked at the keeper, but the man was paying no attention. It was as if Matthew had already gone. The keeper would say nothing, hear nothing. Matthew realized he could be beaten within an inch of his life and the keeper would do nothing.

There was a long painful silence during which Matthew, humiliated by his helplessness, stood watching the keeper as his two confederates waited with insolent smirks. Now he knew his importunities were futile. Surrounded by thieves and knaves, imbeciles and other wretches wanting reason or justice, he would not have Ralph Harbert and he would not have his knife.

All things considered, he would be lucky to get out of Newgate with his pate unbroken and his purse intact.

Coldly, he bade the men good day and had not taken two steps from the lodge when he heard the peal of derisive laughter behind him.

FIVE_____

Denwood Roley had spent most of the afternoon on the Strand, waiting for Sir Jeremy Parr to materialize from one of the great houses that lined the street and proceed to his lodgings in Westminster. Now in the late afternoon, amid the throng of pedestrians, Roley maintained his vigil with a solemn dutifulness. Observed from one of the houses that fronted on the street or by one of the persons of quality who strolled there on warm summer days to admire the occasional view of the river or enjoy its air, Roley would have appeared to be exactly what he was: a nondescript manservant about his employer's business, for he was, after all, a very unremarkable fellow with his thin arms and legs, his long pale face festooned with blotches and pimples, his drab, sweat-strained doublet and patched hose. Yet despite his inconsequential appearance Roley was a man of many talents which his master had been quick to recognize and reward, and one of which he was about to put to good use.

At the moment Roley was tired of walking but because he knew well the cost of displeasing Castell the thought of his simply giving over and returning to the house on Barbican Street never crossed his mind. So he continued to walk, his face set stolidly before him, and his eyes shifting secretly to take in the variety of faces and figures that the gala scene offered to his eye. He had seen the object of his quest on but two other occasions: once in Paul's, once at a bear-baiting in Paris Garden on the Bankside, all melancholy with his arms folded. But he was sure he would recognize the knight when he saw him again. He hoped only that when Parr did appear— as Castell had assured Roley he would—the knight would be unaccompanied. Contact would be easier that way.

Later, about the time Roley was preparing to risk Castell's displeasure and return to the City, he spotted his man, emerging from one of the houses and marching confidently toward Westminster.

Roley quickened his pace, weaving deftly through the mob of porters, serving men, and gentlefolk bravely attired. The better quality of men wore satin suits and short cloaks, and the women, in the height of fashion, gowns with trunk sleeves, bounteous farthingales, and elegant taffeta hats with gold and silver bands to shield their complexions from the rude sun.

When Roley had his quarry within earshot, he slowed his pace to a walk, mopped the sweat from his brow with his silk handkerchief, and ran up to pluck the knight by the elbow.

Parr turned sharply about and glared at Roley suspiciously.

Roley made a very mannerly low leg, bending himself nearly double and sweeping his hat off and through the air in an elaborate flourish. His obeisance done, he stood erect and looked respectfully at the knight, who waited now with scarcely concealed impatience to see what was wanted of him. Parr was a large man with ruddy cheeks and handsome dark eyes and a neatly trimmed beard flecked with gray. He was dressed most elegantly in a brown velvet doublet, white hose, and a black felt hat with a high crown adorned with some rich jewel the size of Roley's thumb. Roley looked at the jewel enviously and then framed an obsequious countenance. He extended the letter he bore in his hand.

"If you please, sir. You dropped this letter some way back."

Parr gave the paper a cursory glance, then looked at Roley contemptuously. "I lost no letter. You are mistaken."

The knight began to turn away.

"If your honor please. I saw it fall from your side, not twenty yards behind."

Parr scowled. "I said I dropped no letter. I had none about me. Be off now, sirrah. You trouble me."

Parr turned away and proceeded at an even faster pace than before. Roley scrambled after him, calling out the knight's name. At that Parr stopped and turned back. He glared at Roley menacingly.

"How do you know my name?"

"The letter, sir. It is signed by you."

"Let me see it," he said, snatching the proffered letter from Roley's hand.

Roley looked about him. None of the pedestrians on the Strand had stopped to notice them. That was good, he thought. Their meeting would appear nothing more than a master conversing with his servant over some trivial domestic matter.

"It is not in my hand," Parr snapped after a moment's perusal.

"But it is signed by you. Sir Jeremy Parr. See, so it does say just here."

Roley showed Parr his signature.

"This is *not* in my hand." Grimacing, Parr began to read the text. His handsome face paled, his perturbation changed to astonishment. He looked hard at Roley. "How did you come by this?"

"As I have said, Sir Jeremy, I found it where you mislaid it."

"You devil," Parr hissed angrily, reaching out to grasp him, but Roley danced out of his reach and at the same instant the knight seemed to remember where they were and regained his composure.

"This is some foul practice," he said. "Who did this, made this copy? Is it money you want?"

"Money, sir?" Roley asked with an expression of calculated innocence. "Why, do you take me for one who peruses the pockets of others for gain? I should hope not, sir, for upon my honor, what so little a serving man may have, I never intended such."

"Well, what is it that you want, then? You do have the original letter, I presume?"

"Not I, sir. However, I can put you in touch with him who would be more than happy to deliver up the lost article."

"For a price?" Parr asked.

"For a price," said Roley.

"You said even now that you didn't want money—you evoked your honor as you called it."

"Why, so I did and do, sir. But you do equate price with silver. Let us say rather that it is a good turn my master requires—for which in recompense you shall have your missive to the Lady Alice to do with what you will and no man, nor woman, shall be the wiser."

"You give me little reason to trust your discretion."

Roley protested. "You will find me in all things most confidential."

Parr laughed grimly. "Well, where can I find this master of yours? What is his name?"

"Our first point of confidentiality will be my employer's name," said Roley.

"As I thought," Parr replied sullenly.

"Do you know the tobacconist's shop in Fleet Street, the sign of the Indian?"

Parr said yes. He knew the shop, and the alley behind it, a filthy lane with an open sewer.

"Come round, then, tonight—say at eight o'clock or soon after. Not to the shop but to the alley. About midblock you'll find a plain door, much weathered, with cross and scepter sign. The sign is faint. You must look sharply for it."

"Cross and scepter," Parr murmured.

"You have it," replied Roley. "Come alone."

"Wherefore?"

"For your protection, Sir Jeremy, as much as mine. The whole matter will be done before you know it."

"I know not why it should not be done here in the open."

"Ah, sir, we must do what we must, not what we would," Roley reflected philosophically, a broad grin spreading over his ruined face.

"Well," said Parr, "I will be at your tobacconist's backsides at the appointed hour, alone as you insist, but I promise you short shrift at the end of a rope if my letter to Alice Farnsworth is not then forthcoming. I make no idle threats. Do you understand?"

"Most assuredly," said Roley without seeming much discomfited by this threat. "Trust me. I have been most plain and open. You shall find him who has the letter of like disposition."

"We shall see," Parr answered doubtfully. Some of the color had returned to his face but his arrogance was gone now. His broad forehead was wrinkled with concern and his eyes smoldered; it was obviously difficult for him to hold his anger in check. "May I have the copy in your hand," he asked Roley in a flat, deadly voice.

Roley handed Parr the letter. Parr took it, shoved it beneath his belt in a sudden violent motion, and turned on his heels without saying another word.

Roley stood watching Parr until the knight was lost in the traffic around Charing Cross. He noticed that Parr did not carry himself as proudly now. The knight's loftly looks had gone; he walked as one ashamed to be seen. Fear had made a mortal of him, a mere mortal, thought Roley with great satisfaction.

Castell's manservant began walking himself, taking his time, back toward the City. He was in no hurry now; he always enjoyed walking on the Strand and at the moment he was experiencing a marvelous sense of well-being that made him much pleased with his little world of service. His employer, too, would be pleased, he thought, and, as important, the jeweler would be generous, for it is a foolish servant that does not come to know the ways and whims of his master, and Denwood Roley was no fool.

Beyond the houses and gardens that lined the south side of the street Roley glimpsed the river. He could see the barges and smaller craft plying the great stream and, beyond, the roofs and towers of the Bankside where he hoped that night to frolic with a pretty little wench he had recently taken upon himself to console for her elderly husband's neglect. As he walked he thought of her face and form: her high arched brows as black as coal, the little mouth and sharp nose he loved to kiss, her lecherous rolling eye. Smooth and plump she was in every part and when the old man should die . . .

Yes, Castell would be very pleased, thought Denwood Roley, and he would be generous.

Matthew had some trouble finding the milliner of whom Ralph had spoken. There were so many shops in the neighborhood of Ludgate, so many signs. He stood before them in confusion. Do you know Margaret Browne, he asked of passersby, she who keeps shop at the sign of the Needle and Thread, she who sells lace and ribbons? But no one knew, or would tell. Most of those in the street were craftsmen of the baser sort—cobblers and curriers and tinkers. They rushed to and fro, had no time to guide a stranger in his way. Finally Matthew was set on his course by a blind man seated cross-legged in the street. Marveling, Matthew thanked the man for that information he had not found among those who could see and put a penny in the tin cup the blind man held before him.

Mrs. Browne turned out to be a plump little soul, neither young nor old but somewhere in between, comely and well spoken, with a round, ruddy countenance and full red lips. She was dressed in a pretty yellow petticoat and kirtle, a white waistcoat, and a clean cambric ruff about her neck. Her shop was small but neat and seemed well stocked. When she heard Matthew's business, she invited him into her parlor, which was a small room just beyond the shop proper. It, too, was well furnished with a handsome cupboard, two fine chairs, and a round oak table upon which Matthew was pleased to see a great store of sweets, arranged with care upon a pewter plate. There were sugar, biscuits, comfits, marmalade, marchpane, and other dainties, and Matthew feasted his eyes while Mrs. Browne explained that these things she had prepared for two neighbors, who having become indisposed with the catarrh, had failed to come. And having said this she invited Matthew to partake as he pleased, since it was a great shame should such banqueting stuff be thrown away.

Then she explained that Mary Skelton was no longer in her employ. As it turned out, she had disappeared.

"Disappeared!" exclaimed Matthew, between mouthfuls of a particularly delicious comfit.

"Indeed," said Margaret Browne, filling Matthew's cup with wine without asking if he wanted any. "Mary slept in a small room in the back of the shop. She had a paltry little bag of things which she kept always about her, and these and she herself were gone one morning. Without a word!"

"She left no note?"

"None."

"You've heard nothing of her since?"

Mrs. Browne shook her head sadly. "The girl was new to London. She had but one friend, a young man whose name she never mentioned."

"Was she satisfied with her employment?" Matthew asked, helping himself to another biscuit and already eying a third.

"Oh, she was most happy in her work," Margaret Browne explained. "Why, many was the day I would hear her from the shop, plying her needle and singing in the loveliest voice. It would melt your heart to have heard her, so sweet a voice she had."

"Ah, what a world this is," said Matthew.

"So I fear that's all I can tell you," said Margaret Browne with a note of finality.

Matthew looked at the table of dainties ruefully. In the matter of sweets he was almost totally without self-restraint. Mustering what little discipline remained after two biscuits, a generous share of marchpane, and the marmalade, he rose, and thanked his hostess for both information and the refreshments. She handed him his hat.

He followed the mistress of the shop to the shop door, appreciating with another quick glance the orderliness of her stock, table, stools, and counters. The room had a very pleasant smell. He looked again at Mrs. Browne. Yes, he thought somewhat guiltily, she was a very neat little woman, unmarried, he presumed, a widow doubtless, and a more than tolerable confectioner, too.

She was smiling at him winsomely and bidding him good day when she suddenly exclaimed: "Jesu God, I almost forgot myself."

"How so?" inquired Matthew, his hat in hand.

"She had a sister. Mary mentioned her but once. The sister was older, I believe, and had some employment here in London."

"What employment?"

"Mary never said."

"What was the sister's name?"

Margaret Browne paused to think. Her eyebrows knitted together in a frown of concentration. She could not remember. Then she could remember.

"Catherine," she said. "I do recall it now. It was when Mary first came to work for me. I asked after her family. She said she had a father somewhere in the country, and a sister, Catherine, who lived here."

"It is strange that she did not live with her sister," Matthew remarked.

"Yes, it is," Margaret Browne agreed. "I remember thinking that, too, but then she never spoke of her again and I supposed the twain did not get along."

"Catherine Skelton," murmured Matthew, as though invoking the girl's presence. "I don't suppose you know where I could find her?"

Margaret Browne began to shake her head, but then she said, "No, but Philipa may. She's my other girl. Philipa and Mary were very thick, being of the same age." Margaret Browne called out and presently a pale young girl with hair the color of straw came into the room carrying a piece of lace in her arms. She looked at Matthew curiously and then at her mistress.

"Philipa," Margaret Browne began, using now the more formal

tone of the mistress of the house, "here is Mr. Matthew Stock, come from Chelmsford, where he is constable, in search of our Mary."

Matthew doubted Philipa had heard of Chelmsford, being as it was a good way off, but the word *constable* certainly took its effect. Upon hearing of Matthew's office, the girl had begun to quake like a sparrow in a wind and her pale blue eyes went wide with alarm. He would have said some words of comfort to her, had he dared to interrupt her employer, who obviously felt herself sufficiently in command of the situation.

"Tell us where he might find her sister Catherine," Margaret Browne continued.

"She lives in London, ma'am," the girl replied after a moment's hesitation during which she seemed hard put to find courage to speak at all.

"Goose," replied her mistress impatiently. "We know well she lives in London. Can you not tell us more particularly *where* she lives—in what street, in what house?"

The girl paused again, seemed to turn even paler than before, and Matthew wondered if she was concealing something, or if she was merely dull-witted. "Mary told me Catherine her sister keeps ill company," Philipa said at last.

"Why, she may keep what company she pleases," Margaret Browne exclaimed with exasperation. "I would know *where* she does keep it."

Reluctantly, the girl named a lane in Bankside, a neighborhood of ill-repute, full, Matthew had heard, of gaming parlors, leaping houses, and theaters.

Philipa's mistress blushed at this revelation and glared at the young girl as though she had said something unseemly. Then Margaret Browne looked appealingly at Matthew.

"This is the first I have heard of this," she announced brusquely, clearing herself of association with the unfortunate Catherine Skelton, who, it now appeared, was a fallen woman. "It's no wonder that Mary would have naught to do with her."

She sent the girl back to her work. "Foolish girl," remarked Margaret Browne with impatience. "As melancholy as a hare. I am most sorry," she said to Matthew. "Under the circumstances I would be much surprised if Catherine Skelton has her parents' name. You might with more chance of success go seek ice in hell."

Matthew sighed heavily. "Yet I must do what I can. I promised my wife and daughter, and my daughter's husband," he said, reciting the litany of his obligations. "I'll go to the Bankside this evening. It will not hurt to make a few inquiries."

The woman looked at Matthew doubtfully. "If you do, you were best home before dark. The neighborhood is a most vile and unsavory place."

Matthew thanked the woman for her help and strode out onto the sunny cobblestone pavement. For a few moments he stood surveying the crowded street and collecting his thoughts. The warm, clear day seemed to have brought everyone out of doors. It was a typical London throng, a mingle-mangle of gender and degree, rushing about in a motion, all intense and purposeful. Matthew alone seemed unpreoccupied, stationary. But then his eyes fell upon a fellow watcher. Across the street and beneath a grocer's sign he observed himself being scrutinized by a young man lounging against a wall.

The young man was slender and hatless and from this distance Matthew could see that he had dark hair. The coat on his back was ill-fitting; the wings on the shoulders came down halfway to his arm and the skirts an equal distance below the waist. The crowd was moving about him, as though he were part of the structure he leaned against.

Matthew returned the young man's stare and for some time, then suddenly the fellow turned on his heels and walked away. In a moment he was lost to Matthew's view.

Matthew knew he had seen the man before. He recognized that the moment the young man had fled. But where?

The question dominated his thoughts as he headed back to his lodgings, but he had not walked a quarter of a mile before he remembered.

The same fellow had been milling around outside the prison that morning. Later, Matthew had seen him again when he emerged from the prison and started out for Ludgate. Now here was this silent watcher, in quite another part of town, haunting Matthew's steps like an old debt.

Parr was aware he might have hired a couple of thugs to take care of this insolent, villainous turd-face, this scurvy blackmailer. That idea was in the back of his mind as he walked toward his lodgings in Westminster, and the idea was there yet when he ordered his manservant to fetch him his supper and he ate it alone in his large room with the window overlooking the garden and the river beyond. But that would have been nothing to the purpose. The cheeky rogue had given him nothing but a copy. What Parr wanted, desperately needed, was the original. Worse, he contemplated between mouthfuls of rare-done beef and dry Spanish wine, he needed to know what the blackmailer wanted of him.

Parr stuffed until he felt heavy and sleepy. It was habitual with him to do so when his mind was at work, and it was working faster now than it had in a month.

His man Furness, solemn-faced and tiptoeing about the carpeted chamber like a laundry filcher, cleared his table. He brought a lamp and some writing materials and inquired, in a whisper that rankled his employer, if Sir Jeremy would want anything else before bedtime.

Nothing else. Parr looked up at Furness, wondering what this decrepit bag of bones knew of his affair with Alice Farnsworth. Furness had yellow skin, tight to the skull, a palsy in the right hand, a long somber face of a churchman. Dog piss coursed through the old man's veins, Parr was sure.

He dismissed Furness with a wave of his hand and a low growl in the throat.

Alice Farnsworth, he thought. Pretty Alice. Round and merry, her lips like cherry, her breasts like what? Like . . . like . . . He fumbled for a simile, for a rhyme. But what she had cost him! He had invested three months of his time and he no longer recalled how much silver in pursuit of her. She had dangled her virginity before him like a jewel. And he had paid a jewel for it—a rich emerald, set in gold, had from Mr. Castell's shop for—he couldn't bring himself to think of the sum. What a fool he had been. Now Alice Farnsworth was nothing to him, nothing. All that flesh, those lily paps, those languid eyes with their moist, heavy lids and subtle promise—all that simpering that had attracted and now repelled—what terrible price was he to pay for his misbegotten pleasures?

It was not knowing that tormented him.

At the stroke of seven he changed into a plain black suit with a very modest white collar and a broad-brimmed hat that made a politic concealment of the upper part of his face. Then, making sure that Furness did not observe his leaving, Parr set out for the City.

Within the hour he had come to the weathered door, the faded cross and scepter sign of some long-failed enterprise, and a back alley whose depressing squalor found no relief in the gathering gloom. He stood for a while before the door, meditating upon his ill luck and listening for noises within, but there was nothing. Finally, heaving a great sigh of wretchedness, he knocked.

When there was no response he knocked again, looking about him nervously for it was dark in the alley and the solitude which first had pleased him now seemed oppressive and threatening. Then came upon him standing there, a feeling to which he was not accustomed, a cringing, womanish fear. He felt himself trembling and was ashamed for it. His bowels ached and he could feel his hair beneath the hat damp with sweat.

He had come armed with his rapier and a dagger. He stood with his back to the door facing the alley, his hand upon the pommel of his blade, alert to any movement or noise. A sudden shrill whine from a shadowy corner caused his heart to leap into his throat, and in the same instant his blade was out and shaking at the dark.

But it was only a cat. The body materialized from the shadows, approached and paused, arching its back, then came toward him on silent feet, mewing and almost apologetically rubbing its furry body against Parr's boot.

Parr uttered a threatening growl and the cat darted off. Then he replaced the weapon in its hanger, turned to the door, and began knocking more vigorously, wondering if he was on a fool's errand.

But no, it was no fool's errand; he knew that even as he kept up the futile pounding. Someone had taken the trouble to steal his letter, copy it, face him down on the street, his reputation for bad temper and a quick thrust notwithstanding.

No, it was no jest.

The door rattled with the increasing violence of his blows. "Hello, hello, in the house," he called, not caring who might hear him in the neighborhood.

But no one came. Only when somewhere between disappointment and relief he gave over and began to walk away did he hear behind him the drawing of the bolt, the groan of a rusty hinge, and his name whispered.

Parr had half expected the scab-faced knave who had accosted him on the Strand and in his present temper molded of fear, shame, and rage he would have welcomed him as a fit object of his wrath. But it was not he. A candle held aloft illuminated this new face, the face of a solidly built man in tradesman's garb speaking to Parr in a strangely melodious voice with the slight suggestion of the north, perhaps Yorkshire or Durham. Fortune had cleanly shorn his scalp except for the fringe of lank, oily curls that fell to the plain collar and broad shoulders. The eyes were small but intense with concentrated energy and separated by a broad flat nose flaring at the nostrils. The man's teeth were ragged and shiny with saliva and his complexion had the yellowish hue and coarse texture of old parchment.

"Come in, Sir Jeremy Parr," said the man again when Parr hesitated, his hand still resting on the pommel of his rapier.

Inside, Parr found himself in a large dusty storeroom full of crates and barrels. Two windows on an opposite wall had been boarded up, and the only light in the room was provided by the candle the stranger held. Parr could detect the odor of malt and something else, stale and deadly like decaying flesh. A brewer's warehouse, he thought, or perhaps a grocer's. It was evident that the building had been unused for some time, and certain as well that the man behind him was as much an intruder here as he.

"I have come for my letter," said Parr, weakly.

"I don't have it," the bald man replied, placing the candle on a barrel head and staring at the knight as though Parr's expectation that he should have it were absurd. "Presently I will take you to one who does."

"Presently," snapped Parr, beginning to feel his old self now that he was in the light and face to face with his enemy. He made a gesture of annoyance. "I was told you would have it."

From somewhere behind the stack of barrels Parr heard a rustling noise. He started, was about to draw, fearing a worse sort of trap.

The bald man laughed softly. "Rats," he said. "We have disturbed their labors. Here, put this on." He held a large handkerchief in his hand and thrust it toward Parr. "Turn around, please."

Puzzled, Parr glared at the man.

"You are to be blindfolded, of course."

"Now see here," Parr protested.

"You *do* want the letter, do you not?"

Coolly, Parr assayed his circumstances. He had the advantage in height and weight, he was armed, and he was not afraid to use his weapon. But he did want the letter, and he believed the villainous knave with the bald pate was speaking the truth when he denied having it about him.

"Very well," Parr said reluctantly. Removing his hat, he turned and faced the door. He felt the handkerchief wrapped around his head, felt it cover most of his nose and forehead. He replaced his hat on his head.

"It isn't too tight?" the man inquired with mock solicitude.

Parr shook his head. In his mind's eye he could see the man's smirking face behind him. Damn his eyes, damn his eyes, thought Parr, struggling to control his anger.

He felt his sword suddenly drawn from its hanger and exclaimed: "What?"

"You'll not need your blade, sir, nor this knife."

His dagger was drawn instantly.

"You devil—to disarm me!" Parr cried out in rage. He was about to rip the blindfold from his eyes and turn to face the man when he felt the other's arm about his neck in a viselike grip and a pointed blade at his throat. It was his own weapon, he knew that. He stood perfectly still, his heart beating wildly.

The man said slowly and with chilling deliberation, "You do exactly what I say, sir knight, and you do it when I say it, or they will find your body in the morn floating in the Thames. Do you understand?"

Before Parr had a chance to reply the man intensified his grip and thrust the blade harder into the flesh. Parr cried out between clenched teeth. He nodded yes, yes, he understood. Blindfolded, disarmed, and within a fingernail's breadth of extinction, he had little choice.

The man relaxed his grip and removed the point of the dagger from Parr's neck. "Now we'll go. Your knife I'll keep about my person, just in case you should prove difficult to handle during our journey. Take my arm. Hold fast."

Parr heard the door to the storeroom unbolted and felt himself being led out into the night. They seemed to cross over to the opposite side of the alley for he felt his boots sink into the sewage that ran down the middle of the alley and his face burned with anger as he heard at his back his guide's low derisive chuckle.

There were several turns; once they seemed to double back. Soon Parr lost all sense of direction. Presently he was brought to a halt, he heard a knocking, a muffled voice, and felt himself pushed forward. He was standing in a lighted room, he knew that much. He could see the light through the handkerchief. There were more whispers.

Parr felt the blindfold being removed. When he could see again he saw that he was standing in a narrow passage at the far end of which was another closed door. He turned to look at his guide and was startled to find himself in the presence of a new face.

"Where—?" he began with astonishment.

The tall, youngish man had the swarthy complexion of an Italian or Greek. He smiled impudently. "One man's as good as another for a guide, if he knows the way."

Parr didn't say anything. The man was armed with a stout cudgel and looked as though he would welcome an occasion to use it.

"Follow me, sir," said the swarthy man.

Parr did what he was told and passed through the door to come to a square chamber without windows or furniture except for a plain stool placed before an ornate grillwork. Beside the stool was a small table on which a candle burned, illuminating the room. The light was very feeble but Parr could see the shadowy form of a man sitting on the other side of the grille.

Parr was ordered to approach and take the stool, which he did, relieved to find himself at last at the end of his strange journey. The man with the cudgel stood at his back.

"Well, speak," said Parr, trying to assume his wonted authority.

There was a pause, a rustling behind the grille, and then a voice. Parr was sure he had heard it before, somewhere; he tried to place it.

"I would moderate your tone with me, sir. I have you at a disadvantage."

"You have my sword."

"I have more than your sword—"

"More?"

The voice responded shrilly. "I have you by the ballocks with this letter, sir knight, and by God I'll yank them hard if you do not moderate your tone."

Parr sat very still now, listening to his own heavy breathing. Behind him the man with the cudgel shifted his weight. The voice began to speak: Parr knew the words. They were his own. His letter to Alice Farnsworth was being thrown back in his face. He cringed. The devil on the other side of the grille. A high-pitched, mocking voice. Parr felt his cheeks and ears flush with anger and humiliation.

"Is that enough for you, knight?"

"It is enough," Parr answered weakly. He sat forward on the stool, exhausted, his arms hanging between his legs, reaching almost to the floor. He removed his hat and wiped the sweat from his forehead.

"What is it you want of me?" he asked in a dry whisper. The voice of some other man, not his, a knight with an income of three thousand pounds a year and a position at court an earl might envy.

"That, later. I want to make sure, Sir Jeremy, that you first appreciate your position. This letter confirms your alliance with a woman not your wife. Indeed, it has adultery written all over it, betwixt each line. Were it to become the common talk, you would be disgraced—especially in the eyes of your father-in-law."

Parr thought of his father-in-law, misshapen old devil that he was, rich as Croesus, clutching obscenely to his life and dangling his money over his daughter's head. No, the voice was right. The old man would hardly take kindly to his son-in-law's perfidy. Parr had no choice but to submit. Whoever was behind the grille had devised this plot with particular care. Parr was in the hands of no mean order of scoundrel. How he would have liked to pull aside the grille, seize his tormentor by the throat and . . .

"Your fellow said—" Parr began. He could hardly talk now his mouth was so dry.

"My servant, please."

"Your servant . . . said you didn't want money."

"Information," responded the voice.

"What sort of information?"

"Facts and figures."

"Pertaining to . . ."

"Your duties."

"My duties—"

Parr felt sick, his brain reeled, and his sweat turned cold; he began to shake.

"You are master of the ordnance in the Tower, are you not?"

Parr could only nod dumbly. The plot was beginning to assume its ugly shape.

"I want a full inventory of what artillery, cannon, musket, and other pertinences are housed there, what number of men, in whose command, and the hour of the watch."

"Wherefore would you know this? Why, I could be drawn and quartered—"

"Indeed, if your cooperation should become known. But consider this, Sir Jeremy. That would do little good to me or my friends. Trust me that we have the best interests of the state at heart. We are not traitors, sir, far from it."

"Who are you, then?"

"Ones who wish their country better governed."

"And you carry on thusly, hugger-mugger?"

"Secretly," responded the voice.

"When I have given you this . . . inventory . . . will you then give me the letter?"

"You have my word on it."

Parr thought about that. Obtaining the information requested of him would be no trouble at all. Within the week he had commissioned such an inventory himself. If his two assistants, Scott and Woodruff, had done their duty, the inventory would be even now in his cabinet at the Tower. But there was no doubt about it, delivering the document to unauthorized persons would be treason, plain and simple. He felt he desperately needed time to think. He decided to agree with the person on the other side of the grille. At the moment he felt he would do anything to get out into the open air.

"Well, what say you, Parr?"

He cringed at hearing his own name without the respectful "Sir Jeremy" he was used to.

"I agree. Where shall I bring the inventory?"

"Take it to your lodgings in Westminster. Place it in your cabinet, the one with the ornately molded top. Leave the desk top unlocked. I will do the rest."

"And my letter?"

"You will find it in place of the document. That's fair exchange, isn't it?"

Parr nodded. Behind the grille the figure moved, seemed to sigh.

"Don't despair, you may find this experience good for you. Improves humility, doesn't it? There's nothing like a good taking-down as a remedy for pride."

When Parr didn't reply, the voice repeated itself: "Don't you agree?"

"I agree," Parr said, in what was almost a whisper.

"Well then, our business is done, it seems. My servant behind you will see you to the door. I trust you will endure the blindfold once again. You'll be delivered at the place from which you came."

Parr was led from the room, down the passage, and out into the night. He allowed himself to be led along now, not listening for the meaningful sounds that might have helped him determine just where he had been, not really caring where he was being led, muddled in his mind, tortured by an aching swelling bladder, and wishing nothing more than to relieve his agony and get himself to bed. When this was over—if it ended—he would sleep, and when he would awake perhaps he would find it had all been a dream or momentary madness such as when he got himself gloriously drunk and had done those things he never would have done sober.

"Watch your step, Sir Jeremy."

He watched his step, but seeing nothing, his care was to no avail. He stumbled forward, landing hard on his hands and knees and feeling his palms sink into mud and something cold and damp through his hose. With disgust, he realized he had fallen into some kind of awful slime. He scrambled to his feet, cursing; he wiped his hands on his doublet while at some distance he heard a low mocking laugh. Brought back to his senses by this assault upon his person, he called out to his guide. "You, you there?"

Another laugh at a greater distance. He could hear that. The bald man's lyrical note of scorn.

He realized that he had been left alone, blindfolded and covered with filth, in an empty street. The fall had been no accident; he had been led into harm's way. Was this to be the last of his humiliations of the evening?

He tore the blindfold from his eyes and looked wildly about him. True to the blackmailer's word he was back where he started, at the weathered door, the faded sign of cross and scepter of a long-failed enterprise, and a back alley of depressing squalor. He started to knock but never touched the door. It would be futile. There would be no one there now. He would not see his sword and dagger again. Or his hat. That had been lost too. It had been a fine evening's work for someone, not for Jeremy Parr.

He took note of the storeroom's location, the adjacent buildings, knowing at the same time that it would do no good. The building was vacant. Its owner, were he found, would claim no knowledge of a bald man in tradesman's garb, would swear that the building had stood empty this twelve-month.

Parr cursed his luck and hurried homeward, hot tears of rage and shame streaming from his eyes and turning the dark streets to a watery blur. When later Furness admitted him, staring aghast at his master's dishevelment, Parr cursed his manservant too and sent him straightway to his bed with a swift kick to his backsides.

The knight gone, Gervase Castell came out from behind the grille and saw that Parr had left his hat. The jeweler wore no such hats himself but he recognized Parr's as a good hat, made of fine materials. He picked it up off the floor. It would, he decided, make a pleasant souvenir of an interesting evening.

He made sure the outer door was bolted and then entered his shop, to which the windowless room was adjacent. In the darkness he glanced down at the long cases displaying his wares, realizing that his eyes surveyed a king's ransom. On the next day the shop would be filled with the quality of the kingdom—knights and their ladies, an earl or two, gentlemen of means from the City, all attracted by Castell's toys like bees to the hive. Castell would wait upon them with pleasure, would listen to all their small talk, and he would suck up a wealth of knowledge more sweet to his taste than any jewel in his shop.

At length Starkey returned to the shop and joined Castell in his watch.

"You saw the knight back to where you found him?" he asked.

Yes, Starkey had done that. Starkey also had another report, about Perryman, who had spent the entire day following Matthew Stock about London. "Perryman kept a fastidious eye on his body from sunup to sunset. The constable will sleep now, like a babe at his mother's breast, full of roast beef and plum pudding and a sense of his own virtue. So says Perryman."

Castell nodded. "Stock had no more converse with apprentices, then?"

"Our friend with the loose tongue has met an accident, I fear, and gone off to a better world."

"Indeed," said Castell. "And who did that work?"

"I did," said Starkey.

"What else?"

"Stock went to see the milliner—about Mary Skelton."

"What could she know?"

"Nothing but that the girl has vanished."

Castell chuckled mirthlessly. "Good Constable Stock will think

80

London is an Irish bog. One no sooner sets foot here but disappears." But then he said with a dead seriousness: "It were better Mary Skelton had gone heavenward, along with that babbling apprentice. Keep a sharp eye out for her. Have Perryman continue to watch Stock. The constable's a fool, yet even a fool may have a day of luck."

Castell's bodyguards had been playing cards upstairs during the long evening. They descended now and prepared to accompany Castell to his house on Barbican Street, to which he presently went, whistling on the way, as much at home in the forlorn, shadow-ridden streets as most men are in the daylight.

SIX

At dusk a surly little boatman took Matthew's penny and ferried him across the river while the constable watched the glow of lamps ashore slip discreetly into the general gloom. The great cathedral church of Paul's, its blunt steeple thrust heavenward like an appeal for grace, was the last thing in the City Matthew could discern with any clarity. Now he looked in the other direction, across the dark placid water to the southern bank. There he could see the vague humps of houses and trees and rising above them the larger shape of the Globe theater, like a beer tun turned upright.

The theater would be dark now, its galleries and stage empty, but Matthew recalled the first time he had seen it. Hot in pursuit of Harry Saltmarsh—murderer, adulterer, madman—Matthew had plunged into that sweating, violent throng, his head swimming with the confusion and color and novelty of it all to him, a plain simple clothier from a small town. It had been one of the great experiences of his life. Next to his marriage. Joan had been his great experience, coming to know her. He thought of Joan now. Later, after Saltmarsh's trial, he and Joan had gone to the theater together. They had seen a play, a wondrous comedy by Will Shakespeare. The play had been rich in poetry and song. And jests, marvelous jests.

When had he seen his little wife laugh so? Matthew could not remember.

He was still thinking about his wife as the finer details of the approaching bank materialized out of the dark and the boat's prow nudged against the stone steps. The boatman held his lantern aloft to show Matthew the way, grumbling and sighing beneath his breath a vague complaint of his lot, as though he had bent his back to ferry the world's troubles across the Thames instead of a single customer. Matthew bid the man good night and felt his eyes follow him as he climbed the stairs and then began to walk down the road to where the houses began.

The air was foul along the bank, his footing uncertain. He had the vague uneasiness of one who has come late to a feast and fears both that he will not be admitted and that he may be, to his regret, but soon he was cheered somewhat by the sound of music and voices and he came around a corner to find himself in a neighborhood of shabby tenements and alehouses lining a narrow, crooked street, illuminated by torches. It was crowded and noisy. Young gentlemen out on the town, apprentices and their masters mingled together, sundry punks and brawlers, all moved, conversed, drank, in a holiday mood. There were women, too, among them, mingling familiarly with the men—women standing in doorways or loitering in the shadowy mouths of alleys, women leaning from the windows of upper stories calling to their mates in the streets below like carrion birds perched in treetops, their throaty laughter audible above the brittle harmonies of a little band of wretched musicians dressed in tawny coats.

He stood for a moment on the periphery of the crowd surveying the scene with his businessman's eye. Trade here was all flesh and drink and the tenements cheap rental property, the landlord doubtless some well-fed and pious merchant or lawyer of the City, a decent family man out to make a quick pound in the stews of Bankside. God knew what went on indoors. No doubt Matthew would find out himself before the night was done.

Alert as Argus with his hundred eyes, he mingled, favoring the side of the street where he could mind his purse and view the interiors of the taverns and alehouses. For an hour he wandered, asking for Mary Skelton—or her sister Catherine—of Sussex, newly come to the neighborhood. But no one he asked knew the sisters, or would admit to knowing them. People responded to his question strangely, as though to ask after a single maid or two was a great impertinence, as though he himself were a suspect—a sheriff's man in plainclothes, or a scrapping hedge-creeper, or sneaking eavesdropper. Did he want some nameless drab or pretty boy? That was well. Did he want to procure the services of a blackmailer or murderer? He had come to the right place. But to ask after a certain girl!

Getting nowhere except deeper into the wretched slum where every lane and doorway began to look like every other, Matthew took refuge at last in an alehouse that appeared more respectable than the others and promised decent refreshment, for he was sleepy and footsore and ready to give over his search. The interior was a spacious hall, girdled at the midriff by a gallery from which hung various limp and tattered flags and pennants, giving the establishment a certain military air. It was dimly lighted as though the proprietor either preferred the dark or was at great charge for oil or torches, meanly furnished with rough-hewn tables and benches, and full to overflowing with a motley collection of townsmen, sailors, laborers, and their women, sitting about at tables, drinking, smoking, and laughing. At one end of a long bar drawers were extracting beer from spigots projecting from several large kegs the size of rainbarrels. At the other end two very drunk women had begun to push and shove each other about and had drawn a little circle of spectators who were egging them on and laying wagers on the victor. A man Matthew took to be the proprietor was vainly trying to separate the women, one of whom had succeeded in doing such violence to the other's gown that the top of it was now in shreds revealing some very pink flesh, the viewing of which was giving the spectators no little pleasure.

Matthew found himself a quiet corner where he could watch the proceedings. At the opposite end of the table where he sat three drunk men were quarreling over the reckoning. Matthew listened. One of them, a great fat fellow with yellow hair and a florid complexion, was haranguing his companions in a harsh guttural tongue. Dutch, Matthew thought, for there were a good many of these folk now in Chelmsford and he had no doubt London would have its share as well. The other two men were less vocal but by their expressions equally resolute. The Dutchman was banging on the table with his fist.

Soon, to Matthew's relief, the Dutchman stomped out of the house with a great show of disdain for the company and then his companions followed, leaving their end of the table a ruin of empty pots and bowls. Meanwhile the tussle at the bar concluded as well. Sheer exhaustion and the persuasion of their friends had made peace between the female combatants and they had separated to different corners of the hall to repair damages and regain their composure. All of this Matthew had viewed without the services of a waiter. Now finally he was observed by a pimply-faced youth in a smock that looked as though it had gone unwashed for a year or more. The young waiter emerged from the confusion of bobbing heads and tobacco smoke to inquire what Matthew would have. The boy did not look as though he cared very much. He slouched and hemmed and stood before Matthew with his arms brazenly crossed and as insolent an eye as Matthew had seen.

Matthew ignored this rudeness and asked for a cup of chilled wine and, because hunger had joined his other discomforts, a plate of apple-johns, dried fruit of which Matthew was very fond.

This order seemed satisfactory to the waiter, who stopped long enough to stroke the miserable few hairs growing from his chin and then vanished into the smoke.

Matthew was served, in time; the waiter thumped the bowl and plate down on the board before him, the wine spilled, the plate was dirty. Matthew was too glad for this meal to complain about the service and the waiter too churlish to apologize. Matthew sent him off, ate and drank happily while the crowd thinned and mellowed. He was about to begin the second of the apple-johns when he observed the woman heading toward him in a purposeful way, toward him certainly for he was alone now at the table in the far end of the room; she couldn't have been steering a course for anyone else. Flamboyant and confident, she wore a flame-colored taffeta gown, a broad kirtle at the waist that accentuated the fullness of her bodice, a dazzling display of rings on her fingers. She had a mass of yellow hair that fell about her shoulders in a riot of wanton curls; large, wide-set eyes, and a semblance of youthfulness that diminished as she drew near. She must have been pretty once; up close, there was something hard and calculating in her countenance. Matthew felt his face flush.

"Norwich," she pronounced confidently as though it were his name, standing over him.

Puzzled, Matthew started to stand and inquire whatever she meant, but she urged him to remain seated, pushing him down with good-natured roughness, and then, taking possession of the space next to him on the bench, she drew very close to him without asking his leave or identifying herself,

"I can always tell a man from the towns," she minced. "You are from Norwich?"

"Chelmsford," Matthew replied awkwardly, feeling suddenly that his tongue had grown very large in his mouth and shifting himself to put a more decent interval between them.

"Are you alone?" she asked.

"Here? Yes."

"Good," said she. "I thought that surely such a gentleman as you would be accompanied, that perhaps your lady had stepped out to do her business in the jakes." She winked. "Chelmsford lies in the same direction as Norwich, does it not?" she continued.

"Indeed it does," replied Matthew uncertainly, anxious not to take up the wrong tone.

"Well, then, I have you," she said, grinning broadly. "I *can* always tell."

She then proceeded to introduce herself as Beth Drury and to identify Matthew as a gentleman merchant. By your dress, she said, and your demeanor—a word she pronounced very oddly, though somewhat self-consciously, as though it were French. Yes, she insisted, Matthew was a merchant come up to London to buy horses at Smithfield and was now sojourning in the Bankside for the quality of the air.

She giggled girlishly at her own jest and then asserted, "I can always tell about men. Where they lie, when they lie, and with whom they lie."

Beth Drury waited patiently for Matthew to appreciate her joke, then she burst into laughter. It was laughter of a very raucous sort and seemed to Matthew to fill the whole hall. He looked about him very embarrassed for them both and was amazed to see that no one else had seemed to notice her outburst.

While she continued to chatter, Matthew studied the woman's face. Sitting as close as they were now, Matthew could see the loose flesh of the woman's neck, the large pores of her face, and the lines in her forehead and around the eyes, only partially concealed in the heavy rouge. She was clearly older than she had first seemed, and then she had not seemed young. There was a kind of cruel mockery in her effort at rejuvenation, and Matthew suddenly felt a surge of pity for her. She had very large breasts that quivered as she talked and she was thrusting them toward him provocatively, so that he found it necessary to avert his gaze. It had grown very hot in the room; beneath his doublet Matthew could feel himself sweating fiercely. He could smell the sweet-sourness of her body too, feel the warm, winish breath in his face as she jabbered. His head began to ache from the tobacco smoke.

The woman lisped as she talked, either naturally or from excessive drink. He offered her an apple-john. She looked at the shriveled fruit, poked it with a finger, laughed and teased.

"I'll give you a sweeter morsel anon," she whispered. She moved closer to him, throwing her arm around his shoulder.

She had lived all of her life in London, she said. Her parents had been gentry, fallen on evil days. She had earned her bread since she was nine. She wiped a tear from one heavily made-up eye as a testimonial to her veracity.

Matthew listened intently, grateful not to have to say anything, but then, abruptly, she wanted to talk about him.

"What is your humor?" she asked.

Matthew did not understand.

"Your will, your pleasure," she said, pinching his cheek saucily. Now Matthew thought she meant his business and was about to describe the clothier's trade when her scowl of impatience made it clear she was thinking of something quite different.

"I am looking for a girl. About sixteen or thereabouts. Her name is—"

"Name me no names," Beth Drury interrupted indignantly. She gave him a long stare of unmitigated contempt. "Young flesh, young flesh," she scolded. "What is it with you men? Will no woman serve your turn but she is half-grown and yesterday a virgin, thin as a bean and all green sickness and mother's milk? I swear it is the new fashion, even among the gallants, to want nothing older than a pup."

She seized a passing waiter by his apron and pulled him toward the table.

"A cup of sack—and within the hour, if it please you, sirrah. And permit our Chelmsford clothier to pay the cost."

The waiter, different from the one who had served Matthew so ill, looked at him dully; Matthew nodded, he would pay for the drink.

Not mollified by this overture, Beth Drury renewed her attack. "You whoremasterly rogue, you corrupter of children," she sputtered.

Matthew was about to take exception to these calumnies when quite unexpectedly her scolding ceased and she flashed a conciliatory smile as though her previous outburst had been a jest. "Sixteen or thereabouts, you say? Five or six of such girls I know intimately; two fair, two dark, one a Moor or African, in this very house. What is your pleasure? A shapely leg? Shoulders white damask? A soft breast cupped by the Queen of Love?"

As she warmed to her theme, Matthew realized it was time to make his intentions clear. He told her he wanted to find a Catherine Skelton for her parents' sake. They were old and infirm, and she their only child, their last hope. It was a pitiful case, which a hard man might weep at just the hearing.

Beth Drury listened. Matthew had manufactured the tale of a sudden and as the words came tripping forth from his lips it was almost as though he could hear them ringing false onto the floor like counterfeit coins. But Beth Drury seemed to believe him. He thought she would be used to believing, a woman like this, who must hear patiently the counterfeit words of many a counterfeit man. He forgave himself the lie because he could not see any good reason for telling the truth. His quest had grown very complicated now, and besides, he was not sure whom he could trust.

She nodded noncommittally, looked pensive. "A narrow face, clear forehead, small rump, and simpering voice," she said. "That's your girl."

Matthew admitted that he had never seen her. She might resemble the Devil's dame for all he knew.

"And well she might, considering the leaping house in which she does her tricks," Beth Drury remarked dryly.

"Which is?"

"A moment, sir," said Beth Drury, scooping up the wine the waiter had just delivered and finishing the most of it at a gulp.

She wiped her mouth on her sleeve and said, "I *am* a woman of business."

"A woman of business?"

"What will you give me for her whereabouts?" she asked now, looking suddenly very old and ravaged.

Matthew ventured again into his purse. His supply of money

was slowly vanishing, but it was true this woman was on the verge of doing him a service. He found a piece of silver and shoved it across the table.

She smiled with satisfaction and swept the coin into some private place in her bodice.

"The sign of the Dove," she said. "It's but a quarter of an hour's walk to the east, on this very street."

Matthew thanked her and finished the last of his apple-johns. Beth Drury did not seem interested now in detaining him, and he left her in the corner in the midst of the flounces of her flaming taffeta, her great breasts sunk into her lap like two weary pilgrims. With great relief, he walked out into the air.

The street now seemed full of whores and their confederates. They accosted him at every step, beckoning him to follow, pleading for money, promising incredible pleasures, half of which he had never before imagined. He shook them off and walked ahead boldly, one hand before him to ward off the appellants and the other close in to his belt to safeguard his purse.

He found the Dove where Beth had said; where the human habitations ended and the flat, dark fields began and the night air was fetid with cattle and marsh grass. The house was tumbledown—that Matthew could discern even in the dark—with crumbling plaster, shutters battered and askew, and a riot of vines scaling the walls and masking the upstairs windows so that the little illumination from within glowed a sickly, pale color. A sign, hung on the crosstimber of what looked like a ship's mast and adorned with the crude outlines of a bird with a sprig of holly in its beak, was the only indication Matthew could see that the house was a place of business. The path to the front door was well trodden; and from where he stood, just outside the gate, Matthew thought he could hear from within the sound of voices and the forlorn pluckings of a lute.

He hesitated to enter; the remoteness of the house, which first had seemed a welcome relief from the crush of humanity farther up the street, now seemed unnerving. He knew well what sort of place this was, and as he looked about him at the other dwellings in the immediate vicinity, he could see how brutish they were too, how loathsome, and he shuddered for fear not so much for his person as for his soul, for he felt he had come to the end of his journey, this last house on the street, this house so inaptly called the Dove.

He stood about a few minutes longer mustering up his resolve and making peace with an intractable conscience that protested his being there, then he proceeded without further deliberation through a wicket gate and down the wide, well-trodden path to the door.

It was a very solid door, and Matthew knocked thrice before hearing any response from within. Presently, however, he could make out the scraping of a bolt being drawn and the door opened a crack and a bent figure seemingly without years or sex and not half Matthew's height peered out at him and without a word beckoned him to enter.

Inside he found himself in a hall paneled in dark oak and furnished threadbarely. On a distant table there was a single lamp and by that Matthew could perceive that the person who let him in was a very old woman wrapped up tightly in a shawl as though it were the dead of winter. She had a long, drawn face, watery blue eyes deeply embedded in a maze of wrinkles, and a little tuft of white hair at the end of a pointed chin. Seemingly incapable of speech, she smiled at him foolishly from a mouth bereft of its teeth and began to push him toward the stairs, making strange clucking noises like a hen in the yard.

Uncertain as to what to do next, Matthew allowed himself to be guided and while the old woman waited at the foot of the stairs, he climbed to the next floor, thinking all the while of Joan and wondering what she might think were she to know he had entered such a place. Indeed, what would he do were he to encounter one of his neighbors here? Good morrow to you, Mr. Stock. A great wonder meeting you here! How travel broadens the mind!

God's eye missed nothing. Matthew had thought of that, too, between the foot and the top of the stairs, as his hand grew sticky on the cold wood of the banister, rubbed to a high sheen by how many sweaty palms. But then he remembered that God saw the heart, read its script no matter how smudged or curious, knew therefore his present intent, a mission of mercy.

At the top of the stairs he found a sort of waiting room adorned with faded wallhangings and furnished with a scattering of high-backed, uncomfortable-looking chairs. In one of these a callow youth with very long legs extended before him was folding and unfolding his hands and staring morosely into his lap. As Matthew approached he looked up from beneath shaggy brows that ran without intermission from one side of his face to the other and then quickly averted his gaze to the opposite wall where there was a woman seated behind a small desk.

The woman smiled thinly at Matthew and told him to be seated. She was not what Matthew had expected. Clearly the proprietress by her demeanor, she was modestly clothed in a simple chaste bodice and a narrow white collar with only a margin of yellow lace. She wore a little white cap, had plain, somewhat stern features, and bare plump forearms, pale as milk curd in the lamplight. By her side an old bitch hound, nestled in the rushes, emitted a long, guttural snarl as Matthew approached, and then rolled over on her side to expose her swollen dugs.

The woman was sewing; her eyes were fixed on her work. The dog began to snore softly and from some distant room Matthew could hear the sound of the lute, quite distinct now, but played without skill by someone who knew only where to place his fingers.

"I am looking for Catherine Skelton, who I have been told lives in this house," Matthew said, looking about him curiously, a prey to unfamiliar sensations of shame, curiosity, and a strange excitement.

"Catherine Skelton," repeated the woman without looking up. "Yes, she lives here. That will be sixpence."

"I have come only to have . . . conversation with her."

"Call it what you will," said the woman brusquely. "Yet that will be sixpence. For your *conversation*," she added.

A gentleman, very heavyset with fat, sweaty cheeks and bushy beard, emerged from a darkened corridor, mumbled good night to the proprietress, and then lumbered down the stairs, breathing heavily. The woman signaled to the string-bean youth and Matthew watched him proceed in the direction whence the fat man had come.

Matthew reached into his purse, found the required sum, and placed it on the desk. The woman swept up the coins into her apron and again told him to sit down. He must wait his turn, she said, as others before him had done.

"It is Catherine Skelton that I want to see," Matthew reminded her, sitting. "I am from the same village. In Sussex."

"Catherine is occupied," responded the proprietress curtly, obviously indifferent to Matthew's place of origin. "Can you not contain yourself this quarter hour?"

"But no other will do," he insisted.

She fixed him in a long cold stare. "You *must* be patient, sir."

The hound, alert now, glared at Matthew suspiciously.

Matthew sighed heavily, resigned himself to wait, while the woman returned to her sewing. She was intent on her task and for a while seemed to forget Matthew's presence. The minutes passed, and Matthew no longer heard the lutanist. It was very quiet in the house and no other patrons appeared. He concluded that the Dove was a poor house, even for a brothel, and that its clientele was no better. When the woman looked at him again she smiled sweetly.

"Mary is ready now," said the proprietress of the Dove.

"Mary?" exclaimed Matthew, rising from his chair. "But I said—"

"You will not be disappointed," she said peremptorily. "Mary is Catherine's sister. She's younger, but they are much the same in form and manner. The chamber is clean and the girl, too."

Mary Skelton. So, thought Matthew, the girl had followed her sister's lewd example.

"Down the corridor," said the proprietress. "Second door to your right. Please knock before entering. The girls appreciate that."

Ill at ease, Matthew came to the second door, knocked softly, and heard in almost the same instant a thin, quavering voice from the other side bid him enter.

Despite the proprietress's assurances to the contrary the chamber was not clean, and it was very small and smelled of mildew. A leaky roof had left the dark wainscoting water-stained and cracked, and the few articles of furniture—a battered chest, two stools, and a bed—were scattered about upon old rushes. Mary Skelton was seated on the bed. A thin girl with long uncombed hair that fell about her shoulders, she seemed at once to Matthew to be more a frightened child than a woman of pleasure. She was holding the stub of a candle in her hand and staring at Matthew with great round glistening eyes. As he shut the door behind him and approached her she stood and he could see that despite her winsome features, her skin had an unhealthy pallor. She was wearing a plain white cambric smock material that hung like a sack on her body and her feet were bare.

She placed the candle on one of the stools and with trembling fingers began to disrobe. Alarmed, Matthew said: "No, child. I'm not come for *that*. I am a friend," he said, in a tone of assurance.

She stared at him blankly, biting her nether lip and holding her thin arms folded across her breasts. He took a step toward her and she shrank from him. He spoke more words of comfort, telling her that he meant her no harm, that he was a decent, honest man come to help her, but his assurances seemed only to confuse her the more. It quickly became apparent to Matthew that Mary Skelton did not know what to make of a friend, not in the Dove, not in the place of business.

He gave an account of himself that seemed to calm her. He told her of his shop, of his office as constable, and immediately regretted doing so for she seemed terrified of the law and he had to inform her that he had no authority outside his own parish.

After more such assurances, the girl's fear began to subside and she listened to him with intelligent interest. They sat upon the bed and he pressed her to tell her own story, which after a few tears of relief she did in a timid little voice a sparrow might have used were it endowed with human speech.

"You're wondering what a maid such as I am doing here," she said between sobs. "I who but two weeks hence was respectfully employed . . . as a seamstress . . . had friends . . . who . . ."

She was unable to proceed, and Matthew felt tears gather in his own eyes. It was not pity. He was thinking of his daughter Elizabeth. Elizabeth was older than Mary Skelton, somewhat stout, and darker in complexion, and their present circumstances were incomparable, yet somewhere there was a man like himself who had watched this child grow, bloom, and now, were he to see how her life had been blasted, his heart would surely break.

He caressed the girl's tangled hair and kissed her on the forehead, sharing her tormented recollection of a life now irretrievably lost while memories of the earlier days of his fatherhood filled him with a bittersweet longing.

"I have a sister—"

"Catherine."

"Yes. You know about her?"

"Your mistress told me."

"She took me in. I had nowhere else to go."

"Could you not have gone home?"

For Matthew it was a logical question: home, place of refuge. She turned deathly pale, and began to shudder and look about her wildly.

"No," she said. "There was no welcome for me there."

"Why not?"

93

She hesitated, unwilling to answer. Matthew decided not to press her. She said she was afraid, afraid of the men. What men? Matthew wanted to know. Who had threatened her?

She shook her head. No one had threatened her. But she had been followed and watched.

"At first I thought they only wanted *me*. In an unlawful way, I mean. A girl gets used to *that*. But then I realized it was something more they wanted."

"What men?" asked Matthew again.

She did not know. Some stared at her as she passed; others dogged her footsteps through the streets. She had not told her mistress, for fear of losing her place. No employer wants a girl who causes that kind of trouble. But then it became more than she could bear.

"So you came to your sister?"

"Yes."

"But you did *know* the men, did you not—I mean why you were being followed?"

She turned to him, then suddenly she buried her face in his shoulder and began to weep again.

"Easy, easy." Matthew fell into the father's part without difficulty. This strange, helpless girl.

She continued to weep; when she came to herself again, she wiped her eyes on a thin woollen shawl she had taken up from the bed and took a deep breath as though she were about to launch into a bitter truth.

"I knew a boy—"

"Thomas Ingram?"

Her eyes grew round with surprise; she nodded and continued.

"He ran away from his master."

"Thomas told you why?"

Yes, he had told her.

"Tell *me*, then," Matthew asked reassuringly, fearing that she wouldn't.

"Your life will be in danger if you know."

But he shrugged this off with comfortable resolution, feeling himself safe enough at the moment.

"Thomas told me his employer, Gervase Castell, the jeweler, was a thief."

"A thief?"

"A purse snatcher."

Matthew laughed without wanting to. All that wealth, a king's ransom. "Why, what could Castell have found in a pocket he could not have discovered amidst his own stock of goods?"

She ignored his laughter. She said: "He cared nothing for the money. He wanted letters, notes, jottings on paper." She hesitated, searching for the other word Tom had said. "Documents," she said, finding the word. "He had used documents to get these great ones to do what he wanted them to do."

She didn't know what that was, what Castell had wanted from his victims.

"How did Tom come to know of this?"

"By accident. He overheard, saw things. He was curious, made a point of listening. He wanted to know what he had got himself into."

"By Christ," exclaimed Matthew, marveling at this.

She continued: "Tom never went to the house. Few if any of the apprentices have been there. Even Castell's bodyguards only accompany him to the threshold. He found out about Castell by overhearing his master converse with one of the gentlemen whose pocket Castell's men had harvested. It was all hugger-mugger. The gentleman comes very late, after the shop is closed. There's a chamber in the back of the shop, very private, Tom says."

"What were they conversing about?"

But Tom had not told her that, only that it was clear Castell was blackmailing the gentleman. "Tom wouldn't lie," she insisted defensively as though Matthew had said he would. "He's honest and he's clever."

"I know him to be so," Matthew replied. "He is the brother of my son-in-law, William Ingram."

"Why, then," she said, "you are Matthew Stock himself, constable of Chelmsford!"

"The same," Matthew said, realizing that he had forgotten to tell her his name.

"Tom spoke of you," she said. "The day before he left London he said that he was returning to Chelmsford and that you would know how to proceed against Castell and the Basilisk."

"Castell's shop?"

She cast him a confused sidelong glance, and he hastened to make his own confusion clear. "The Basilisk—what you said just now. *Proceed against the Basilisk.*"

"That's the sign of his shop to be sure," she said, wiping a lone

95

tear from her pale cheek. She looked at him very seriously. "But the Basilisk is more than that."

"I have seen the jewel. Castell himself showed it to me, mounted on a velvet cloth."

"The Basilisk of which I speak is neither shop nor stone," she said, gazing at him now intently. Her lips were set in full resolve. "He is a man. Mr. Castell's employer."

"His employer!" exclaimed Matthew.

"The jeweler is nothing more than an agent himself. Though he has underlings enough, he is himself an underling to a great one."

"To someone in the City—or about the court?" prompted Matthew.

She shrugged. She knew only the name. Thomas Ingram himself had known no more. Matthew thought her story an unlikely turn. A man named the Basilisk? It *was* a most unlikely name and he said as much to her.

"I doubt he was born with it," she replied, without seeming to have paid attention to Matthew's tone of incredulity. "Tom told me himself. Castell, said he, goes regularly about the business of this Basilisk. Those were Tom Ingram's very words."

They sat pensively on the edge of the bed while Matthew thought more about the Basilisk. He remembered the creature as it had been depicted on the jeweler's sign—the monstrous round eye, the brutal claws. Not merely a freak of nature but a tool of Satan— vicious, predatory, and insatiable. If this Basilisk of whom the girl and Tom Ingram had spoken was well named, what had Matthew got himself into?

He thought to ask: "So it was Tom Ingram's intention to return to Chelmsford?"

"Oh, yes," she responded. "He was sick enough of London. He told me he never wished to see it again, but for me," she added, and even in the half-dark Matthew could see the girl blushing at this admission of mutual affection. "He left the jeweler's because, having denied his service to his employer, he feared for his life. Somehow Castell found out that Tom *knew*. There was nothing else to be done."

"Then the men who followed you were doubtless seeking Tom?"

"Yes, when Tom left, Castell must have ordered him followed . . . and killed to keep him silent."

She swallowed hard and began to whimper again. Matthew took her hand and tried to comfort her, attempting to mask his own anxiety about the boy's fate.

"We have no reason to believe Castell succeeded," Matthew said. "Indeed, the fact that the men were watching you proves he did not, for they doubtless supposed Tom would try to see you. I would wager my purse that Tom is alive."

"I love him," she said in a thin voice between sobs. "Were he to know how I pass my time—"

But now she had touched upon the thing that for sometime waited in the back of his own mind.

"I didn't dare return to my home. My father is besotted and brutal. Six beatings a week is the welcome I'd have from him. My sister, Catherine, is the only friend I have. At first Mrs. Smalley who operates the Dove let me stay with Catherine. For my keep I swept the parlor, changed the rushes in the bedchamber; then, presently, she demanded of me work—of the sort that is done here."

The girl stopped speaking for shame, but Matthew encouraged her to proceed.

"I refused—at first," she continued. "But Mrs. Smalley has two stout young men to do her bidding and take a share of the house. One plies the lane of nights and draws gentleman hither; the other dwells below and keeps the girls in good order. His Christian name is Samuel. The latter threatened to beat me. I gave in, because I was afraid of the pain. He said he would break my nose . . . blind me by thrusting a burning candle into my eyes."

"Could you not escape? Surely you could find opportunity during the day?"

"They keep a close watch on us. There are six girls in the house, all beneath the age of twenty save for one who is twenty-eight, although she seems more like forty, so gray is her hair and lined her face. Catherine would like to leave, too. She fears for her life. Samuel threatens her, too, and has twice beaten her upon some trivial matter. He has his way with her when he will."

"Your mistress permits this?"

"I think she is half mad herself for fear of Samuel."

"Well," said Matthew fiercely, "we must have you out of here and at once. It is only a matter of time before you are found by Castell's men—and I fear I may have led them here myself. I, too, have been followed. I am certain."

She looked at him with dread. "Then if they know I have spoken to you it will be my life."

"If they find you, said Matthew.

"They will find me."

She thrust her face into her hands and began to wail. In a stern voice, Matthew bade her be silent. He himself cared nothing for fate or destiny. There was no misfortune that could not be escaped—if one were clever enough. Or God merciful enough. That he believed as firmly as he believed in anything. He tried to comfort the girl but it was no use. She would not be comforted now. Fear had dissolved her will.

Then Matthew seized her and shook her hard until she stopped weeping and stared at him blankly. He had heard something and he wanted her to listen, too.

Footsteps. Running. On the stairs, he thought, where there were no rushes to muffle the sound.

Now Mary Skelton was listening, too, her eyes wide with concern. Suddenly there was a urgent knocking at the door. Mary said, "Enter," and another girl rushed in, bolting the door behind her.

The newcomer did not have to identify herself to Matthew. Catherine Skelton was an older version of her sister—their eyes, noses, and mouths were cut from the same mold. She was obviously much agitated.

"You are the gentleman from Sussex?" she asked, gasping for breath.

"I said as much to your mistress," Matthew replied, staring at the girl in wonder now. "I did so that I might speak to you and your sister. The truth is that I am of Chelmsford."

"Well, whoever you may be, some men below seek you out. They're in an ugly mood, half drunk, and armed with cudgels. And they say they have sworn an oath to make mincemeat of your brains."

"It's about Tom. I know it," cried Mary Skelton. "It's Castell's men for sure!" She turned to her sister. "This is Matthew Stock. Thomas's brother is married to his daughter. You remember, I told you of him."

Catherine Skelton glanced quickly at Matthew in light of this new information, and flashed a hurried but agreeable smile. She was a pretty girl and had been prettier. At the moment she was wearing a cheap taffeta gown that exposed a good deal of her white flesh and she had made up her face with bright rouge and painted her lips crimson. Despite this, her face shone with courage and resolve.

Suddenly there was a rumble of footsteps on the stairs, a deal of swearing and blaspheming, and soon a woman's piercing scream from the chamber beyond. It was the proprietress. Terrified at the prospect of strange men invading her establishment, she had cried out and incited the hound who, now, fully awakened from her stupor, was barking savagely in response to the threats and curses of the invading men. Other patrons of the Dove, equally alarmed by the uproar, were pouring into the corridor in a mindless panic. Matthew could hear their clamor and for the moment he was grateful for Mrs. Smalley's hound. Unlovable creature that she was, she would surely hold the invaders at bay until he could determine what to do.

But Catherine Skelton had already decided that. "The bolt will not hold," she cried. "There, there's the window. You can climb down by the vines."

"But I can't leave you two behind," Matthew protested.

"Go, man," said Catherine, "it's you they seek now. They'll rush to the window and heigh-ho after you when it's clear you've escaped that way. We'll conceal ourselves and be safe enough. Look to yourself, Constable. For God's sake go and be quick about it."

"Very well," said Matthew dubiously as vigorous pounding and snarling voices indicated his pursuers were now directly without. Matthew rushed to the window, threw open the lattice, and clambered up on the sill while the sisters crawled beneath the bed. Unsteady, he seized a handful of leaves, relieved to find the stem thick and sinewy like rope, and hung precariously there until a moment later the door to the chamber yielded with a splintery crash. Matthew waited only long enough to be sure the two menacing shadows in the doorway had seen him. Then he made an undignified descent, dropping the last half-dozen feet to the ground and nearly breaking his ankle in doing so. Sure he was being pursued still, he fled through the garden, favoring his injured ankle as he could, and then scrambled through a break in the hedge and limped down a long lane of dark cottages.

The men did not catch him. He thought he must have lost them somewhere in Bankside, somewhere before his arrival at the river. It was after midnight by the time he got back to the Blue Boar.

There he found a message awaiting him. It had come from Abraham at the prison and said simply that Ralph Harbert was dead.

Two whores had been clubbed to death in a Bankside brothel. A quarrel over the reckoning, the authorities would say, if they investigated the deaths at all, if they bothered to trace the two ruffians with cudgels who witnesses said did it.

By dawn the word had got back to Castell through a long chain of intermediaries, few of whom knew the ultimate destination of the word, or for that matter, the identity of anyone in the chain beyond his immediate contact. The jeweler had just finished his breakfast.

"What about the constable?"

"Pyncheon says he fled through the window."

"It was Stock, then?"

"Without a doubt. Pyncheon got that out of one of the drabs he found concealed beneath the bed."

"It's likely he knows all now," Castell murmured, almost to himself.

"All?" queried Starkey, standing just before his employer's chair as though he were preparing to remove the trencher, greasy napkin, and table wastes.

"Well, Stock probably does not know all—but he knows enough. There'll be no stopping him now. His nose is to the scent, that's for sure," said Castell, very melancholy. "Tell me, Starkey, were I to complain of a pebble in my shoe, between the soft inner sole and the flesh of my foot, and were this pebble to become a great vexation, rubbing raw the flesh, cutting it to the quick at last, what course would you recommend?"

"Why, to remove it forthwith," said Starkey, a glint of amusement in his little eyes.

"Then see to it, Starkey, and the quicker the better. Be my surgeon. Do you get my meaning?"

Starkey did.

"And Starkey," Castell continued, "make the constable's death appear by misadventure. I have made inquiries. Evidently he has friends of some stature in London, although I cannot begin to imagine why he should. I would not want to encourage their interest in his reasons for being here."

"No," said Starkey, "we should not want to do that."

Starkey went about his business, while Castell remained at the table, thinking about Starkey and how the man did good work. How fortunate he was to have come upon him, gallows-bait at Tyburn, not half an inch from the rope and damnation until Castell, sensing the man's talent by pure intuition, greased the palms of the jailers and brought him away. Since then, Starkey seemed to have no private life; he was always available, and Castell trusted him as much as the jeweler trusted any man, referring to him—to himself but never to Starkey—as his familiar spirit.

Then he thought about the dead whores. He had never seen the one sister, but Starkey had told him she was a puny thing, with breasts no bigger than apricots. Her sister must have been much the same. Now they were dead, and whatever they had known would be preserved in the silence of the grave. A very discreet place, the grave. A dead man might babble all he liked but as long as he who listened was four or five feet aboveground there was no harm done.

Matthew Stock would be the next to die.

Castell pushed back his chair and rose from the table. A mastiff dog that had lain at his feet slunk over to the corner and began to lick its paws. The animal made loud slurping sounds, and Castell stared at the dog. Presently, as if aware it was the object of its master's attention, the creature's face broke into a silly dog-grin, its tongue extended and pink like an old menstrual rag.

The whores, the constable.

Where would it end?

The question no sooner took its place in his mind before it was joined by an answer. It would end when Castell had what he wanted. It would end when he had evened the score.

SEVEN

"Tom Ingram!" Joan Stock exclaimed as she held the candle aloft to illuminate the unfortunate creature before her in the street.

He was half naked and filthy, top to bottom; he wore a kind of loincloth for modesty's sake, his feet were bare and bleeding, and he smelled strongly as though he had been keeping company with swine.

He didn't say a word at first. He just stood there gaping at her as though he had expected someone else to answer to the pebbles thrown against her upstairs window. But of course, she supposed, Tom wanted her husband.

It was sometime after midnight, and there was a pale full moon hovering listlessly over the town like thin gold dish flung upward and adrift on the wind. Joan was wearing her nightcap and her gown and was still half asleep. She flushed self-consciously at the thought of how she must appear to him. A haggard, forty-year-old woman in her bedclothes.

But there was no time for her little vanities. Perceiving his distress, she ushered him through the dark shop, and then into her large kitchen and to the iron tub in which she bathed herself once a week—and more, if it was a holiday.

She sat him down on a stool, knelt at the hearth, and in a moment the tinder was aglow, and a warm smoky smell filled the room. She lit a lamp and placed it on the table between them, and then she went back upstairs to waken Betty, who shortly thereafter came unsteadily, noisily down the stairs, her hands flat against her sides as though to hold her great girth in, complaining in broken sentences as she descended of the wretchedness of them who weren't allowed to sleep a full night as God had ordained.

When Betty saw the naked man hunched forward on the stool she emitted a little cry of alarm and stared at her mistress disapprovingly.

"It's Tom Ingram, William's brother," Joan hastened to explain. "He's come home at last."

"And brought the barnyards of Essex with him," Betty murmured, but loudly enough for her mistress to hear. Joan reproved her sharply, telling her to fetch water, bucketsful, for the great tub and straightway.

Ruffled by the reproof, Betty went reluctantly into the dark yard, continuing her complaint at a lower volume. She made several round trips, for it was a large tub, and when it was half filled Joan told her that would do and sent her galumphing off to bed again. Meanwhile Joan removed the water she had heated over the fire and poured it into the tub to mix with the cold. Then she tested the water with her finger, declared it suitable for bathing, and ordered Tom to remove what little he wore and wash himself while she went upstairs to fetch some suitable clothes. When she returned, Tom was in the tub, lathering. The noisome odor was gone, replaced by the scent of fresh herbs.

The clothes were Matthew's. They would not fit, she knew, but they would make Tom decent again, not a naked savage. He dried himself with a towel, mumbled thanks, and put on the clothes, a plain cotton shirt and loose-fitting breeches that came down to his calves and gathered loosely at the waist. He appeared to be in a daze, looking about the kitchen as though he had never before seen such furniture: the great stone hearth, the long racks of iron pots and pans gleaming in the somber lamplight, the rows of pewter plate, the trencher table with its benches, the several stools, the samplers with their wisdom adorning the white-washed walls.

She sensed him watching her while she cut the turkey cock into thin slices, laid butter to the bread, and poured the claret into a wooden bowl. The wine she watered, not wishing to see his torpor encouraged with drunkenness, and then she set it all upon the board and bid him eat to his heart's content.

This he did, and with a will, as though he had not eaten in a month. She watched with satisfaction and then noticed for the first time the ghastly wound at the hairline, a pale strip of raw swollen flesh. She wondered how he had come by it, if the blow had done violence to his brains. How relieved she was to find he could speak and was not like Israel Goodwin, who had fallen into a well and been rendered a simpleton as a consequence.

When Tom had finished eating at last he looked up at her gratefully. "God bless you, Mrs. Stock," he said.

"God be thanked you know me," Joan replied. "I feared your wound had made you dumb."

"My wound?" he asked.

"On your forehead."

"Oh," he said, probing the wound with his finger. "It quite put me out of my memory—for a long time, I think. What day is it? What month?"

"July," she said. "The thirtieth day."

He shook his head in amazement.

She asked him how he came by the wound.

"I don't remember," he said.

"What do you remember?"

An expression of puzzlement fell upon his face, then cleared. He remembered. "I woke up, not an hour or so hence, and found myself bedded in filthy straw. I was in a wretched hovel. An old woman and her man snored in a corner. I didn't know where I was or how I came to be there. I wore no clothes but a rag about my private parts, felt my chin to find it well beyond the beginnings of a beard, thought myself on the verge of death for want of a full stomach. My mouth was dry as dust. I searched about for my things, careful not to waken the old folks. I didn't know who they were but thought they might cry out to someone who'd prevent me from leaving. I couldn't find anything—no shirt or hose to cover my nakedness. The hovel had not a stool to sit upon, nothing but a dirt floor, and a solitary window covered with an old rag let in just enough moonlight for me to keep from stumbling over myself. Then I crept out into the night and looked about the hovel for most of an hour before heading off into the woods. Presently I came to Thompson's Oak. I had climbed to the top of it as a boy—I and William. Then things began coming back to me. I knew where I was—not three miles from Chelmsford, and it came to me of a sudden where I should be bound."

"To your brother's house," she said.

"To yours," Tom said. "My business is with the constable."

"Well, he's gone to London."

The boy's face fell. "To London!" he exclaimed. "That's a piece of ill luck."

"He went seeking you," she explained.

"I?"

"When you did not return, nor could be found in London. Your brother would have gone himself but we thought my husband could be better spared. Besides he knew the city, as William didn't."

"How did you know I left the jeweler's?"

"Mr. Castell wrote to William. William showed his letter to us."

"What did Castell say—that I had filched some ring or bracelet?"

"No, only that you had broken indentures and fled. He suggested you may have run away to sea."

"Run away, indeed!" he said, his eyes flashing with indignation. "Well may a wise man hightail it from the Devil and be called a runaway."

"God's body!" she exclaimed wonderingly. "Then your master did abuse you."

"Yes, he abused me, and a good many others as well. The man is up to his elbows in vice and worse, were the truth racked out of him, and as it yet may be if your husband will aid me."

"Trust him to do so," Joan replied earnestly. Then she urged him to tell his story, as much as he could remember, and he proceeded, beginning with his first employment at the jeweler's, then his discovery of his employer's wrongdoing—about which he first spoke very vaguely—and then about the two men in the woods and the merciless cudgel that had come near braining him.

She listened, fascinated, but between his beating in the woods and his awakening a few hours earlier he could recall nothing.

"They must have taken care of you—the old folks," Joan ventured.

Tom shrugged. "Maybe they found me as I found myself—

105

filthy naked. Or maybe they made me so for what a shirt of good linen, a fair pair of hose, and a patched jerkin would bring at market. By the looks of his yard, the old man was a wood gatherer. Poor as a widow's wen, I'd say, not a chicken nor dog to call his own. It was no trouble escaping them—they snored on most discordantly. I won't be missed for another hour at least."

"You've been much in the sun," she said.

"Probably toting wood for the old man," Tom said bitterly. "It's not likely they would have fed me for charity's sake."

Joan asked him to tell her more about his employer. "This conversation you overhead. Its purpose, you say, was to blackmail the gentleman with some amorous discourse found in his purse."

"Stolen from his purse," Tom corrected her.

"Indeed, as you say. Letters, memoranda, notebooks, and the like. But how would he know which purse to pick? What if he were to find only money?"

"He knows," Tom replied confidently. "I reckon he first gets wind of some naughtiness from his gossips, then sets his toadies to harvest until he reaps just the right sort of confirmation. The day I interrupted his labors, Castell sat himself behind a grillwork, squat like a heathen idol, whispering through a long tube so as to distort his voice. The shop had been closed an hour earlier and all the servants and apprentices sent to bed. Castell thought he had the place to himself."

"How came you to be there?"

"Marry, I had spent the day running my legs off for him, delivering goods and receiving payment. From one gentleman I had ten pounds sterling, and having come upon the donor late in the day and fearing to keep such a sum overnight, I thought I would secrete it in one of the cabinets."

"The cabinets were not all locked?"

"Not all. I knew a hiding place. I thought I could retrieve the money the next day."

"What did you do when you returned to find the shop locked up for the night?"

"I knew another entrance. I doubt that Castell himself knows of it. It was shown to me by my friend Ralph—some loose stonework around the foundation which a slender man can crawl through and from thence beneath the building and up by a trapdoor in one of the closets. This journey I made, the rats notwithstanding, had concealed the ten pounds, and was about to leave when I heard voices in the rear of the shop where there are several empty rooms. At first I thought to ignore the voices, but then my curiosity had the best of me. I tiptoed close, found a door ajar by an inch, and peered in.

"There was Castell, behind the screen as I have said, his back to me. Beyond was someone, a gentleman, well dressed in black silk stockings and looking very dumpish, I warrant you. I listened for the gist of the talk, half guilty at putting my ear where it didn't belong."

"That's when you heard all of the blackmail."

"I heard enough. When the gentleman was led out, I betook myself straightway from the shop, waiting in the shadows to see who might emerge. Anon comes this gentleman, blindfolded now as in a child's game, led by John Starkey, one of Castell's toadies. Off the two go down the alley, Starkey in the lead. The alley's pestilent dead after dark, being too narrow to receive coaches or carts and too dangerous for a man without twenty stout fellows to second his action, but I followed them to see the outcome."

"Which was?" Joan asked intently, now completely enthralled in his story.

"They came presently to the back parts of a warehouse, in a neighboring street. Starkey had led the poor gentleman in circles— to make him think he had traveled a great distance. Then Starkey made off like a rabbit, leaving the poor gentleman standing there in the alley, his legs astraddle a puddle of horse piss, calling out, first in a thin piping girl's voice to him who had deserted him, but now to no avail for he was as solitary as the nose upon your face. Soon he cries out more boldly, begins to curse, finally comes upon his manhood and rips the blindfold from his eyes. Then you should have heard the man! His words before were but a maid's oaths. Now came the curses in torrents. He stamped upon the ground and reached for his sword, only to find it gone. More curses followed, then silence."

"Poor man. How did he fare thereafter?" Joan asked sympathetically, although she had been amused, too, by the colorful manner of Tom's narration.

"Marry, having no dog to kick, servant to beat, nor curses yet in his store, he stomped homeward straightway to nurse his much-abused pride."

"How was it you did not go up to him?"

"Curiosity again, I think. I wanted to see what would happen next. Also I feared he might know me again when he saw me and tie me in somewhat with my master's plot. I thought his wrath might fall upon me were I to have removed his blindfold."

"Doubtless it would have," murmured Joan, reflecting now on the dangers of the city and beginning to worry about Matthew.

"Wonder of wonders, two days thereafter I see my master conversing with this same unfortunate gentleman of whom I spoke, comes this very John Starkey whilst I am polishing some of the plate and inquires would I like to make something a little extra to bloat my purse. Bloat my purse, say I? Well may you ask, for my purse is a scrawny one and much in want of nourishment. Good, says Starkey. Then he leads me into one of the back rooms very privately and begins to praise my industry, my wit, my prospects—all very fulsomely. Indeed, he would have continued on to praise my points and garters had not the hour prevented him. All these, says he, my master has observed. Castell, he says, has been eager to advance my fortunes, but discreetly so as not to kindle the jealousy of the other apprentices."

"What did he want you to do?"

"Well may you ask," Tom replied ironically. "For it was to my task that all his compliments were an idle preface. He wanted me to turn cutpurse for the master."

"He said as much?" Joan exclaimed.

"Not in those words, of course. I abbreviate them for the sake of time and honesty, for such was their sum. Starkey put it thus: The jeweler's trade depends, said he, on a knowledge of the market, the market being the well-to-do, those with money in their pockets and lust, vanity, and folly in their hearts. By this he meant, I suppose, the comings and goings of the court and the circumstances of certain great ones in the city and so forth. Presently he made it very clear in his knavish way that intelligence was got by a kind of judicious pilferage of purses."

"Did he explain what Master Castell did with the intelligence so garnered?"

"He was very woolly about that. He assured me all this went on with his master's blessing, that certain purses were prized above others, and that he, his master's agent in this side of the business, should direct my labors. First, however, I must learn the trade, which amounted to understanding just how to create a distraction in the street, to slip my hand most privily in and out, and where about my person to conceal the harvest."

"So you were to be put to school. What did you say to this Starkey?"

"To go to the Devil, I told him," Tom Ingram replied with a scowl. "My words he must have reported to Castell within the hour for afterward I had many frowns from the both of them. I had the message then. Though I am honest, yet I am no fool. That night I packed my belongings and was off to Chelmsford."

"To see my husband."

"I thought he could help me. Castell's undertaking is no simple thievery."

"How so?"

Thomas Ingram hesitated before responding, long enough to make Joan wonder if his memory were slipping again, but then he said solemnly, "Castell's schemes touch upon matters of the Queen."

"Her Majesty!" Joan exclaimed.

Tom Ingram nodded and bent forward conspiratorially in the lamplight. "This gentleman who came to my master's was in exchange for some indiscreet letter to provide Castell with certain agenda of the Queen, where she might be in such and such an hour, who in attendance, who regularly admitted to her person, and so forth."

"But why should the jeweler be concerned with such matters?" she asked.

Tom shrugged. "I don't know—only that it's very unlikely they are any of his business and he risks his life and fortune to know them."

"Why didn't you go seek out the authorities in London? It would have saved you a journey and undoubtedly sped up the courses of the law."

"I didn't know whom I could trust," Tom said. "Castell has many friends. Besides, it would have been easy for him to deny everything, since I had no more evidence than a good memory and an honest nose for infamy. Well might he have charged me for the crime and then who would prefer my story—the story of an apprentice—to his? I would have ended my days in Newgate or been split up the middle by one of his ruffians."

"Would the jeweler go so far?"

109

"Has he not tried to kill me?" Tom protested, pointing to his wound as evidence.

She mulled over this story while Tom finished his meat, believing it all and fearing now very much for her husband. She knew Matthew was too good-hearted to see the other side of a politic smile, and if Tom's description of his employer was accurate, this Castell could assume a pleasing shape.

Somewhere in the neighborhood a cock crowed. It was dawning.

"I must go," he said, wiping his mouth and gulping the last of the claret.

"To your brother's?"

"To London again, after the constable."

"Very foolish," she cried with alarm, "given the danger to you there. Castell thinks you're dead and rotting. You're safe from him now and will remain so if you stay out of his way."

"But I can't let Castell continue his—"

It was a firm protest, but Joan interrupted, "No, *we* cannot let him do so." She laid her hand on his and looked at him with maternal authority. "Be ruled by me. I'll go myself and convey to Matthew all that you have said. I will not be at risk—Castell does not know me. In the meanwhile, you go to your brother's farm and keep your presence there confined to William, Elizabeth, and the few servants. Stay out of Chelmsford, for even here someone may carry to London the word that you live still."

Tom considered this advice, raised several more objections, but could not sustain them in face of Joan's determination. Finally, he conceded. He would go to his brother's, though it vexed him sorely to have to play the woman's part when there was a man's work to be done.

"Woman's part!" Joan cried with mock ferocity, for now that she had her will she was in good humor. "See you then how a woman does a man's work, for if I am not gone for London by midmorning you may have my husband's shop lock, stock, and barrel."

"Agreed," Tom replied, grinning now for the first time since he had appeared outside her window. He leaned toward her so that the wound in his forehead gaped in the lamplight like a second mouth, and whispered urgently, "You tell your husband, Mistress Stock, to beware of the Basilisk."

"The Basilisk, you say?"

"A fabulous beast that has set his foot in London."

She looked at the boy uncertainly.

"I'm not mad," he explained, seeming to perceive how his words had confused her. "I heard Castell speak of someone *named* Basilisk. It's a password at least, a person very probably, and if so, I warrant you this same Basilisk is Castell's master."

"Where might Matthew find this Basilisk?"

Tom shook his head. "I don't know. I wish I could tell you more."

"Well, never fear," she said, rising from her stool and gathering his empty cup and plate. "An ounce of mirth is better than a pound of sorrow and, yes, makes a good weight, too. Here's a goodly day before us with you home safe again. Go to William's and wait word from me. I will find Matthew and warn him of Castell's treachery and his danger to the state. My husband knows Sir Robert Cecil, the Queen's Principal Secretary. He'll be quick enough to take notice of the jeweler."

"I'll go, with all my heart," Tom said, smiling again.

Joan bolted her door behind him and hurried up the stairs. The whole house was awake now, and within the half-hour the men would be at the looms and the shop a beehive of industry. She knew she must take time by the forelock. She called to Betty to prepare her things for the journey. It would take the day to travel the thirty or so miles to London and she must dress herself and repair her face from the spoilage of the night. Every minute lost increased her husband's danger.

Matthew awoke from sleep fully intent on seeing Cecil first thing that morning. And he would have done so had he not found a second message, stuck with a glob of pitch to the door of his chamber and scrawled on cheap paper as though the writer could not spare more than a half minute to the writing of it. It said that if Matthew wanted to converse with Tom Ingram he might do so by showing his face at Paul's Cross, at the foot of the fountain there, at nine o'clock.

Matthew didn't know what to do. After his escape of the previous night, he knew it was well past time to invoke the aid of his powerful friend Cecil, now that the danger to himself was clear and that to the state sufficiently implied, at least by hearsay. But then, too, he hated to lose the chance of seeing Tom Ingram, of discovering Castell's treachery first hand. And so by nine o'clock he was standing at the appointed place in a drizzling rain. He waited for an hour. Finally he noticed a baldheaded man dodging puddles in the yard to come to where Matthew stood.

"You are Matthew Stock of Chelmsford?" asked the man.

Matthew said that he was and the man introduced himself as John Starkey.

"I expected Tom Ingram," said Matthew.

"Indeed," replied Starkey. "You shall have him, too, but not here. It's much too dangerous. Come, let us seek a roof whilst we talk."

Matthew thought this was a good idea, and although he was curious as to just who this fellow was, he felt sure that question could wait. He had seen an alehouse opposite them not twenty paces, and hither they went without further ado, found themselves a bench, and ordered ale. The Morning Star, as the house was called, was crowded and noisy; the proprietor was running around in great excitement, calling to his assistants in a strident, shrewish voice. He was obviously delighted by the rain. It had caused his house to fill.

"You're a friend of Thomas Ingram?" Matthew said, raising his voice above the din.

"Oh, indeed, sir, a very good friend," replied Starkey, without amplifying on their relationship. Starkey took in the room with an interested gaze. "He wants to see you," he said without looking at Matthew.

"And I want very much to see him."

"Good, then. It's settled."

Starkey finished his ale in a long swig. Matthew was unsure as to what had been settled.

"Where is Thomas?" he asked.

"He's in a safe place, sir. Oh, yes, a very safe place."

"You will take me to him?"

"Of course. We'll go presently. See, now, through the window, the rain is ceasing."

"Is he near here?"

"No, I'll take you by boat to where he is."

"By boat!"

Starkey laughed. "It will be all the quicker and I'm sure you'll agree that haste is in the interest of both of us."

Matthew paid for them both and then followed Starkey out into the street. It had been a typical summer storm: a furious downpour one moment, a placid drizzle the next. The paving stones were shiny and many pedestrians had returned to the streets. Starkey walked slightly ahead of Matthew, briskly, maintaining a steady stream of discourse concerning the local antiquities, a subject on which he was apparently an expert. He could tell during whose reign such a building was constructed, give a name to this church or that inn, identify the present proprietors of this place of business or that. The man's energy seemed as inexhaustible as his discourse. Matthew could hardly keep up and when they at least reached the river Matthew was breathless, but Starkey seemed fit and eager to continue on what he assured Matthew was the last leg of their journey.

"There now, not more than a middling time from the Morning Star to here, just as I said."

Matthew looked out over the broad expanse of river. It was somber and peaceful. There were boats upon it of various sizes—barge, lighters, the ubiquitous wherries carrying passengers to this place and that, and there was a tilt boat, an elegant craft with a long canopy running its length and uniformed men with halberds standing at attention on its deck. The boat was towed by a smaller craft manned by a half-dozen oarsmen who were straining at their work. The tilt boat was obviously heavy and the river ran against them.

"I have a wherry at the foot of the stairs," Starkey said proudly when they had come to Paul's wharf. He pointed down to the riverbank where a stone landing jutted from the shore into the stream. "She's a small craft but very tight."

Smiling, Starkey scanned the river. The tide was right, he said, and then he asked if Matthew was a sailor and Matthew replied that indeed he was not, that he had been upon the water only a few times before in his life and had not thought much of the experience.

"Brace up, man," cried his guide cheerily. "You'll be reunited with your friend in no time at all."

"In God's name, where is this place you're taking me to?" Matthew asked, casting a cold eye on the file of skiffs and wherries tied up at the foot of the stairs.

"Downriver, just beyond Wapping," Starkey replied, beckoning Matthew to follow as he clambered down the wet stones.

Matthew knew Wapping. It was some distance from the Tower, down a long street with alleys of poor tenements and cottages occupied mostly by sailors and victuallers.

Matthew hurried to catch up with his guide, who had already

arrived at the wharf's end and was presently staring down into the river below. It was still drizzling. Some boatmen were huddled under a tattered canvas at the end of the wharf cooking their dinner over an open fire. Matthew could smell the smoke and their dinner, trout or sturgeon, fresh from the Thames. The men looked at him curiously as he walked past them.

Below, crowded among a good many other small boats, was Starkey's wherry. Matthew looked at it doubtfully. Pointed at each end, the length of two men, maybe three, it was much in need of paint. Starkey told him to board; Matthew descended the ladder and stepped cautiously in, startled by the little boat's giving beneath his feet, the lateral slipping. On water now, not on land. He sat down with a thud amidships. Starkey, watching from above, laughed good-humoredly. He untied the line and cast it into the boat, then descended the ladder, told Matthew to move to the stern, and took the place amidships Matthew had occupied. He took an oar and used it to shove the bow of the boat into the stream, then he picked up the other and began to row with long even strokes, his smile gone, replaced with an expression of grim determination.

Matthew watched the City glide past, solemn and gray in the drizzle. There went Bracken's wharf, there the three cranes, then ahead, Stilliards. On the south bank of the river he could see the Liberty of the Clink, the theaters, and the steeple of St. Mary Overie's Dock. Soon they were in midchannel and Starkey ceased rowing, letting the oars trail in the water like broken limbs. The current carried them now. Matthew stared down into the water. Its surface was pitted by rain and its depths further obscured by the overcast sky, yet occasionally he glimpsed the fugitive shadows of fish, debris, and once the remains of a dog, bloated and ghastly, floating along beside the boat, just beneath the surface.

Ahead was London Bridge. It was one of the sights of the City— a little city in itself with its many-storied, timbered houses, stretching across the river like a dam on a millpond. The arches of squared stone and the narrow passages between permitted the coming and going of only the smallest craft. Matthew had crossed the bridge once upon foot, but he had never seen it from this angle before, and he made a note to himself to tell Joan of it as soon as he was home again.

"We'll be shooting the bridge betimes," announced Starkey, who had been silent all this while and whose presence in the wherry Matthew had nearly forgotten in his fascination with the bridge.

"Shooting the bridge?"

"Passing beneath her," explained Starkey.

Matthew had not thought about that. But of course they would have to go beneath the bridge. He looked ahead at the great piers and the starlings, the pedestals upon which they stood.

"Is there no danger?" Matthew asked uncertainly.

"None to one who knows the river."

Starkey wiped his forehead, raised the oars, and began to maneuver the boat toward one of the arches. Matthew noticed theirs was the only craft moving toward the bridge. The others were either standing idly in the water or rowing upstream. "By the way, Master Stock, can you swim?"

"I? No, not a whit," responded Matthew, looking uncertainly over Starkey's shoulder toward the bridge. They were so close now that he could see the faces of pedestrians, make out the signs of the shops, perceive the gruesome outlines of the heads of malefactors stuck upon spikes above the gates as a warning to others so inclined.

"Marry, a man must learn many a skill in his life," Starkey commented philosophically, drawing a sleeve across his sweaty face, rowing with longer strokes, so that the wherry moved even faster than the current.

Matthew heard the sound of churning water ahead, not from the narrow passage between the starlings but from somewhere beyond. He looked up at the approaching bridge. He saw faces peering down at the river at him and Starkey in their boat. Arms waved, voices called, a tone of warning without substance. What did they want? What was the danger? Matthew looked at Starkey for an explanation, but the man's concentration was complete; he rowed rhythmically, staring at his shoes as though the bridge were not there at all, as though he didn't hear the roar of turbulent water at his back.

"Is it safe?" Matthew shouted, alarmed, knowing that it wasn't, that it couldn't be.

"Some of us shall be, pray God," Starkey replied through clenched teeth, breathing heavily, not breaking his rhythm.

Then the bridge was upon them, over them, and suddenly Starkey was gone, gone into the water without a word or warning, swimming for safety. Matthew watched dumbfounded as the pilotless wherry swept between the starlings, and he saw the danger, why theirs had been the only craft shooting the bridge. It was a controversy of currents, the river and the sea—the tide rising to counter the energy of the Thames, just where the great river emptied into the Pool.

Terrified, Matthew gripped the gunwales as the bow of the wherry smashed against the starling and the stern swung violently forward. For a moment the little boat thwarted the stream in bold defiance, then suddenly it capsized, hurling Matthew into the foamy turbulence. Before he knew it he was under the water, thrashing about helplessly in the powerful current, the river twisting and turning him at its will. His lungs bursting, he reached above him, pushed upward against the burden of his clothing, his heavy body, and then, miraculously to him, he broke through to the surface, his head striking something hard and foreign to this watery element. He grasped for the thing, caught it, clutched it to him, knew almost without looking what it would be, the wherry or what remained of it, a fragment of wood, splintery, but a solid plank. The plank saved him. He did not go under again; he held on, gasping for air, knowing that he had come as near to death as ever he had, deafened by the roar and half blinded by spray, seeing once and once only the bridge looming above him, but no faces concerned for his fate, no hands reached out to save.

He held onto the plank until he thought his hands had grown fast to the wood. He was too weak to cry out; he knew it be futile anyway. No one would hear. Lost in the churning, he would not be discerned from the bridge, for the tidal conflict had drawn all manner of debris into it. His head, bobbing in the foam, would be one object among many.

How long was it before the violence waned, before the power of the river overcame that of the sea and he and his plank began to move slowly into the Pool? He could not say whether his terror caused time to collapse or expand, but it seemed to him hours since he had exchanged the relative security of the boat for the watery grave from which he now struggled to resurrect himself. When he looked at the bridge again it was past hailing. He and the plank were moving, downstream again. The tide had turned, and it was raining harder; the world had turned to water, the waters above and the waters below were converging, he thought, floating, floating.

Downriver the stately, tall-masted ships stood like permanent fixtures. He could see smaller craft but they were beyond hailing, too. He continued to drift, past the Tower, past the ships, noticing after a while that the south bank of the river seemed nearer than before. He began to kick his feet to propel himself in that direction. Success helped him find new strength, and within a few minutes he felt his shoe touch the bottom, felt the long stands of river weed caressing his legs.

It stopped raining. The clouds passed to reveal generous patches of blue sky. The sun shone on the water, on the ships standing in midriver, and on Matthew Stock's salvation. He cast the plank aside and began to walk, the water at waist level. Ahead between him and the bank a half-dozen boys were standing about knee deep in the water throwing stones at a flock of swans. The birds fluttered their wings and chided their attackers with their frantic bird voices, moving quickly out of range. Ragamuffins by their tattered clothing and dirty faces, the boys took no notice of Matthew, a half-drowned man wading ashore. They were still throwing stones even though the swans were long past. One of the boys wore only a shirt; below he was naked. He stood ankle deep in the river on thin, white legs, urinating in a steady yellow stream and watching Matthew out of the corner of his eye.

Matthew passed him by, breathing heavily, struggling up the slippery embankment and then collapsing, never in his life so utterly weary. For a long time he lay there like a dead man, face down in a clump of sweet-smelling grass. He was grateful to be alive, grateful to be free from John Starkey who had tried to kill him.

EIGHT_____

By suppertime Joan had arrived in London and had found her way to the Blue Boar. When the innkeeper informed her that he had not seen her husband since early morning, she went up to his chamber apprehensively, inspected the handful of personal articles he had left there, and sat down to wait.

There was nothing else to do. She felt idle and useless.

The evening air was mild and fresh after the morning's rain. She opened the window and looked down at the street. Even at this hour it was a fast-moving stream, a feverish scramble in the failing light—folk of all conditions rushing homeward, concluding the day's business, anticipating the night's rest, labors, merriment, or mischief. In Chelmsford, life was a leisurely amble of generous days. London, however, was a kind of mad riot of activity, coming and going, getting and spending in a fury as though it were always the eleventh hour, the last minute.

She felt a surge of homesickness, thought of her husband.

Now it was quite dark, the passersby were ghostly figures illuminated by torches; she could hear their voices, vague and diminutive in the gloom. She was far removed from them, looking from her window, dumpish.

Matthew?

The black pall of melancholy overwhelmed her, and she fell into a reverie in which she saw her husband, his face pale and his hands cold and limp and lifeless.

Death by water.

The image confused her sense of place. She looked about her; yes, it was still where her husband had lain. His impression on the bed, his wallet with his second-best suit, pushed beneath. But then, willful thing that it was, the vision recurred. There was a great expanse of gray water, a horrid stagnant smell, and Matthew floating just below the surface, his face upward toward her, dreadfully stark.

He had drowned. She knew it, although she could not explain how, and the grief engulfed her suddenly and she began to weep slow hot tears. She was not sure she could go on without him.

She returned to the bed and, without undressing, lay down upon it. She did not bother to light a candle or lamp. She lay brooding in the darkness, listening, feeling her thoughts as though they were tangible things she could take from her purse and put back again, show to Matthew, or secrete in her bosom.

She smelled the herb-scented pillow, the country freshness of the rushes on the floor, the faint acrid odor of the chamberpot in the corner and she began to weep again. The tears ran down her cheeks, down the sides of her face.

Matthew drowned.

She could not rid herself of the impression.

In time she fell asleep and dreamed. Strangely, she did not dream of her husband, but of the odd serpentlike creature of which Tom Ingram had spoken. She was wandering through woods. The trees and bushes seemed familiar to her. A rain had fallen earlier, for the leaves glistened with moisture and she could smell the strong earthy odor of growing things. It was very pleasant where she walked. She looked up and saw that the branches of the trees were full of birds of all kinds, singing joyously. Joan longed to join them in the air, and no sooner experienced the desire but found herself floating upward. Floating, floating, floating. She felt wonderfully light and contented.

She drew near the branch on which the birds sat.

But then suddenly they ceased singing. They turned their little heads and looked at her oddly with their pinched faces and little round black eyes.

119

Then, at once, there was a flurry of wings, screams of alarm. The wings beat furiously about her head. She raised her hands to protect her face and eyes. Wings, white wings, everywhere she looked. "Don't . . . don't," she heard herself cry in a strange voice not her own.

When as suddenly it grew quiet, she looked around her to find the birds gone and she was hanging in the air without support. The sense of floating which had so delighted her earlier now terrified her. She reached out to grasp at the limb, pulled herself over to it, and more secure now, stared down at the ground. She wondered what had happened to the birds. A deathly silence had fallen over the woods.

Presently she had the feeling that she was not alone. Someone or something watched her. In time she heard the crackle of twigs. She could see in the distance something moving through the trees; it was all misty to her now, the wood. She couldn't see clearly and yet she needed to see, for she sensed powerfully danger.

Trembling, she looked around her. The limb to which she clung was a great distance from the one above it. She could go no higher, and the ground was too far below her. There was an unpleasant smell too, something like an animal's. Was it the thing in the wood or her own fear?

Then through the mist she saw it—not its shape, its visage, but its eye, large, round, glaring at her. The Basilisk. She was seized by a paralysis of dread.

She might have screamed. She wasn't sure. Suddenly she was sitting upright in the bed in the room and her gown was soaked with sweat and her hands were shaking uncontrollably.

That she had been dreaming made no difference to her. Her presentiment of Matthew's death and this bizarre dream had unsettled her completely and now made sleep impossible. She got out of bed and walked toward the door and listened. She heard footfalls, a heavy, weary tread, someone mounting the stairs, stopping outside her door.

Her heart was all aflutter from the dream, the abrupt awakening. The fear that someone was approaching *her* door sent her blood racing at even a faster pace.

The door rattled, and she recoiled in fear.

"Who's there?" she called in a thin frightened voice.

"Joan?"

"Who is it?"

"It's your husband. Pray let me in."

Quickly she pulled the bolt and a second later Matthew was in her arms, smothering her with kisses. They held each other for a long time, like young lovers enjoying a first embrace.

She fastened the door behind him and hastened to light a candle. In a moment it illuminated the chamber and her husband, who was pale and damply bedraggled.

He walked over to the bed and collapsed upon it.

"In God's name, what happened to you?" she exclaimed, holding the candle aloft so that she could inspect him for injuries. "Are you hurt?"

"In pride for the most part," he muttered. "I was near an inch to drowning this day."

Death by water. She shuddered at the recollection. So her terrible vision had some substance after all. She stared at him. He was lying there massaging his left foot. Obviously he had walked a great distance, and just as obviously, this was an exhausted man, no ghost come to pay a final visit.

When he had recovered some of his strength he told her of his near-drowning, about Starkey, and about his other experiences since he had last seen her. "I walked back," he said. "I lost my purse in the river and had nothing left about me but my good name, which will buy very little here."

"It was a great distance, then?" she inquired.

"Nay, not so much as I might not have walked in two hours, but I remained concealed by the river until dark, and then did not dare enter the inn until the house was in bed. Castell and his ruffians think me dead. May they continue to think so."

"As well they might, after the wherry sank," she said with a mixture of pity and indignation. "This Starkey, then, did not see you afloat upon the plank?"

"I think not. After he scrambled ashore I doubt he would have remained about the bridge to have onlookers inquire into the incident."

"You took a great chance returning to the inn."

"I had no other course," Matthew said, inviting her to sit by him upon the bed. "I had no money and no clothes, was a marked man should I show my face in any public place, and my feet would not carry me home again, not to Chelmsford."

Then she told him her own news. "Thomas Ingram turned up outside my window this morning early."

"Tom Ingram alive, then!" Matthew exclaimed. "Heaven be thanked!"

"You may well thank heaven," she said, "for if he say true, this Gervase Castell is up to more mischief than you thought. He's a blackmailer and, it would seem, a traitor to boot."

She provided a full version of Tom Ingram's story, upon hearing which Matthew sighed heavily; he sank back onto the bed. "This is even as Mary Skelton said. I must go to Sir Robert at once."

"Rest. Now, at least," she said. "When you have recovered your strength we will lay our plans."

"I think I'm too weary to sleep," he said. He was slowly removing his wrinkled, soggy clothes.

"My poor dear heart." She bent down to kiss him on the cheek. She undressed, too, and soon got into bed beside him. He put his arm around her and buried his face in her hair.

"I'm so glad you've come," he murmured drowsily.

"You could not have kept me at home once I knew what danger you courted, Matthew. Matthew?"

But he was already asleep. His chest was rising and falling rhythmically. She blew out the candle and lay thanking all the saints for her husband's delivery, until she heard the chimes of midnight. One, two, three, she counted them. She did not make it to twelve before she herself drifted away.

When they awoke, their room was already suffused with the soft yellow glow of morning. They could hear footsteps and voices in the passage without their door. Matthew's second comment of the new day—the first having been a greeting to his wife—was a declaration of the state of his stomach. It was powerfully empty, he said. He had not eaten since yesterday's breakfast and was less a man by a good ten pounds or more.

"You cannot go down to breakfast," she said.

"No," he agreed, looking very pitiful with his unshaven cheeks.

"I'll have something brought up. I'll order enough for us both."

Within the hour, a maid had brought a rasher of bacon, a half-loaf of bread, and some good quality wine to wash it all down with. Matthew remained concealed beneath the covers, he and his wife having agreed in the meantime that it was best if no one at the inn knew of his return.

"First we'll eat, then we'll talk," she announced decisively.

Matthew ate the bulk of the food; the rest they secured for later in the day.

"Here's where we stand," she said, examining her face in the tiny hand mirror Matthew had given her upon her last birthday. "It's plain you are a marked man. If Castell or his toads discover Starkey has bungled his work they will lose no time in arranging another misadventure."

"Very likely—if not certain," Matthew agreed.

"Then you must stay hidden," she said.

"But where? I can't remain in the room."

"Indeed you cannot," she said. She put her mirror in her bag and looked him up and down as though the answer to their dilemma were to be written upon his forehead, breast, or legs. "Were you not so plump, husband, we could fit you out in my second gown and send you forth as a woman."

"God's body!" Matthew exclaimed. "You will send me forth as my own corpse before I'll don a woman's garb."

"Tut, tut, tut," she chided. "This is serious business, Matthew. There's no time for your japing now."

"I do not jape, wife," Matthew said sternly.

She gave him another searching look, sighed, then smiled with satisfaction.

"Be it as you will," she said, her mouth now having that peculiar expression it had when she had made up her mind about something. "You shall retain your precious manhood and escape the Blue Boar at the same time."

She collected the cup, plate, and bowl that remained of their breakfast and put them on the tray. "I have a new calling for you, husband, if you're up to it."

"You will put me to service?" Matthew inquired, guessing her intent.

"I will," she said with determination.

Within a half-hour she had her husband dressed out in shirt and breeches, had combed his thick black hair forward so that it came near to covering his eyes, and tied about his waist the remains of her smock so that it very much appeared an apron.

"But they know me below," Matthew protested, futilely.

"Indeed, the innkeeper does, and his daughter, and one or two else, and perhaps a Chelmsford merchant or tradesman lying here presently. But if you move quickly none will see you leave, and they that do will not look twice at a portly serving man bearing the remains of breakfast below to the kitchen. Look you now, here's money for your pocket. Find lodging elsewhere—the Bell on the Strand. Assume a false name—say of our neighbor, Miles Merryweather. I'll have your luggage sent after you and depart myself, telling first the innkeeper that I despair of your return and have gone back to Chelmsford to bewail the loss of a good husband. Should one of Castell's men come inquiring of you, the innkeeper may convey to him so much of this story that will confirm your death and put the villain at his ease, whilst we—"

"Whilst we do what?" Matthew wanted to know.

"Whilst we—"

She hesitated, unsure herself. Then she remembered Cecil. "Whilst you call upon Sir Robert," she continued, confidently now. "Tell him every whit. Including what Tom Ingram conveyed to me."

Matthew thought about this. Joan was right. Cecil was the next step. Treason was afoot and who knew its stride? And who could stop its advance but Cecil? But what did Matthew really *know*, know for himself? His ignorance oppressed him. He said, "It's a poor little tale I have to tell—all second- and third-hand save Starkey's mischief at the river and Starkey will say that was an accident."

"An accident," she murmured in disgust. But she realized her husband was right. What did they *know*?

They sat on the bed, hunched over and thoughtful. Joan rubbed her forehead, trying to clear away the mist of her ignorance.

"It's proper evidence that we lack."

"Evidence," returned Matthew. "And it will not be easy to find. Castell's no fool. His courses are subtle and treacherous. Had Tom not stumbled on the plot by mere chance it would be known only to the jeweler."

"And to his victims," Joan added.

"Yes, to his victims."

"They know well enough his treachery," Joan said, thinking harder, making headway against the mist.

"Yes," said Matthew, "it's a tight little circle."

"A what?"

"A tight little circle," Matthew repeated, not looking at her. He was staring out the window. The morning sky was flat blue and clear.

The figure of speech surprised her. Her husband was ordinarily not of a poetic turn. But how apt it was. A tight little circle. The blackmailer and his victims. The circle ever widening as the jeweler's victims increased in number, but it remained tight, impenetrable. Only Thomas Ingram had glimpsed its workings, and he didn't even know the identity of the victim. Castell would deny everything, the victim would deny everything. Blackmail was the most private of crimes. The victim had as much reason as the blackmailer to want the circle kept intact, for he had much to lose.

If only there was a victim who had nothing to lose—one who might come right out and say, this thing the jeweler *tried* to do, this thing the jeweler wanted in exchange for his silence.

How to penetrate the cirlce? Find the right victim?

And then it came to her, full-blown in an instant, sprung from her forehead all nimble and ready. What was needed was a new victim—one who had nothing to lose although Castell thought he did. Someone Castell would risk everything to enclose in the circle. And someone whose testimony would be unimpeachable.

To Joan the idea seemed absolutely perfect.

Turning to face him, she grasped Matthew's hands and pressed them eagerly, her heart fluttering with excitement. "Look, the jeweler doesn't know *me*."

"So?" Matthew looked at his wife guardedly. Why was she smiling at him that way, the way she did when she was on the verge of triumphing over his better judgment? "Now wait—"

"He doesn't know that I am your wife."

"I'll not have you mixed in this. Castell is dangerous."

"Yes, all the more reason for us to act speedily."

"Why us? Now it's the business of Cecil and the Council."

"But you agreed we needed evidence," she protested.

"I said so, but let Sir Robert secure it."

She stared at him as though he had just said a foolish thing. "We—you and I—can secure the evidence."

He shook his head sadly.

"Look," she pressed, "your life remains in danger. What, do you think to remain Miles Merryweather? Our good friend will want his name back. And you, husband, will want to show your face in London again without fear of Castell or Starkey or whatever other devil he keeps about him."

"But Cecil, the Council—"

"No, Matthew," she said firmly. "You yourself have said it. We *know* very little, but only we can find out much more and quickly, knowing what little we do."

"No," he said firmly, crossing his arms, asserting his maleness. But she could be firm too. "Matthew."

"No."

"I have a plan," she said. "If you will bear the hearing of it."

"No."

"You will not even listen! What, will it hurt you to listen?"

Matthew had to agree that it would not hurt for him to listen, but he feared to listen. Already he felt himself losing ground, the prospect of safety slipping away as Starkey's boat had slipped away from the safety of the shore. Yet a terrible curiosity drew him on.

"I will hear it," he said at length.

Matthew listened skeptically while Joan outlined her plan. She spoke with quiet confidence, waving aside his interruptions and objections. The plan was bold and risky, but he marveled at her ingenuity and conceded at last that the device might work after all. But he forced her to make concessions, too. She was to involve herself in no unnecessary danger, and he was to inform Sir Robert Cecil of their stratagem as quickly as possible.

They agreed that Matthew should go quickly to the Bell, from thence to Cecil, and that they should meet at evening. They took leave of each other warmly and then Matthew, groomed and aproned, hoisted the tray to his shoulder, made a wry face at Joan, and vanished into the passageway.

Since it was nearly eight of the morning and most of the inn's patrons were already about their day's business, Matthew had little trouble going downstairs unobserved. He hurried past the taproom and slipped into the kitchen where the innkeeper's daughter was sitting in an open doorway sewing. She didn't see him approach, she didn't look up from the stitchery in her lap. Matthew backed out of the kitchen cautiously. He would have to leave now through the front door, worse luck. He returned to the taproom whose door let out on the street and looked in to see one of the tapsters behind the bar and two men he didn't know seated at a table playing cards. Placing the tray on a table at hand, Matthew walked softly across the floor trying not to call attention to himself. He was nearly out the door when he heard the tapster call out behind him.

"Hello! You, boy!"

Matthew broke into a run, burst through the door to the street, and in a moment was mixing with the crowd. Discarding the apron in a convenient alley, he proceeded to the Bell, took a chamber under the name of Miles Merryweather as he and Joan had agreed, and having quieted his agitation with a cup of wine, waited until later in the morning when his luggage was delivered. Then he shaved, dressed in his one remaining suit, and proceeded to Cecil's office, thinking all the while of just how he was to present his curious story to the Principal Secretary.

Gervase Castell looked out into the dim interior of the shop and was pleased to find it full of customers, although it was near closing time. As he did so, he noticed a plump, dark-complexioned woman peering into one of the display cases. She was well but not elegantly dressed in a green satin gown with a lace collar and a pretty white cap upon her head. Since at the moment she was unattended and Castell was weary of sitting he decided to serve her himself.

She smiled graciously as he approached, and he smiled in return. No, she was no great lady, he discerned, but neither was she mean. He put her down as some merchant's wife, or perhaps a lady in service. She carried herself well, with an air of self-importance, and what little jewelry she had about her person—a good ring, a chain, and an opal pin to match the green satin—she wore with taste.

"Is it for yourself?" he inquired, looking with her into the glass case.

"No," replied the woman in a discreet whisper.

"For your husband, perhaps?"

She simpered, looked down shamefacedly.

"For a . . . friend, then?"

"Oh, no!"

Castell grew impatient. Here was a giddy goose indeed. He began to look around for one of his assistants to take her off his hands.

"The truth is that I have something to sell," she said.

"What, may I ask? Some jewel or ring or chain like that you wear about your neck?"

"A ring," she said.

Castell waited expectantly.

"Oh, I don't have it on my person. Only this description." She pulled from her handkerchief a folded paper, which she proceeded to unfold and read.

"May I read it for you?" suggested Castell. "The light is better by the candle."

The woman looked aghast at the thought and clutched the

letter to her bosom. "Oh, no. I couldn't do that. It's a letter, you see, a letter from my daughter. It's very private."

"I see," said Castell, nodding gravely. "Well then, perhaps you can read the description to me."

She took some time to glance through the letter and then came upon the portion she sought. "Spanish gold, very heavy, mounted with an orient pearl."

"A pearl, you say?" replied Castell, interested.

The woman screwed up her face to read the letter again. "It does say a pearl."

"I might advance myself as a buyer of the ring," said Castell, nonchalantly. "I would have to see the ring before I could give you a price."

"Yes, I understand that. You would need to see it," she murmured absently but with obvious disappointment. "It was a gift, you see, from a friend."

"This ring . . . your daughter has it now?"

"Yes."

"And it was a gift from her . . . friend?"

"Yes, a gift."

"May I ask the gentleman's name?"

Castell's question occasioned another expression of dismay. No, she couldn't reveal the gentleman's name. That was impossible. Castell explained that if he knew the name of the original owner he might better gauge the ring's worth.

"Well . . . no, I couldn't say it."

"Of course, if your daughter's friend is that sort of friend," said Castell, baiting her.

The woman looked this way and that. She protested. "I assure you their relationship is most honest."

"I'm sure it must be," replied Castell, hiding his amusement.

The woman continued, "He is a well-known gentleman of the City—a knight, if the truth were known, and he has done great honor to her to make her acquaintance. He has sought to advance my son-in-law . . ."

The woman rattled on about her daughter and this gentleman without revealing any particulars of the relationship. Castell began to pay close attention.

"She is married then, but not to her . . . friend?"

The woman's dark eyes regarded him uncertainly, as though to determine whether Castell could be trusted. What a foolish creature, thought Castell, framing at the same instant an expression of concern. A fool might draw the whole story out of her now and Castell knew himself to be no fool.

"Madam," he began soothingly. "Please be assured that I have the greatest respect for you, your daughter, her husband, and this duke—"

"Oh, he's not a duke, only a knight," she said, tittering.

"A knight," murmured Castell.

"And yet no mere knight," she added. "He's a Privy Councillor, he's—"

She put her hands to her face. "Oh, but I have said much too much."

"Nay, lady," Castell said, "it is impossible to say too much to a man who's the soul of discretion." He bowed again, this time more graciously, and reached for her hand, holding it for a moment above the glass case, noticing that the palm was cold and damp.

"You may trust me," he said. "Were I to know of this knight I might by such knowledge be able to give a better estimate of the value of the ring. But pray, tell me first why your daughter wishes to sell it."

She looked about her as though to ensure her words would not be overheard, and sighed.

"Her husband has discovered her friendship with—"

"With—"

"This knight."

"And?"

"Well, he has grown unreasonably jealous."

"I see."

"And she desires to rid herself of any evidence of—"

"Wrongdoing."

"Exactly."

"And so she desires to sell the ring."

"Yes."

"But pray, why does she not merely return it to—"

"Sir Robert? Well, because . . . because . . ."

"Because that would be impolitic—might offend the knight."

"Yes."

Sir Robert—so that was the name. The woman had let it slip and now prattled on, ignorant of what she had done. Well, Castell

129

would not embarrass her by calling attention to the slip; in an instant he ran through the Sir Roberts he knew of in the city. Sir Robert Gordon, Sir Robert Fitzhue, Sir Robert Davies, Sir Robert Cecil. Sir Robert Cecil. No, that was too much to hope for—that he should somehow find a way to get that pious upstart Cecil in his pocket along with the other bloated lordlets he had blackmailed.

"She's such a fine girl. I was overjoyed at the match . . . at first. But her husband treats her abominably and has gone half through his inheritance in six months. And of course when this knight showed her the slightest attention . . . It was, not, to be sure, one of these common entanglements. The knight is the soul of honor."

"I do believe it," Castell assured her. "But tell me now, does this knight reside in the City?"

"In an apartment at Westminster," the woman said expansively, warming to this theme. "Most magnificent, my daughter tells me, with a great four-poster bed laid with silken coverlets. *And* he has a new house abuilding in the Strand. But I *have* said too much!" she exclaimed. She turned to go.

"Now, wait," Castell said, trying to control his own excitement and thinking at the same time of that apartment in Westminster, the new house in the Strand. Who should it be but Cecil? That hunchbacked devil, spewing sweetness to the old Queen out of one side of his mouth whilst his privy member burrowed its way into a young wife's smock. Oh, beautiful! Oh, wonderful!

"Let me see now. A pearl, you say, about the size of fingernail?"

Joan's eyes widened. "Oh, larger, sir. My girl said he had it of an Indian prince."

"Well now, perhaps I can name a price." Castell paused, calculating. He named a sum, a very generous one. "Would that serve your daughter's needs?"

"Oh, admirably, sir!" replied the woman.

"When can you come again? When can I see the ring?"

"Friday."

"Early?"

"Yes."

"Well, it might be more, you know, than what I have said, considering its origin—from a knight's collection."

"Do you really mean it?"

"Most assuredly. And, if I were but to know the knight's name . . ."

The woman shook her head vigorously. "Never," she said. "My daughter has sworn me to keep secret his name—and indeed, everything in her letter."

Of course, if the silly girl were anything like her garrulous mother she would have revealed all in the letter. Castell looked at it greedily. The woman refolded it with elaborate care and replaced it in her handkerchief. This she then stuck within her bodice. She smiled shyly.

"It's a pleasure doing business with you," she said.

"Oh, indeed," Castell replied. "Pray take care. I'll look forward to our meeting Friday."

The woman had no more walked through the door than Castell seized one of his assistants and sent him to fetch Starkey. Within minutes the man came in from the back room, his eyes brightening with anticipation as they always did when his employer had work for him.

"She has it about her now?"

"Yes, yes," replied Castell impatiently. "In her handkerchief, tucked in her bodice nigh unto her left breast."

"Shall I kill the drab?"

"No, fool, kill only when you must. But get the letter and straightway." Castell described the woman in great detail.

"Snatching the letter will not be easy," said Starkey.

"She'll doubtless pass nigh unto Waterlane."

"Very crowded this time of day."

"Well, I trust that will present no great obstacle to one of your talents," Castell inquired with heavy irony and a little irritation, for he was very eager to peruse this letter which he hoped would be every bit as incriminating as the woman's reluctance to display it implied.

"Hardly, sir. I know my business, and if you do not have your letter within this hour I'll go hang myself."

"A foolish boast, Starkey. A foolish boast. Pride goeth before a fall. *After her, man!*"

"Well, I'll not fall, nor fail. You'll see."

It was seven o'clock and Castell ordered the shop closed. Then he went back into his office to wait. But waiting was very hard for him. Essentially he was a man of action, and to sit while there was the possibility, no, the likelihood of such glorious plunder in the offing, caused him an almost physical pain. Cecil. He prayed it was Cecil and not some other. Already he yearned to see Cecil crumple before him, struck dumb with astonishment when the evidence of his liaison was waved under his nose, as foul as a black toad's crotch. Now what might Cecil give to have the letter returned, the scandal hushed up?

That would be the theme of Castell's reflections for the next hour.

Joan walked at a leisurely pace, looking behind her from time to time to see who followed, half hoping that no one would and knowing at the same time that were she not followed and robbed, her performance in Castell's shop would have been for nothing.

Her imagination had run riot, amazing her with its fertility once her plot had been born. She had distilled the counterfeit history in her letter, writing it out with great care, the vain and foolish mother of a vain and foolish daughter, the pearl to please Castell's fancy, and the entanglement with Cecil, the irresistible lure. Castell had responded as she had expected. All her instincts told her he had swallowed the bait. Cecil would know firsthand what deviltry the jeweler practiced.

She had been frightened to death in the shop, in the belly of the beast, with its fabulous treasures gleaming in the dim light. But she had been caught up in her part at last and, like a good player, had kept a constant decorum of foolishness, wagging her tongue just enough to make the jeweler curious and then letting him know the setting of her course. All the while her heart had kept up such a thumping, as though the poor thing were beating to be let out.

It was late but she was not alone in the street. Most of the shops had shut up for the day but the alehouses, tobacconists, and brothels were just beginning to come alive. As she walked, she thought of Matthew. By now she hoped he had been able to see Sir Robert Cecil, explain their plan, and ask the knight's aid. If Sir Robert required evidence, he would have it all right. Yes, he would have it by direct involvement with the blackmailer, as a victim himself.

She had traveled a dozen yards into a lane when she became aware of someone behind her. She stopped to turn and look and there was nothing, yet she was sure she had heard steps. She proceeded, pausing from time to time to listen. There was no sound of steps, yet she felt sure a threat was concealed in the shadows. She began to regret that she had not done what she had promised—let the letter slip from her handkerchief as she departed the shop. Castell would have found the letter. But she was afraid that would be too obvious. Well, she was in for it now; there was no going back. She prayed when he took it from her he would not hurt her.

She prayed he would not kill her.

She quickened her step. Behind her she could sense the man's presence. She felt his hostility, his violence, as surely as though these had already demonstrated themselves in his assault upon her.

And then it came. Suddenly. But in front of her, not from behind as she had expected. The man was there before her, grabbing her by the throat and pulling her into an alley. His hand muffled her scream; she heard the rending of cloth, felt the smooth chastity of her bodice violated. The handkerchief, the letter, she thought numbly, *he's taking them. Dear God, let him do it quickly.*

He threw her upon the ground. She heard the quick patter of his escape. Blinded by tears of pain and indignation, she struggled to her feet, leaning against a wall for support and fumbling with the torn bodice. At her feet she saw the handkerchief. She bent over to pick it up, finding it empty as she had hoped. Her assailant had got what he wanted, what she had wanted him to have. He had also carried off her gold chain.

She thought of crying for help, but she knew it would be futile. This was London, not Chelmsford. A cry in the street at this hour was more likely to arouse suspicion than elicit aid.

Dazed, she walked the last mile to the Bell. The porter at the door regarded her curiously. Was Matthew—no, Miles Merryweather—lodging there? The porter told her where to find the room, looking at her bruises and her gown. "Are you well, lady?" She nodded, dumbly; she climbed the stairs, came to the room, and then there was Matthew. She rushed into his arms.

NINE⎯⎯⎯⎯⎯⎯⎯⎯⎯⎯⎯⎯⎯⎯⎯⎯⎯

It was very late in the day when Matthew finally gained an audience with Cecil. All morning the anteroom of his office at Westminster had been crowded with visitors—lawyers, clerks, counsellors of state, burgesses, reverend churchmen, several ambassadors, and not a few humbler petitioners anxious to secure Cecil's goodwill in some cause. The visitors waited on benches or stools, or stood around in little clusters whispering. There was a great deal of bowing and scraping, and an atmosphere of urgency and expectation, as though something momentous were about to transpire. Whenever the door to Cecil's inner office opened, to let someone in or out, a solemn hush fell. Heads turned abruptly, ears cocked for the great man's voice, and eyes followed anyone who came or went with mingled curiosity and envy.

Because Matthew had arrived late and was of no great importance, his name had been placed at the end of the waiting list kept by the pale, indolent young man seated at the desk near the door. Matthew waited and waited; while the long afternoon waned, his concern for Joan's safety intensified. Finally he approached the clerk.

"My business with Sir Robert is most urgent."

"Everyone's business is urgent," the young appointments clerk replied coolly, surveying Matthew with contempt.

The clerk had spoken loudly enough that Matthew was sure others in the room had overheard. A quick glance about him confirmed his fears. His special pleading was attracting stares of disapproval.

Much abashed, Matthew sat back down.

During the next half-hour only a bishop was admitted. Matthew thought his garb quite splendid and wondered what matter he would take up with Cecil. Shortly after entering, the bishop came out again, smiling with satisfaction. In the meantime many of those waiting with Matthew departed in frustration while others indicated to their friends or to the clerk their intention of returning the next day. It was nearly suppertime. Soon only Matthew and three others remained in the outer chamber—the appointments clerk and two elderly gentlemen Matthew took to be lawyers, for all their talk was of citations, appellations, allegations, certificates, attachments, and convictions. He couldn't help listening.

At six o'clock the appointments clerk rose from his desk to declare that his master would see no more petitioners that day. The lawyers departed chattering, without seeming to mind not having seen Cecil. Matthew remained seated.

The clerk emitted a loud "ahem" to indicate his displeasure. Matthew looked up slowly, pretending not to understand, sure that within moments Cecil would emerge, recognize him, and invite him into his office.

"I said Sir Robert's conferences have concluded for the day. He will see no more petitioners. You must leave." The clerk glanced anxiously at the closed door.

And at that moment the door opened and Cecil came out. Matthew leaped to his feet. "Sir Robert—"

"By my soul, Matthew Stock, is it?"

"Sir Robert, this man would not leave—" sputtered the clerk in a great state of consternation at this irregularity.

Cecil dismissed the protest with a wave of his hand. "And very well he did not. I should have been most sorry to miss him. Come in, Mr. Stock."

The clerk, much annoyed but wisely silent, resumed his chair and began to shuffle his papers nervously. Matthew followed Cecil into the office.

The room in which Cecil conducted the business of state was a very grand one, with a high, ornately carved ceiling, a marble-faced hearth, and a magnificent writing desk that dominated the center of the room so that everything else seemed organized around it. The heavy oak paneling was almost hidden by rich tapestries depicting various scenes: some gentlefolk at hunt, a landscape of sorts featuring scrawny sheep and one Matthew took to be their shepherd, a slight, effeminate figure holding a staff in one hand and a pipe in the other. The tapestry directly behind the desk showed Our Lord surrounded by his apostles. Christ had a sorrowful face, the apostles mean countenances. Which was the betrayer? Which was the beloved? Matthew could not tell. He had but a fleeting glimpse as he crossed the room and took the chair Cecil had indicated by a graceful wave of the hand.

Cecil was dressed in a handsome suit of purple velvet with a white lace collar and cuffs. He wore a chain of office. He was sitting with his legs crossed, his long fingers wrapped around the arms of the chair, and he was leaning slightly forward and looking at Matthew with an expression of intelligent interest.

"Well then, Constable Stock, pray what is this urgent business of yours? Were it any other at this late hour I would have dismissed him at once, but I have not yet exhausted my debt to you. So, then—"

Matthew took a deep breath and began his story. He told Cecil about Thomas Ingram, his disappearance, and his return. He told him all that Thomas had told Joan about the jeweler, and how Starkey had tried to drown Matthew in the river. Then he explained Joan's device for securing proof—the counterfeit letter and its slanderous implications. He spoke very quickly and confusedly, despite the practice he had given his account during his long wait in the anteroom, but Cecil was content to hear him out. The knight sat erect, and his expression of interest did not alter. When Matthew finished, Cecil nodded and folded his hands thoughtfully.

"Now let me understand this. This fellow you speak of, this jeweler—"

"Gervase Castell."

"Indeed, Castell."

"His shop is in the City," Matthew said although he had already conveyed that information and Cecil seemed to know the man, at least by reputation.

"Will think to blackmail *me*?"

Cecil seemed more amused than offended, but Matthew continued with caution.

"Most likely."

Cecil laughed self-confidently, a rich resonant laugh that did not seem entirely to belong in this chamber with its dim religious light and august decor. "For which of my crimes and misdemeanors?"

Matthew took another deep breath. "A liaison, sir," he said softly, "with a married woman."

"Oh, my," answered Cecil, his eyes round with dismay. "Your wife has laid *that* upon me in her forged letter?"

Matthew admitted it, wondering at the same time that he should have allowed his wife to persuade him of this scheme. It seemed madness now, a gross slander and imposition, more likely to offend Cecil than to secure evidence from Castell. Matthew searched Cecil's face, looking for signs of scorn, contempt, outrage. But Cecil's expression remained calm, even amused.

"Well, I suppose there are worse crimes," the knight said after a prolonged silence during which he seemed to weigh the cost of his reputation with the possibility of discovering a traitor. "But pray, do you think this trout will take to tickling?"

"Most assuredly," Matthew responded, with more confidence now. "The man feeds on scandal."

Cecil thought some more. It was very quiet in the room. Matthew watched the knight's face. The man had a broad, high forehead; his hazel eyes were wide-set and penetrating under the perfectly arched brows.

Then Cecil said, "Your good wife is a marvelously clever woman—a greater jewel than this Castell has in his shop. I would hold on to her, Matthew Stock, hold on to her, I say. She will make you rich yet—and wise."

Matthew was very pleased with this compliment to his wife. But of course Joan was marvelously clever. He had always known *that*. He looked about the chamber. It really was a splendid room. He had never before seen the like. He had come a long way since his days as an apprentice to his cousin, when all his industry was sweeping and carding and his ambition only to some day be his own master.

"So then," Cecil continued after another moment's reflection, "the plan is that I wait to see what proceeds from Castell and attempt to ferret out his motive from the price he puts upon his silence?"

"Exactly," Matthew replied.

Cecil pondered this, staring into a middle distance. His handsome features looked thoughtful, yet alert. Matthew could well understand how the Queen could put such great confidence in this man. Although small and crookbacked, he had a commanding presence.

"As you surmise, Mr. Stock, there may be a good bit more to Castell's treachery than a lust for money. Her Majesty the Queen is in good health—for her age. But even so glorious a sun must set. It is very likely she will name her cousin James of Scotland her successor, but between her death and James's succession may appear a moment of opportunity to them who wish our country great harm. Do you understand me?"

"You mean Spain," Matthew said.

"Not only Spain. English politics is very complicated, Mr. Stock. There are many factions, many ambitious persons. There's the Essex crowd, for instance, mourning their lost leader and conniving still. There's Ralegh and the wizard Earl Northumberland. God knows what they're up to. Most of our domestic Papists are loyal, but not all. I could name you a dozen Catholic lords who would fain see a Papist succeed Elizabeth and a good many of the landed gentry of the same persuasion. We must do all that we can to ensure that the next occupant of the throne is a Protestant."

"Then you suspect this is Catholic plot?" asked Matthew.

"Very likely."

"And who is this Basilisk?"

"Ah, yes," replied Cecil, "this Basilisk. I cannot say, but I don't like the name. Basilisk—a creature of legend with a fatal breath and glance." Cecil rolled the word around on his tongue, giving it various pronunciations. "Basilisk, basiliscus, basiliskos, basileus. Greek, Mr. Stock," said Cecil, seeming to notice Matthew's bewilderment, "a diminutive form—a word meaning 'royal king.'"

Matthew didn't understand. England had no king.

"Not our king, Master Stock. But one who *would* be king, perhaps."

The idea hung suspended in the air, and Matthew contemplated it, as best he could, being unfamiliar with matters of state, succession, treason, and the like. But Cecil had obviously been moved by his own speculations. Now he sat perfectly erect, his slender legs uncrossed so that his lean knees and shanks, encased in dark silk, were pressed tightly together. He was staring in the distance again, lost in a kind of trance. Matthew waited expectantly, sensing that the moment was significant but quite unsure of how to interpret it.

Then, abruptly, Cecil shifted his posture, smiled somewhat mechanically at Matthew and rose from his chair. Matthew hastened to do likewise. "Would you and your good wife were in my service, Constable. Should we not then clear England of malefactors within twelve months! But, pray, tell me where do you lie in London? We must keep in close touch."

Matthew gave him the name of the inn. He also explained that he was using the name Miles Merryweather, for safety's sake. Cecil nodded approval, made note of the name. "We thought it the most politic course," said Matthew.

"Yes. You *are* at risk, aren't you? You are safe as long as Castell thinks you dead," said Cecil, absently.

The knight's mind was elsewhere; Matthew waited, fearing to disturb Cecil's meditation. Then abruptly, Cecil was attentive again. He rose and extended his hand.

"You have done your Queen a service, Constable Stock, and if this jeweler plots as I suspect, you may live to understand as well that you have saved your country."

Later, Matthew remembered the knight's words exactly. The praise they implied did not so much flatter him as overwhelm him. Could it be true? Could he have done anything to merit such praise? Must he do something yet?

He walked from the office, past the sullen clerk, without word or glance, feeling somehow taller and larger, but also more threatened. Had Cecil's farewell been generous praise, or ominous prophecy?

"Cecil! *Madre de Dios!*"

Castell tipped his head to acknowledge the implied compliment to his skill before realizing that the Spaniard's outburst was more an expression of alarm than of admiration.

"You really intend to blackmail *him?*"

Castell regarded Ortega coldly. "Why, what else should I do with the wench's letter? The style is not worth imitating." He said this very archly. His supply of courtesy had suddenly been exhausted in the face of the Spaniard's timidity. It was no wonder Spain had never succeeded in vaulting England's walls. The Spaniards were a race of pygmies, of precious manikins. Now he was ashamed of his very association with them.

The look of dismay remained on Ortega's face. His dark eyes burned intensely against the pallor of his skin. "It would be risky, very risky."

"Of course it would be risky. That's what your master pays me for. Yet the risk is mine, not yours."

"Not entirely," said Ortega, worriedly.

"You and your master will not be compromised in any way, I promise you. Look you now, do you think me a fool? A novice in this business? I know Cecil's power. It is for this very reason the foolish letter is a godsend, more than any of your priests could have fasted for."

Ortega shook his head. Castell watched, waiting.

Then the Spaniard's eyes fell, almost shyly. Castell smiled to himself. He had won.

Ortega looked up and asked, in a different tone now, "How do you propose to go about it? You won't bring him to your shop—or here to your house?"

"No," replied Castell.

"Nor would you deal with him directly? Surely you have someone—"

"Yes, someone among my employees."

Employees was the word, impersonal, very businesslike, very discreet. Why should Ortega know more than he needed to know, deserved to know, after his craven display of faintheartedness?

"You really must let me manage things, Count. I know what I'm doing. Believe me."

"Very well," Ortega answered wearily, rising from his chair. "I'll await your report. When may I hear from you?"

Castell thought. "Thursday at the latest."

"Thursday. Good. Yes, we shall see. A most dangerous man, Cecil," he murmured as an afterthought.

The two men exchanged farewells, without warmth, and Castell prepared himself for bed, thinking all the while of his coming encounter with Cecil. Send one of his servicers in his place? He almost laughed aloud at the ridiculousness of it. Ortega would think of that. A timid man at heart, all caution and concern. Of course

140

Castell would do the job himself. Whom should he trust in so delicate a matter? Besides, why should he deprive himself of the pleasure of seeing the great man helpless before the threat of revelation of his private affairs?

Castell had concealed the young wife's letter carefully, but not before making an exact copy. He would not need to show the document itself. The names and circumstances would be enough to turn Cecil green. The question in his mind as he snuffed out the candle was where the meeting should be held. The shop would be too dangerous since it would require the transport of Cecil at too great a distance. Neither would his house be safe and of course Castell would certainly not even consider using his house on Barbican Street. Some neutral ground would have to do then, but a place that Castell knew well, a place private and secure from the threat of intrusion. Well, he knew of such a place. By this time tomorrow he would call the hawk to the lure.

Now it was Matthew's turn to comfort her. She was very pale and disheveled. The bodice of her gown had been ruined, her chain stolen, her arms and face bruised. A moment before he had been startled by the urgency of her knocking, telling him there was trouble even before he opened the door and saw her standing there so pitifully in the passage looking up at him, blubbering. He took her into the room and into his arms and between sobs she confessed that she had not dropped the letter as she had promised, but had allowed it to be snatched from her to add credibility to their stratagem. Matthew was about to scold her, but he did not. The villain had roughed her up badly. She hardly needed to be told now how dangerous this alteration in their plan had proved.

He led her over to the bed and helped her remove her tattered clothing.

"The gown—it's in shreds," she wailed, looking to where it lay now on the bed.

"I care nothing for the gown. I'll buy you another. You're safe, that's all that matters."

Was she hungry, he wanted to know. No, she had not thought of food. How could she think of eating at a time like this? Some wine, then, or ale? Yes.

He went downstairs to fetch a bottle of wine and two bowls. When he returned, he looked at her with concern. She was still pale and trembling. It was clear that only now was it coming to her how close to death she had come.

"What manner of man did this?" he asked, pouring for her.

"I didn't see his face. He was very strong."

"I'll wager it was Starkey," Matthew said, pouring for himself. "You spoke to Sir Robert?"

"Late this afternoon. I told him everything."

"What did he think?" Joan looked at him hopefully. "Pray God we gave no offense."

"Why should he be offended?" asked Matthew casually. But he had uttered the same prayer a thousand times since she had proposed her plan.

"Why, at the slanders I put upon him," she said.

"He thought your letter was very clever. He admired your courage."

She sighed with relief. "He believed what you told him about Castell, then?"

"Every whit."

"Well?" she said.

"Well, what?"

"Thomas Ingram shall be avenged for his hurt."

"And you for yours," said Matthew.

"And you for yours, husband."

She looked at the bruises on her forearms with a cold dispassionate gaze, as though they were someone else's injuries now. She drank some of the wine, complained of its strength and bitterness, but then admitted that it was restoring. They drank to each other, to the success of their stratagem.

"Sir Robert promises to inform us when Castell approaches him."

"Good," she said. "That's very good."

Matthew refilled her cup, then his own. "To Sir Robert Cecil."

She joined him in this toast.

They were very merry for an hour, finishing the bottle. Matthew bolted the door and blew out the candle. He removed his clothing and crawled under the covers beside her. She snuggled under the crook of his arm, whispering softly as though she were afraid someone else might hear, "I wish we were home again, Matthew. Home and all well."

"So do I," said Matthew, sadly, "so do I."

TEN_____

Cecil rose early of mornings, ate sparingly, and then, as was his custom, was at his desk by daybreak poring over letters, minutes of the Council, or documents of state. He worked long and obsessively, with a furious dedication to an ideal of statesmanship he had inherited from his father, the great Lord Burghley, and with the conviction that what he lacked in appearance he could redeem through intelligence and industry. His chief amusements were gambling and hunting, but he also enjoyed music, read widely, and was no mean Latinist. He had the gift of wit which his age adored and which, for a courtier, was virtually everything. But for all of this he was not a popular man. The common rout distrusted him and most of the court envied him, for he was essentially a private person, holding himself aloof, given to inexplicable fits of melancholy and sensitive about his physical appearance although he took pains not to show it. He was short and crookbacked, and he walked in a curious, awkward manner as though he were trying out his feet for the first time and was not as yet certain they fit at the end of his legs.

Though still young, he was old in experience and his countenance was somewhat weathered by public care. Growing up in Cecil House, he had a firsthand view of great men and matters and his father had thrust him early into the thicket of English politics. At eighteen he had been a member of Parliament, at twenty-eight a Privy Councillor. Now, just shy of forty, he was the Queen's Principal Secretary and the most powerful man in England.

He had struggled to win his place in his monarch's esteem, for though Burghley's influence had facilitated his rise, it had not guaranteed it, as the fortunes of his elder half-brother Thomas demonstrated. Thomas was a spending sot, meet to keep only a tennis court, Burghley had complained to a friend. Robert, on the other hand, was the true son. The dashing Essex and the warlike Ralegh, his chief rivals, could not at last compete with Robert Cecil's unflinching loyalty, his solid competence. Yet when Cecil thought of his rivals his emotions always became turbulent. Ralegh lived still, a burr beneath Cecil's saddle. Essex was dead, almost the worse, a living ghost. Cecil had attended the handsome earl's trial, concealed behind a curtain, emerging at the climactic moment to refute Essex's charge that *he*, not the earl, was the traitor. Cecil had given him the lie in his face, and stayed to watch while the earl crumpled before the truth and the court found him guilty of treason as charged.

In consideration for Essex's high birth, the executioner had taken but his head, leaving his bowels and privates intact.

Anthony Bacon and the other partisans of Essex's cause grieved still for their lost leader. They heaped abuse upon Cecil, schemed behind his back, calling him Robertus Diabolus—Robert the Devil. They could call him what they chose; the names would not hurt him. Elizabeth herself called him elf and pygmy but with such evident appreciation for his talents that the epithets on her royal lips turned to golden compliments.

On this particular morning he had just finished a very long letter which had it been to any other person and about some less consequential matter he would have dictated to his secretary. But this was no routine missive. He wrote in his own hand, larding the text with classical and biblical allusions and flattery of a sort that under ordinary circumstances he would have disdained. The letter would be touched by only certain hands, travel in secret, open at last to a single pair of eyes. Unbeknownst to the Queen, for whom all talk of a successor was as a death knell, Cecil had been regularly corresponding with the Scottish King for the past year. The epistle at hand was a comprehensive report of the affairs of the kingdom, with special attention to Her Majesty's health. James, it seemed, had heard rumors. They were the usual calumnies. Elizabeth was dying of cancer or some other fatal disease. She was already dead and the fact was being concealed by her ministers. James wanted to know if any of this was true. He had also heard that she had chosen another as heir and that had put him quite beside himself with grief.

Cecil wrote to reassure him. The Queen was alive and she had regained some of her wonted vigor. Of course, she was an old woman. How much longer could she live? Although she played the virginals, ate largely, rode horseback, yet she could go in an instant. Such was life. As for the possibility of another heir, well, that was a lie, propagated by her enemies. Cecil assured James that he would look out for his interests. Had not Burghley admonished his second son in their last interview to have regard for the tottering commonwealth after the Queen's death? To invest the true and lawful successor?

An obedient son, Cecil often recalled his father's exact words. He would indeed steady the tottering commonwealth. At the same time he would, like any wise man, advance his own fortunes. James, who Cecil was sure would succeed his royal aunt, would be a monster of ingratitude were he not to reward him appropriately when the impoverished Scot came into his affluent southern kingdom.

For, to Cecil, James was the only logical successor, despite his unprepossessing figure and the tedious pedantry Cecil had taken pains to indulge in in his letters to him. James was Elizabeth's choice as well. He was a Protestant and a man, and even Elizabeth did not want another woman to wear the crown. There were other candidates, of course, but they could not be taken seriously. Lady Arabella Stuart, a descendant of the elder daughter of Henry VII, was a weak-willed insignificant woman with little or no support among the nobility and less among the commons. Lord Beauchamp, the eldest son of the house of Seymour, posed even less a threat. His legitimacy was questionable and his claim rested entirely on an obscure provision in the will of Henry VIII. Now, after fifty years, who cared? Then there was the unthinkable—the Infanta Isabella of Spain. Although strongly favored by the radical Catholics, her succession would mean not only capitulation to England's worst enemy but the destruction of the English Church.

No, Isabella was unthinkable.

That left James.

Cecil signed the letter with a bold flourish, using the code name he and James had agreed upon, and then sealed it. As he did so he remembered Matthew Stock's visit of the previous day.

Blackmail—a dastardly practice, not unknown, however, in the court despite Elizabeth's strict probity and supervision. Cecil thought of Joan Stock's clever forgery and marveled again. Mrs. Stock was a damnably clever woman for a clothier's wife. Her device had shown all the right instincts. A widower of some half-dozen years, Cecil had often been accused of unchastity by his enemies and the letter was all the more fit for its plausibility. Cecil was a man of power and power attracted women. But the truth was that although he was not naturally celibate, few women attracted him now. A casual flirtation perhaps, with some gentleman's wife, discreetly carried on and platonic, but he abstained from brothels and the looser women about the court, those who invited seduction with their bare bosoms and bold stares, their simpering and mewing. Besides, politics, like an unsatiable mistress, tended to drain his energies. He understood well that love was what one sacrificed at the altar of greatness.

He placed the letter in a leather pouch and rang for one of his secretaries. Then, as though he had been waiting all morning for his signal, a callow young man named John Beauclerk, whom Cecil had recently appointed to this office, entered and stood before his master expectantly. Cecil delivered the pouch to him, and Beauclerk took it. James would have the letter by the end of the week if the weather held and the courier managed to avoid the thieves and brigands that plagued the north country roads.

Toward noon, just as Cecil finished the last draft of a long report touching upon the dangers of Jesuit conspiracies, Beauclerk came again with the day's mail. As usual it consisted of a good many pieces, for Cecil maintained a large correspondence. He dismissed Beauclerk and then glanced through the pack, selecting some to read at once. As he did this, one letter in particular caught his attention because it was oddly addressed—to Robin Cecil.

Robin? A few intimates called him that, sometimes the Queen in a jocular mood, more often his enemies. Sensitive to the insolence of the address, he broke the seal and found inside two letters. One was written in a fine hand. This he read first. It was a mere fragment beginning in midsentence and ending likewise, like a snatch of conversation overheard as one passed from one room to the next. A phrase caught his eye: *Sweet Robin hath promised advancement and cometh daily to the house when Henry lieth abroad.*

Do I? thought Cecil with quiet amusement. He was relieved that Joan Stock had not been too specific as to just what advancement he had promised. He would leave that to Castell's imagination. What was at issue then was not merely Cecil's alleged adultery, but the sale of office. That was a serious business indeed.

He read the fragment through. The rest was in the same vein as the first, the style direct and lusterless, which made its composition by a foolish, semiliterate woman (not Joan, but the poor hapless wench she had invented) all the more probable. The effort at discretion was a total failure. The fact of the adulterous liaison was as obvious as the price of the woman's virtue, a promotion to some lucrative office for her poor cuckold of a husband.

The other letter was scrawled on foolscap, wretchedly penned as though it had been done by a scrivener or, more likely, his apprentice, eager to demonstrate legibility rather than art. It read:

> Right Honorable,
> I have come by this letter, a piece of which you shall find enclosed, in the street and have copied it with pains. None hath set eyes upon it but I, who am most anxious to deliver the whole of it to you again, since in perusing the contents thereof I find much that would compromise your high and mighty station. Your honor, the expectation of your friends, the trust of the Queen, are all at stake in this.
>
> Yet if you were to stroll in Paul's Yard and linger before the bookstall of P. Winter, inquiring there for a copy of Tacitus, bound in buff leather somewhat worn, you might find therein a strong hope of recovery.

The letter was unsigned, as he had expected. He put it down on his desk and examined the enclosed fragment again, feeling the texture of the paper between his thumb and forefinger, while he contemplated what he should do. He had enough evidence now to move against the jeweler. What remained to be discovered—the full scope of Castell's stratagem and its purpose—might be wrung from the man by threats or torture. In a civil matter something more circumstantial would have been required, but when treason was abroad one was driven to take extraordinary measures.

He was about to call for Beauclerk and set in motion the arrest when he suddenly changed his mind. Why should he act precipitously? This was an intrigue of the sort with which, if anything, he was overly familiar, but always before as a detached observer, never as a direct participant. That was the daily work of his undercover agents—clandestine meetings, cryptic messages, artful disguises. Had one of his agents been involved to the degree Cecil was now, the First Secretary would never have preempted the game with an official arrest. He would have let the agent play on and catch the plotter somewhere further along when the plot and its end were in plain sight. Why should he lose the opportunity now? Besides, there was something about this business that appealed to his sense of adventure, his gambler's instinct. He would show Castell he was the cleverer. Cecil thought a walk in Paul's might be refreshing after the long morning at his desk. Outdoors it was a fine summer day and, besides, he had always admired Tacitus.

By two o'clock he was in his coach and being driven toward the City, secure in the visible invisibility the coach afforded. It was a magnificent vehicle, the coach, very well designed and crafted, capacious and elegant with its team of six horses, its two drivers and two footmen in livery and its doors blazoned with the Cecil crest. It had cost him a fortune and had aroused much admiration and envy in the court. Ordinarily, on such a pleasant afternoon, he would have enjoyed a leisurely drive through London. Today, however, his impatience undermined his pleasure. How slowly the coach moved through the crowded streets, and yet for all his eagerness to get to Paul's and the bookseller's, when he peered from the window to view the city he loved he experienced a surge of patriotic feeling. He had traveled widely. He had visited the courts of European princes and viewed the great churches of Christendom. But for him there was no city to be compared with this. In its diversity and richness, it was the whole world epitomized. Its citizens were the finest; its churches the purest; its court all courts, made more splendid by its compression. All this Castell and his fellow conspirators threatened. Just how he had yet to discover. But whatever the plot, Cecil knew he must uncover it. It all depended upon him, and realizing that, he suddenly saw himself in heroic perspective, meet to stand with other defenders of the faith who had kept England free. Would he not be worthy to receive as they had received?

Cecil counted on being made an earl at least or duke.

When he arrived he left the coach on a side street and approached Paul's Yard from the west on foot. He found P. Winter's bookstall very quickly. The books were set out upon a table under a crimson canopy and the fastidious eyes of a stocky, robust-looking man dressed in a shabby black suit. Cecil himself had dressed plainly for the occasion. He had left his great chain of office at home and wore instead a dark gray doublet, silk hose of the same solemn color, and short cape of any ordinary knight. Yet though in the throng of Paul's Yard no one approached him begging for a handout, he was aware of the studious regard of those about him. All this he had come to expect as his due, and as he pretended to be absorbed in the general scene he realized the futility of his disguise. His crooked back and splayed feet went before him like a herald and trumpeter.

The bookseller had seen him coming. He rushed forward, hat in his hand, greeting Cecil by name. The handful of other customers drew aside respectfully. Cecil smiled an austere smile of acknowledgment. But of course the bookseller would recognize him at once. If he were part of the conspiracy he would have been waiting all morning.

Cecil glanced cursorily over the book table. Everything was in great disorder, greasy with handling; the covers of many of the books were tattered as though they had been exposed to the weather. Penny broadsides and pamphlets were heaped in stacks with stones on top to keep them from flying off. Learned tomes and collections of sermons rubbed shoulders with jestbooks and travelers' tales.

"I have your book, Sir Robert." The bookseller rushed away to another table. In an instant he was back again, book in hand and grinning wolfishly. The man had large protruding teeth. Several were missing. His breath stank like the Thames at low tide and Cecil recoiled with disgust.

"Tacitus," said the bookseller.

"Tacitus?" murmured Cecil, as though the Roman author were the furthest thing from his thoughts.

"Comes one—a gentleman—this very morning with the book. He said you'd call for it today and I was to give it to you."

Cecil examined the book. The buff leather cover had been slightly stained with water and one corner looked as though it had been chewed. He wondered why the blackmailer had chosen this particular book as vehicle for his next message and wished very much to peruse it at once. But that must wait until he was alone.

"What manner of man was this?"

149

"Sir?"

"He who told you to give the book to me?"

"As I said, a gentleman. He didn't mention his name. He said only that you would come for the book and I should give it to you."

The bookseller's face was round and florid, his eyes close-set like a bird's; his full lips and heavy chin gave the impression that the top and bottom of his face belonged to two different men. Yet although it was not an intelligent countenance there was that about it Cecil would have called honest. Cecil decided that the bookseller was not himself a conspirator. He asked him to describe the gentleman in question in more detail.

"Of middling height, running to tall. Head and face square. Eyes wide apart."

The bookseller could not remember the color of the eyes or of the hair, or whether the man was thin or heavy. His description of the man's clothing was muddled, but he remembered that whatever the man wore it was of good quality.

"Well, I think I know the gentleman," said Cecil, taking the book.

Cecil drew his purse from his belt, opened it, and plumbed it for a coin. He handed the money to the bookseller.

"For your pains," he said.

The bookseller, obviously made nervous by his august patron, thanked Cecil and bowed awkwardly. "May I show you something more?"

He searched anxiously among the store of volumes and withdrew a large one, in better condition than most. "This book of poems by Mr. Spenser. *The Faerie Queene*, it is named. These are the second three books, most suitably dedicated to Her Majesty and much approved by the gentlemen of the city."

Cecil frowned and shook his head impatiently. He already owned a copy of the work. His father had been the subject of one of Spenser's commendatory verses. Cecil knew the lines by heart. They had compared Burghley to Atlas, bearing the burden of government on his shoulders. Now the burden was Robert Cecil's own; it would be greater still when the Queen was dead.

He tucked the Tacitus beneath his arm, thanked the bookseller, and turned into the crowd. A little circle of onlookers had formed to watch the transaction. Now that it was concluded they quickly dispersed and made a path for him, gawking at him. He

150

might have been a trained monkey dancing upon a string, or a savage brought from the Americas. He looked at the faces as he passed. Some of the eyes were merely curious, others suspicious. One of the faces was undoubtedly the blackmailer's—or perhaps one of his confederates—waiting to see if Cecil would follow instructions.

He walked straight across the yard, the cynosure of eyes. When he came to where he had left his coach, the two liveried footmen roused from their stupor and stood by, one to hold the door open, the other to hold his arm as he ascended into its comfortable interior.

Inside, Cecil pulled the velvet drapes across the window and began to examine the book; he held it by its covers and shook it until a small piece of yellow paper fluttered into his lap. Its message was brief: *St. Michael's Cornhill. Eight o'clock tonight. Alone.*

"You will be pleased to learn, Count, that the great little manikin has come up to the bait."

Castell didn't say that to Ortega; he said it beneath his breath and to himself as he mused on the next step in his stratagem. He was in his house in Barbican Street, and the day was waning with the painful slowness of a tiresome conversation that shows no prospect of ending. Ortega would have called him a madman and complained to Spain about the perverse recklessness of their English agent were he to know just how dangerous an interview the jeweler contemplated at the moment. But the Spaniard was a timid soul, and he would sing a different tune when Castell had Cecil where he wanted him, tucked away securely in some compromising agreement with England's enemies.

The clock struck seven; the summer evening mellowed and cooled, and from his window Castell looked out over the back parts of his house and inhaled the heavy fragrance of vegetation run riot. Thinking of Cecil again. Cecil, Cecil, Cecil. The man had never deigned to enter the jeweler's shop, but of course Castell had seen him many times: in the Strand, in Paul's, at other fashionable resorts. Wherever the man appeared now he stirred men's hearts, gathered their attention, as though the pygmy were a king.

Castell wondered that the old Queen could tolerate such a fellow, maugre his honors, most of which he owed to the influence of his father. What a fine thing it was to have a well-heeled, well-allowed father, upon whose graces one could rise easily into royal estimation.

The shadows of the houses and trees lengthened solemnly. Before his glass, Castell put on a large, floppy hat that concealed most of his face, an old leather jerkin and loose-fitting breeches so that he looked like a carpenter or stonemason. He regarded his own image with curious detachment. The humble clothes had quite transformed him, made him a stranger to himself. The creature reflected was poor, downtrodden, therefore practically invisible, and invisibility was exactly what he wanted.

He began to review his plans with the cool deliberation of one who knows he must not err. This was to be the most daring of his plots, and despite his contempt for Ortega's timorousness he had taken the Spaniard's warning seriously, and made elaborate arrangements for his own safety. He had stationed his spies around the church to signal alarm if anyone but Cecil approached, planned his avenues of escape should his spies fail him. He had provided witnesses for the interview with the First Secretary, and conceived of a plan to keep his own identity concealed—from Cecil and the witnesses. He had planned for every contingency: should Cecil come with a troop of guards, or should he not come at all.

He went downstairs, where he found Starkey and Perryman playing cards in the hall. They were dressed as he, in laborers' garb. He beckoned them to follow, and the three men went out the back door, through the garden, and into the alley. Anyone seeing them now, arms linked, singing, would think them simple fellows homeward bound, perhaps a little drunk. Boon companions, the three of them.

The parish church of St. Michael the Archangel was in the Cornhill ward, not far from the Royal Exchange. It was an old church and had once been fair, but now its appearance was blemished by the construction of lower tenements immediately to the north, which had left the church dark and uninviting.

At dusk, Cecil came alone as directed. Between that afternoon and the present moment he had had his second thoughts, as might any man. What if the blackmailer's motive were assassination, the meeting a reason to get Cecil into an obscure place, fit for murder? His going would be a great gamble. Yet, he considered, he could, after all, be murdered anytime. The Queen herself had been the victim of any number of attempts on her life, and she had survived them. So might he.

He had come on horseback and he tied the black gelding that was his favorite mount to a post outside the iron gate surrounding the churchyard. Then he waited. Inside the yard he could see the scaffolding rising against the north wall. Repair work, proceeding very slowly. Soon some stonemasons bearing a chest passed through the gate. They did not look at him, an obscure figure now in the fading light. A few more stragglers departed—an old woman in her shawl, several clerics with their books. Last the sexton came to close the gate and then return to his cottage within the church grounds.

Now the setting sun bathed the church in a rosy hue, illuminating the western windows as though the interior of the church were afire. A holy conflagration, thought Cecil, not a little awed by the spectacle. St. Michael's Church. The Archangel. The Final Conflict. Was this the apocalyptic irony of a madman, Cecil wondered, or the symbolism of a traitor more clever and dangerous than he had supposed? But the illumination was brief. The intensity of color faded and the church became gray and flat against the darkening sky, like a great mound of earth or a rock thrust up from the sea.

The church bell struck the hour in deep, masculine tones, carrying over the neighborhood now enveloped in gathering darkness. Cecil walked through the gate into the yard. At the center of the yard was a pulpit cross much like the one at Paul's. He paused beside it, looking around him. There was no one beside himself. But he had confidence in the blackmailer; he knew his solitude was an illusion.

He found the main doors of the church locked, and he continued on around the side of the building to the east end. There he came upon a small door standing ajar, as though it had been left open purposely for him. He felt for the rapier at his side, withdrew it from the hanger, and slipped inside stealthily.

For a moment he stood there on the threshold, waiting for his vision to adjust to what seemed at first almost total darkness. But it was still dusk, and slowly he saw. Alert for any movement, any object foreign to the sacred precincts, his eyes swept the nave, found the sanctuary deserted. He breathed easier. He could smell the faint odor of incense and marble, could feel the cold trapped in the stone from the past winter, the cold emanating from the dead buried in the vaults beneath the floor. He proceeded down the short aisle of the transept, past the baptismal font, and stood respectfully before the chancel where a wooden Christ floated ghostly in the vacant expanse above the altar. He could not see the face but he knew how it would appear in the light, twisted in agony, knowing, the knowledge more terrible than the physical suffering—like the face of a prisoner on the rack, listening to his bones snap like dry twigs and knowing at the same time that his suffering had only commenced, that the worst was yet to come.

He knelt before the altar, laid the naked blade before him crossways on the floor, and made a sign of devotion. He prayed futilely for he was too preoccupied to concentrate. His pulse was racing with excitement, drowning his piety in the rush of blood.

"The church is closed."

He seized the rapier at the words, twisting, pointing the weapon in the direction the words had come, somewhere before him in the gloom. "I have come to pray," Cecil explained to no one he could see, despising the quiver he heard in his own voice.

A round circle of light approached from the chancel. It was the bellman. He had taken his time descending from the tower. He seemed unsteady, too, terrified doubtless by this specter before him in what he thought was an empty church. Cecil lowered his weapon and stood.

He was a bent old man. A shock of white hair covered the forehead like a cap. Breathing heavily, he approached Cecil and held the lamp above him. He seemed to take notice of Cecil's condition for he bowed respectfully and explained that if a gentleman wished to pay his devotions to the Almighty then who was he to forbid it.

Cecil pulled a coin from his sleeve and tossed it toward the bellman. It fell from his grasp, ringing on the stone floor. The bellman stooped to pick it up.

"Shall I leave a candle with you, sir?"

"I prefer the dark," said Cecil.

The bellman nodded and withdrew, leaving the church by the door Cecil had entered. Cecil sat down. He did not have to wait long. He started at the voice, coming as it did from behind him, hoarse and insolently intimate like a whore's beckoning from a dark alley.

"You've come alone, Mr. Secretary?"

"As you can see," Cecil said. He turned toward the voice, saw the shadowy form of the visitor standing in the middle of the main aisle, halfway toward the back of the church.

"Very prudent. Turn around, please. Imagine that the preacher is in his pulpit and your eyes are where your heart should be, fixed upon the holy altar."

Cecil did as he was told.

"Very good," said the voice. "I have a very uninteresting face really. I think you can understand why I should want to keep it to myself, and while you have come alone, be assured that I have not. I know you are armed, but please don't be so foolish as to think you can use that rapier of yours with impunity."

Cecil listened to the voice, husky and well spoken. London, definitely, not one of the towns. He was dealing with an Englishman and conceivably someone he knew. One of Bacon's crew perhaps?

"Do you have the letter with you?"

"Mrs. Mallory's?"

"Yes, yes."

"Do you think me mad?" replied the voice. "You will have your whore's missive in good time."

"How do I know I will ever have it?"

"You do not."

"Then why should I not get up and walk out of here?"

"Because while you do not know you will have it, yet you hope you shall. Also, you know that I would not have arranged this interview were I not serious about this business."

"This is business, is it? A scurvy sort of business it is."

"Perhaps, but a business nonetheless."

"How much do you want?"

"Not how much, *what*."

"Well, say it."

"For this woman you were prepared—"

"Yes?"

"To advance her husband to what?"

Cecil took his time answering, knowing that the invention must be a plausible one. But it came to him at last. "Some trifling post in chancery court, not worth more than four hundred pounds a year including bribes."

"Indeed," responded the other, with equal cynicism. "Well, since you were of a mind to appoint for no more than what pleasure you had of the wench I suppose you would recommend again to suppress publication of the same."

"To the chancery court."

"No."

"What office then . . . and what friend?"

"Sir Thomas Bampton."

"Bampton?" Cecil knew him, a soldier of modest attainments. The family was Catholic, a mark against him. "He's a Papist."

"Oh, sir, be not overly hasty. Remember that tolerance is the child of mercy, mercy a Christian virtue."

"I am not tolerant of those who bow and scrape to the Roman pontiff."

Chuckling came from behind him, low and humorless. "Let me entertain you, then, with an account of what will transpire if you do not cooperate. First, your affair with this woman becomes a public scandal, giving your many enemies no little pleasure and a great lever to dislodge your worship. By your promise to sell office for amorous favors you lose all credit with the Queen, for comes another recommendation from you and she will ask, what whore does he favor now? You will also lose credit with her successor."

"Her successor? What—"

"Now, Sir Robert, it is common knowledge that you favor the little Scots King, he who drools and loves to surround himself with theologians and pretty boys. What will His hypocritical Majesty say of a counsellor more earnest to obey his lust than either the King of Heaven or the King of England? You'll be out on your ear, sweet Robin, out on your ear, along with Wat Ralegh and the other white boys with a codpiece too small for their cod."

"Why should she believe you?" Cecil responded sharply, outraged at the threat.

"First, there is the letter. The woman who wrote it is a fool, doubtless, who would blab before she'd keep her peace. Oh, I promise you it would be a great scandal. Remember Ralegh's fall, Sir Robert, and take heed. A wise man knows when there's no door in the wall and doesn't batter his brains by making one with his head."

Cecil said, "All right, to what post would you have this Sir Thomas Bampton preferred?"

"Warden of the Cinque Ports," said the voice with steely determination.

"Warden? Absolutely not. Henry Brooke—"

"Yes, I know, your brother-in-law, Lord Cobham, holds the post at the moment, so you must shift him elsewhere."

"Have you thought that out as well?"

"I'll leave it to your discretion, sir. No one will be surprised if you recommend your brother-in-law. Why, how else is a man to get ahead in the world but through influence and—"

"Blackmail!"

"I was about to say money. Surely none is advanced through merit—not in this world."

"Perhaps not, but this Sir Thomas Bampton—what will be thought? The Wardenship is no mean office."

"And Sir Thomas is no mean man. He's of good blood, a family of soldiers, can handle a sword, and men. Prevail upon the Queen for his appointment and you'll have your letter again—not the copy but the original—a piece of paper for peace of mind."

Cecil asked cynically, "How can I have peace of mind—or for that matter how could you? How can you be sure that once the letter is back home again I'll not arrest this Thomas Bampton?"

"On what charge, pray? He knows nothing of this. Besides, for you to reveal him as having had his office by extortion would be to admit *your* part and the gross sale of office. There now, Sir Robert, think about it and tell me if you can think of an alternative to doing as I suggest."

"Who *are* you?" Cecil asked.

"One who would do his country a service."

"That's not much of an answer. No scoundrel but he proclaims himself a patriot."

"Perhaps, but that's all you'll have of me tonight. Now tell me, what is your answer? Will Bampton have the post and you your letter or will the Queen have intelligence about her chief minister that will cause her ears to burn and lose you your place in her esteem? Think how much pleasure your fall will give your enemies. Think what harm it will do your country."

Cecil thought, suppressing his rage, his inclination to seize the rapier and rush the man. Who was this Bampton? A Papist. The whole thing was some sort of Roman plot, then, just as he had suspected. But as yet he could not discern its scope. The Warden was the chief military officer in the east. His responsibility was to guard England's flank from invasion, to police the coming and going of persons, some of whom were spies.

"Very well, Sir Thomas Bampton it shall be."

"When?"

"Soon."

"How soon, Sir Robert? Name the date, for you shall not have your letter before Bampton has his appointment."

"Oh, very well," Cecil responded with feigned exasperation. "I see the Queen Wednesday. I will recommend Lord Cobham to another office. There's a vacancy on the Privy Council. Yes, it would please him greatly. Bampton shall have Lord Cobham's place."

"How soon will the Queen issue the letters patent?" inquired the voice.

"These days the Queen usually confirms at once, unless there's some difficulty, but I doubt there will be."

"You'd better pray there won't be."

"Bampton's appointment will satisfy you, then?"

"It will. When the appointment is made public, we will do our part."

"Good. Then how can I get the letter?"

"It will be delivered to your residence, never doubt it. Thank you, Sir Robert. You have been most cooperative."

Cecil made no reply. Presently he heard footsteps. The other man was leaving. The raspy voice called from a greater distance. "Meditate awhile longer, Sir Robert. With your permission I'll leave first. You may follow thereafter at your leisure."

Cecil said nothing. He listened to the footfalls of the blackmailer on the stone floor, he heard the door he had entered open and close, and then there was nothing except his own breathing in the dark. Yet he listened, not to his breathing but for the eyes and ears that shared the darkness, Castell's witnesses. They would be there, somewhere, the witnesses, hiding behind the altar or beneath the pews or in the choir where even whispers were magnified fivefold.

But they did not appear and presently he grew weary of waiting. He carried his naked sword from the church, its hilt moist in his hand, slippery like a snake, a thing of shame to him now that it had not been used as it should have been to strike dead this thing with whom he had conversed.

Castell watched Cecil leave the church and then reentered the sanctuary where he was presently joined by two other men. One of these was the youngest son of a famous earl, exhausted into submis-

158

sion now from his long struggle on Castell's hook and willing to do anything. Besides, the young man detested Cecil. His family had supported Essex and were now suffering for it, so his part to join the present conspiracy was more like a golden opportunity than another obligation to a blackmailer. The other witness to the proceedings of the evening was Sir Jeremy Parr. He had no particular desire for Cecil's fall but Castell had him now exactly where he had wanted him from the beginning. In the dim light Parr looked very wretched indeed. He looked like a man who realized that a debt he thought he had paid had now turned into an even greater one.

"Did you hear it all?"

"Every jot and tittle," said the earl's son, not without satisfaction.

"You, Sir Jeremy?"

Parr nodded glumly.

"By the mouth of two or three witnesses shall every word be established," Castell intoned with wry amusement.

"Will he appoint Bampton?" asked the earl's son in a high clear voice.

Castell looked at the young man. He was tall with narrow shoulders and long wispy hair. In the dim light his oval face was almost featureless, like a half-finished mask with only the eye-holes cut. "Doubtless he will, or we have spent our time here in vain."

"And what happens when he does?" Parr asked, still glum.

"You tell me, Sir Jeremy. Bampton is one of your co-religionists. What follows if a Catholic is appointed Warden of the Cinque Ports?"

"Nothing, if the man loves his country and his Queen," Parr replied defensively.

"Indeed, but I fear it may *appear* otherwise."

"You mean it may be *made* to appear otherwise," said Parr.

Castell chuckled humorously and regarded the knight. Parr was no fool. Perhaps he had taken too great a chance in selecting him for a witness. If that were the case, the fault could be undone. Accidents could happen to anyone. "Right you are. But as it turns out Bampton is no traitor. When he receives the appointment I shall reveal all."

"That will be the end of the little monkey," said the earl's son.

"That will be the end," agreed Castell, smiling.

ELEVEN_____

He was again in the river and he knew he must be dreaming because he was swimming and, awake, he did not know how to swim.
He was propelling himself with great ease as though the water were
no more substantial than thin winter air, moving his arms in great
arcs and experiencing an exhilarating weightlessness that left him
almost giddy.

The water was green and vibrant with bright shoots of sunlight.
Beneath its shimmering surface Matthew could breathe, miraculously, and he could see down to the bottom where eels with colorful stripes and long sinuous bodies undulated in the current and the
sand was white like salt crystals. He glided past the wrecks of
sunken ships, fully rigged, their decks strewn with treasure, and
over the ruins of submerged cities. He was delighted, entranced; he
wanted to keep swimming forever, exploring this undersea world.

But then at length the water grew murky. His breathing became labored. He was conscious of his extremities now, his cumber-
some arms and legs, ill suited for this watery world. They felt
heavier and heavier. How heavy the garments were, how heavy his
shoes. He struggled to remove them, but found himself unable. He
was seized with a sudden fear of drowning; he gasped for air, grew
dizzy. The beating of his heart was deafening.

Balump, balump, balump.

Bump, bump, bump.

He started from sleep. The river vanished. He was sitting up in his bed, and he could hear Joan's soft breathing next to him.

Joan stirred and sat up, too. "What is it, Matthew?"

"Somebody at the door." He was still not fully awake. The dream had shaken him. What had it meant?

"Shall you see to it?"

"Who's there?" he called.

The knocking continued.

Matthew felt Joan's hand upon his shoulder. Without speaking he got out of bed, struck a light, and walked toward the door. They had retired early, exhausted, even though they had done nothing the previous day but stay within doors and wait. Joan had worked at her sewing, Matthew had sung and read from his Hakluyt with much pleasure. They had talked and stared from the window to the narrow street below, but they had not expected news of the conspiracy so soon.

But here was news now certainly. From behind the door their visitor had identified himself. It was John Beauclerk, Cecil's secretary.

"Sir Robert's secretary!" Joan exclaimed with excitement. "Pray, admit him. It's what we've been waiting for."

"But this early," Matthew protested, thinking not so much of the conspiracy as of the hour, which seemed to him most improper for callers, regardless of their purpose. He set down the candle, unbarred the door, and opened it. Beauclerk looked cross and disheveled.

He said: "Sir Robert says you are to come now. Both of you."

"Now? Pray what hour is it?" Matthew picked up the candle and held it aloft so that it illuminated the bedchamber and a good deal of the passage without.

"Two, perhaps three of the clock," replied Beauclerk. He was a tall young man with fair hair, a long scholar's face, and very pale eyes. He was standing in the passage with his arms akimbo, and his resentment at having been commanded to this nocturnal errand was as evident as his contempt for the country constable before him.

Joan rose and joined the men at the door. "What news from Sir Robert?"

Beauclerk regarded her sourly and shrugged. His master had

given him their names, the sign of the inn where they lay, and directed him to fetch them. He had not inquired into his master's purpose. It was not his place, Beauclerk added, looking askance at the chamber's shabby furnishings, for Matthew had chosen a mean room, so as to make their presence at the Bell less noticeable.

"It's certain the jeweler has approached Sir Robert," Matthew said to his wife. "The plot is afoot, just as you said. I'll wager my life upon it."

Joan agreed, smiling nervously. She was standing there in the doorway in her nightgown and cap, feeling much too old, immodest, and uncomely before this virtual stranger to take much pride in Matthew's praise of her wit. Out of his pale eyes, Beauclerk stared at the couple with new interest.

"Give us ten minutes to make ourselves decent in," Matthew said to Beauclerk, who, scowling, agreed and said that he would wait at the foot of the stairs.

While the Stocks made themselves ready, they talked in excited whispers. Joan had brought two gowns from Chelmsford in addition to that which Starkey had ruined and was unsure which was the more suited to this unexpected audience with the First Secretary. Beauclerk had told them they would ride horseback to Cecil's house on the Strand, and Matthew suggested therefore that she wear the poorer gown, thinking she would have less to lose from the chafing of the saddle or the dust of travel. Besides, he reminded her, it was the middle of the night. What in the way of preparation could even Sir Robert Cecil expect at this hour?

But Joan made up her own mind and chose the newer gown, declaring that she would not appear before Cecil a beggar's mistress, no, not if it were midnight and the inn afire and not a drop of water in the Thames to quench it in.

The gown she had worn but once and the cloth still smelled new and felt rich and fine in her hand. It was a deep purple and had trunk sleeves, a neat little bodice embroidered daintily with gold thread, and a ruff collar that accentuated the oval shape of her face. Upon her head she wore a velvet cap of the sort then much in fashion and upon her finger a gold ring marked with her initials. Donning this ensemble required a full thirty minutes which Matthew endured because he knew no manner of insistence would hurry her.

From below, Beauclerk pleaded with them to hasten. The matter was urgent, he said.

Finally Joan was dressed and she looked to Matthew for his approval. This he gave readily with a sigh of relief and they joined Beauclerk.

"In good time, marry," Beauclerk muttered in exasperation.

"You'd have me go naked, then?" replied Joan sharply.

"Nay," returned Beauclerk, "but while my master yet lives."

Joan brushed off the secretary's insolence and motioned him to proceed. Beauclerk led the way down the stairs and to the stable of the inn where he had left the horses with a hostler who was in a foul mood for having been awakened and seemed little merrier for the pennies Beauclerk handed him.

Beauclerk asked Joan if she could ride. She said that she could, wondering at the same time what he would have done with her had she answered otherwise. She looked uncertainly at her mount. It stomped its feet nervously in the straw, its nostrils inflating and deflating with excitement, its muscles taut with energy. The mare was fitted with an elegant saddle of the sort great ladies rode upon, of fine-tooled leather and silverwork. The mare looked at her with its great brown eyes and she thought, what if the beast bolts, throws me on the stones?

Joan saw herself bloody, her new gown in tatters.

Sensing her anxiety, Matthew led her toward the horse, patting her elbow comfortingly. He bid her hold fast to the pommel and helped her up while her gown spread out over the horse's flank. With her free hand Joan reached forward to stroke the mare's neck and withers. The gentle stroking seemed to calm the animal. The mare ceased stomping and looked about at the other horses. Matthew was mounting now. Was it her imagination or did his horse, a bay gelding, seem more docile than her own?

Beauclerk was watching them, saying something to the hostler, his face still and expressionless. The horse he sat upon was large, black, and powerful. In his left hand Beauclerk held the torch that would illuminate their journey. Then he nodded for them to follow and led the way out through the inn yard into the street.

Quickly they advanced to a canter. Above them the moon was sailing between large billowy clouds. The street itself was deserted, the windows shuttered, the doors bolted. It was a city of shades now, and the solemn glow of moonlight and the shadows of the riders against the walls of houses gave Matthew an eerie feeling that did not leave until they arrived at Cecil's residence.

The house sat back from the street, and was in the shape of a quadrangle with one side lying along the Strand from which it was entered through an archway. Opposite to this, only partly visible to Matthew, were the main living quarters, rising a good three stories with a noble roof bristling with chimneys. There were many windows, all dark, and Matthew watched them curiously as a serving man shook from his lethargy to admit them through the iron gate at the archway. They passed across the cobblestone courtyard where another servant materialized from the shadows to help them dismount and led the horses away.

Beauclerk motioned them to follow and they entered a side door and began walking through a succession of rooms of increasing size. Matthew had been in Cecil's great house of Theobalds and so to him this habitation seemed modest by comparison but to Joan, who had hardly uttered a word since leaving the inn, this was a palace. Knowing his wife as he did, Matthew knew just how she would be taking in all of what she saw.

Presently they came to what seemed a smaller apartment. Beauclerk stopped and knocked softly at a door and announced them. At once Cecil's voice could be heard from the other side of the door beckoning them to come.

Robert Cecil was dressed in a shirt of fine Holland silk opened at the collar and was standing behind a desk in the center of the chamber. He welcomed them, then dismissed Beauclerk, pointing at the same time to chairs in which the Stocks were to sit. Then he began to apologize for his quarters. They were small and dark and cluttered, he said. He explained that he was in the process of building a new house in the Strand and everything was at sixes and sevens. Matthew made a sympathetic face in response, and as Cecil talked Matthew cast his eyes about the room furtively. A high molded ceiling arched over a room almost too full of furniture. There was a great store of books on one wall; the floor was laid with carpet, not strewn with rushes, as in most houses, and in one corner there was a magnificent sideboard, draped with a Turkey carpet, upon which shone a magnificent collection of silverplate that acted as a reflector to the candles on the board. Behind Cecil an elegant tapestry covered what was probably one of the mullioned bow windows Matthew knew would overlook the river. In daytime the room would be well lighted. He imagined Cecil sitting there, reading one of his books or staring from the window, shaping England's course, dreaming her future greatness.

Intently curious, Joan saw first the man himself, correcting the impressions she had made from Matthew's description, finding him smaller in stature than she had imagined, the body that of a large child. She could see the hunched back, but she noticed that his face was fair, his brow generous and calm, his eyes penetrating and intelligent. An altogether handsome man, she thought, were one to consider only the head. Cecil stood behind his chair, upon the back of which his right hand reposed lightly, as though he were upholding the chair and not the chair supporting his hand. For all the knight's courtliness and delicate frame, there was strength and energy in his carriage.

While Cecil welcomed them both and then very flatteringly paid court to her, she half listened and half gawked at the splendid chamber. Upon entering she had quickly taken in its more conspicuous features. Now she focused on the details with that alert interest of one whose life is spent with rooms and their furnishings. She observed that the books that filled the high shelves and burdened his desk were for use, not for show as in other men's houses. Some were laid open, many were stacked at angles, as though they had been quickly taken up, perused, and then cast aside again. Through an open door to the adjoining room she spied a large four-poster bed. Cecil's bed. This was his private apartment. She felt honored and humbled and estranged all at the same moment, for there was an undefinable masculinity about these quarters, although there was nothing she could see that was exclusively a man's.

Her attention returned abruptly to the conversation, which had now involved her husband. Cecil invited them to sit. He took his chair behind his desk. In the candlelight the secretary's eyes were intent with expectation.

"Your letter abusing my virtue has had great success, Mistress Stock," Cecil said, while Joan blushed fiercely at his phrasing. "Gervase Castell has come out to the lure, I have met with him, and am now well on the way to discovering his purpose."

Cecil quickly summarized his meeting with Castell at St.

Michael's. When he had concluded his narrative, Joan asked: "Then the plot does concern the state?"

Cecil nodded. He made his hands into a steeple and rested his upper teeth on his fingertips thoughtfully. "As price for the return of the letter and Castell's silence I am to recommend a certain gentleman to an office of considerable strategic importance."

"Will you do it?" asked Matthew.

"Absolutely not. The gentleman in question is an able soldier, but the family has Papist sympathies. His appointment would be most unseemly under ordinary circumstances, but in this critical moment it could be disastrous. The office in question commands England's coastal defense, her soft underbelly."

"What is the next step?" asked Joan. "Seize Castell?"

Cecil paused before replying as though he were still working the next step out in his own mind. "In due course. First, I wish to investigate both Castell and the man I am to appoint more thoroughly. I see the Queen Wednesday. Castell will not expect the appointment announced until later in the week. That gives me two good days and possibly a third to determine the extent of the conspiracy. It's most unlikely Castell's alone in this, and I still have to determine the identity of this Basilisk, but I'll root them out, never fear."

"Three days is not much time," observed Matthew, amazed at Cecil's coolness in the face of the jeweler's treachery.

"Yet it is time and we must use it to advantage," replied Cecil.

"What can we do to help?" asked Joan.

"Your testimonies will be essential, for as of now only you can connect Castell with this plot."

"You did not see him?" asked Joan.

"No. My back was to him while we talked! Moreover, you can *also* identify some of Castell's men. This person who came very near to drowning you, Mr. Stock, what was his name?"

"John Starkey."

"Yes, Starkey, the beggarly knave. Doubtless there are others at his shop who are equally involved. I shall have them all rounded up in good time."

Cecil suppressed a yawn and smiled. "Forgive me. I've been up all night with this business. The spirit is willing but the flesh, the flesh, eh?" Cecil smiled amiably and rose from his chair. "Return to the Bell and wait there until you hear from me again," he said, leading them to the door and pulling a long silken cord. "But take care whom you admit to your chamber. We have yet to discover the blackmailer's fellows and, given the nature of blackmail, he may have a good many of them and in very high places, too. When Castell's in the Tower I'll call for you. Beauclerk will escort you back to your beds. You'll make it just in time. It will be dawn in an hour or so. Remember, caution is the word. Castell thinks you dead, Mr. Stock, let him think so still."

Presently Beauclerk returned to escort them home again. They said their farewells, greatly excited by the interview with Cecil, and then followed the young man out of the house where they found their horses waiting.

It was dawn. They had not been back to the Bell for an hour when they were startled by a furious pounding at the door.

"What now?" exclaimed Matthew. He had been sitting thinking of breakfast, suffering a gnawing hunger for he had eaten poorly the day before. Joan had resumed her needlework. Although weary, both realized the futility of going to bed again, not after their visit with Cecil. It was all too exciting.

She looked at her husband as he rose to see what was the cause of this new commotion. "Faith," she said, "it is Beauclerk come again with fresh news, though I would not have thought it to fall so hard upon our visit to Cecil."

"Most likely," Matthew grumbled as he unbolted the door.

And there before him was John Starkey, looking very grim. Behind him were two stout fellows in the buff jerkins the sheriff's men wore. Matthew gaped, his jaw falling in amazement.

Starkey and the officers shoved Matthew aside and strode to the center of the room. Joan had dropped her stitchery into her lap and was looking at Matthew for an explanation.

"Arrest them both," Starkey commanded.

Matthew protested. "What charge, my masters?"

One of the officers, a great burly fellow with a square jaw and blank angry eyes, seized Matthew by the arm and threw him against the wall. Joan shrieked and ran toward her husband but Starkey blocked her course, pinching the soft flesh of her upper arm until she cried out in pain.

"Be still, vixen," Starkey hissed, looking at her dangerously.

The other officer, a ruddy-complexioned younger man, had drawn his sword and was brandishing it in the air threateningly.

"See if he has the chain about him," said Starkey, addressing the officer from whose grip Matthew was at the moment struggling to free himself.

The burly officer shoved Matthew against the wall again, ordered him to hold or die, and prepared to search Matthew's person. In vain Matthew protested this rough handling, declaring that he had no chain—either his own or any other man's or woman's about him—but the officer paid no heed. He conducted his search with a ruthless methodicalness, while Joan viewed these proceedings with her eyes round with anguish and bewilderment.

When the officer had satisfied himself that Matthew had no chain upon him, he declared the same to Starkey, who, undeterred by this, commenced a long litany of curses directed at the Stocks. Finally, having exhausted his repertory, he said, "This is the man and this is the woman," casting Matthew a venomous glance. "I saw him steal the chain with my very eyes, as God is my witness. I would have apprehended him myself had he not quickly escaped into the crowd. And this woman here—" Starkey turned threateningly to Joan—"was with him. Search her as well."

Starkey seized Joan again and flung her into the arms of the younger officer. Joan shrieked and then regarded Starkey fiercely, hot with rage now by this impending assault upon her person.

"Should we not search the room and their gear first," suggested the younger officer, apparently hesitant to commence hostility with a woman who appeared able to defend herself.

"Oh, very well," answered Starkey, with obvious reluctance. He began to search about the bed himself, pulling off sheets and coverlets and then dragging Joan's chest from beneath the bed and struggling with the lock. He broke it with the butt of his knife and began plundering the contents, strewing Joan's garments about him in a great flurry of rage and indignation. When it seemed he had plumbed the bottom, he suddenly cried out in great excitement and held up in his fist a slender gold chain.

Matthew and Joan exchanged looks of wonder, but Matthew, knowing Starkey's perfidy all too well, knew also what had happened. With his back to them all the while he searched, Starkey had cleverly planted the chain where he could find it.

Starkey gave the now empty chest a sturdy kick and waved the chain in Matthew's face triumphantly. "See, see," he sputtered, spraying his saliva about him, "what more evidence is needed? The thief has given the chain to his whore to conceal for him. Is it not after the fashion, sirs? Do not these whoremasters practice these devices more regularly than a cock his crowing?"

At this Joan exploded. "Whore? Whore? Whom do you call whore, you bursten-belly knave! You whoremasterly rogue! You, you . . ."

At the same instant Matthew freed himself from the burly officer and rushed at Starkey, swinging awkwardly at his jaw. Starkey dodged the blow deftly and gave Matthew a solid jab to the stomach that set him down hard in the rushes and left him breathless and gasping for air. Nonetheless he managed to cry, "The chain is not mine! Nor is it my wife's. I have never until this minute set eyes upon the cursed thing. It was he," said Matthew, gathering fire now and pointing a shaking finger at Starkey, "who practices upon your credulity. It was he, Starkey is he called, who within this week has tried to drown me in the Thames."

Starkey pointed a derisive finger at Matthew and laughed scornfully. "See, sirs, how an honest man is served. I see a crime, I accuse the criminal, and I am accused. But who accuses me? Who accuses me? A thief, sirs! A proven villain, as our discovery of the evidence makes plain!"

"I am Matthew Stock of Chelmsford, clothier and constable," said Matthew, struggling to his feet.

"Matthew Stock he says! But see the porter below, or the innkeeper," Starkey declared. "They know him as Miles Merryweather. Lo, now, an honest man with two names. Does this deception not reek of villainy?"

Matthew began to explain why he and Joan had registered at the Bell under assumed names but it was futile. How could he explain it? It would take time, more persuasiveness than he had at his present command. Wht a clever devil this Starkey was, what an incredibly clever devil.

"Why do you wait?" asked Starkey, turning from Matthew to the officers. "Bear them away to the prison."

"We must go to the magistrate first," said the younger officer.

"Go then," answered Starkey, "and take the wench he says is his wife with him."

But this insult was more than Joan could bear. She ran toward Starkey flailing her arms wildly; her blow was truer than her husband's had been. She landed a resounding slap upon the man's face. Starkey gaped in astonishment. But the astonishment lasted only a

169

moment. Quickly he seized her and began to shake her violently, his little beady eyes smoldering with hate. She struggled in his arms, struggled to claw his face. Matthew joined the fray and for a moment the three of them were locked in combat until the officers joined to separate them and order them to keep the peace at peril of their lives.

"See now if she be not a witch as well as a thief," Starkey bellowed in rage, holding a hand to his face to which Joan's fury had added several vertical scratches.

"Leave my wife alone," shouted Matthew at them both. "We will go to the magistrate and happily, knowing our innocence, but allow my wife to be."

This concession seemed to quiet the tumult in the room, which had by this time awakened the house and brought a large crowd of spectators to the open door. Joan glared at Starkey. Starkey glared back. Matthew looked at them both. The burly officer took a pair of manacles from his belt and proceeded to bind Matthew, but he did not do the same to Joan. "She'll follow," he said. Starkey protested. He wanted both man and wife bound, but the officer told him he had only manacles for one. "She must follow unbound," he repeated, giving Starkey a look that implied that he had had enough of this uproar. The younger officer attempted to clear their way from the room, but this proved difficult. The crowd had enlarged, had filled the passage without and the stairs, and the curious gathered to view the arrest had difficulty retreating. Finally a path was made and the younger officer with Joan in custody led the way. Matthew, manacled and humiliated, followed with the larger officer, and then Starkey brought up the rear. As he emerged into the passage, someone spit upon Matthew's boots and cried, "Bloody thief." Another gave him a solid poke in the ribs. Up front of the procession the younger officer was commanding the crowd to make way and threatening to call out the watch. But the crowd took these threats very lightly, guffawing and threatening, making obscene gestures at the sheriff's men as well as at Matthew and Joan.

Matthew tried to put on a brave face. Bruised and indignant at this outrageous treatment, he attempted vainly to call out comfort to Joan, who with her officer companion was so far ahead of them that he was in danger of losing sight of them altogether. The crowd pressed in on them, shouting "Thief, thief" and "Let the villains hang." The onlookers seemed unable to distinguish the bound from the unbound, for Starkey was receiving as much abuse as was Matthew.

Matthew was relieved when they finally reached the street and the tumultuous assembly dispersed. Matthew's officer walked at a fast clip, looking neither to the right nor to the left. Matthew could see Joan and her officer in front of him now, and he was happy when they caught up with them again. Soon they came to a gray stone building, very filthy inside and out, and apparently some sort of gathering place for the disreputable persons of the city. He had never seen such a display of sordid humanity, the twisted bodies and countenances of those whom life had made brutal and mean. Some were chained to pillars or posts. Others sat around in groups on their haunches or leaned idly against the walls, spitting in the dirt and leering at the women passersby who were every whit as disreputable as they, whores, thieves, vagabonds, riffraff.

They were brought into a long hall at one end of which was a dais. There Matthew saw the magistrate, robed and deferred to by the cluster of officers about him, a motley collection of men and women in bonds, and a larger number of witnesses and onlookers, clerks of the court, warders of the prisons, and various friends and family of the accused persons present. The magistrate, an old bearded gentleman whose mannerisms suggested he was both hard of hearing and hard of seeing, half dozed as two angry women exchanged slanders before him while the bailiff of the court vainly tried to restore order. Compared to the restlessness of the yard outside the building, the interior seemed distressed. When the women's acrimony was finally stilled, a solemn hush descended over the company, and the business of justice resumed.

It was a good three hours before Matthew and Joan were brought before the magistrate. They had been made to sit upon a hard, stone floor, isolated from others of the accused, forbidden to speak to each other much less prevail upon some passerby to carry an appeal for help to Cecil. In the meantime their accuser, Starkey, came and went, strutted about importantly, and whispered to the two officers and various other persons with whom he apparently was acquainted.

"What have we here?" inquired the magistrate, looking up at the arresting officers and then at Matthew and Joan, as though he was unsure just who was officer and who prisoner. But the burly officer who was in charge of Matthew resolved his doubt with a thunderous denunciation of them as thieves and impersonators, elaborating the charge to such a degree that Matthew was forced to protest. But the protest was censured very severely by the magistrate, who for all of his torpor rose at once to the occasion and told Matthew that if he opened his mouth another time without begging his honor's permission he would be confined to the stocks forthwith.

The officer held the gold chain aloft for the edification of those present. The crowd at their backs drew close to view it and there were various estimations of its worth heard, murmurs of approval and disapproval, and then the shrill voice of the bailiff calling for a restoration of order.

"What says the accused of this?" inquired the magistrate, looking at Matthew sternly, as though the very existence of the chain made Matthew's guilt a foregone conclusion.

Matthew declared his innocence, said that he had never seen the chain before this day, before the moment Starkey produced it from his wife's chest.

"Do you mean to say that you were never in my master's shop, the sign of the Basilisk?" interrupted Starkey.

"Well, yes, I have been in the shop."

"See, sir, he admits it, then," answered Starkey with satisfaction. But Matthew had no time to quarrel with the logic of this inference before Starkey led him into a more damaging admission. "And you told my master your name was Miles Merryweather, did you not?"

Matthew hotly denied this, asserting that his name was Matthew Stock, clothier and constable of Chelmsford, that he had used the name of his neighbor only to protect himself from the threat of murder. But his explanation somehow managed to come out sounding like a palpable lie. Disputing every word, Starkey lost no time in pointing out to the magistrate that a man who registered at an inn under a false name was very probably a thief or worse, and certainly no honest constable. He ridiculed the idea *he* should want to murder Matthew. "What," he exclaimed, "a murderer, I, standing here before this assembly? Do murderers then keep company in the halls of justice and press their suits before magistrates? Sir, I beg you have no regard for this man—or his wife—but to administer speedy justice to them both."

The magistrate, who had seemed content to allow Starkey to undertake the role of prosecutor in this business, now sat back in his chair, stroking his white beard, and looking from Matthew to Joan and back to Matthew again as though the evidence presented left nothing more for an epilogue than the confession of the crime. During this interrogation Joan remained silent by her husband, too mortified to speak, fearful of her own violence should she be slandered again. She knew they were in enough trouble as it was.

But now it was Matthew's turn to lose his temper. He denounced Starkey as a liar and a traitor; he denounced Castell as the father of Starkey's treachery; his indignation even spilled over onto the magistrate, whom he called an old graybeard, more suited to drowse the while than administer justice. These remarks sat poorly with the magistrate, who leaped from his chair, and ordered Matthew and Joan removed to Newgate prison to await the next assizes.

He had no sooner pronounced this sentence than Matthew noticed a familiar face among the spectators. It was John Beauclerk, Cecil's secretary, standing by a pillar observing the proceedings. Matthew pleaded with the magistrate to hold his sentence; there was one in the hall who might testify on their behalf, he said. The magistrate was in no mood for delay, but then he said he would countenance it, should Matthew apologize for his words.

Reluctantly Matthew did, although he knew them to be true, and then he pointed out to the magistrate where Beauclerk stood and the magistrate called the young man forth.

"Who are you, sir?" asked the magistrate.

Beauclerk spoke very calmly and with much dignity, identifying himself as John Beauclerk, secretary to Sir Robert Cecil, information which seemed to impress the old magistrate greatly.

"Do you know this man and his wife?" asked the magistrate.

Beauclerk turned to look at the Stocks.

"I have never seen them before in my life," he answered.

"What!" exclaimed Matthew and Joan in unison.

"I do not know them at all, either the man or his wife," repeated Beauclerk.

This new development caused much commotion in the assembly, which the bailiff moved to quell.

Then Beauclerk asked the magistrate if any more were wanted of him, and the magistrate said no, expressed the wish that his testimony had not inconvenienced either Beauclerk or his august master, and wished him good day.

Stunned by this new treachery where they had least expected

it, Matthew and Joan exchanged looks of bewilderment as Beauclerk disappeared into the crowd. Then Matthew cried, "The man is lying in his throat!"

"Indeed," mocked Starkey cruelly, "we are all liars here, save for this goodman chainswiper, this Mr. Stock-Merryweather-or What-you-will."

There was a great explosion of derisive laughter from the crowd at these words, and then Matthew felt himself being led off again. He caught a glimpse of Joan behind him. Her face was ghastly pale and her eyes drooping, as though she was about to faint. Faint she must have done, for when he saw her later outside, the younger officer was carrying her in his arms.

"Then there is no woman named Susan Mallory at court?" Castell asked again, well knowing the answer now but still clinging to the hope that somehow the old man would say that there was.

"None, sir . . . not in this Queen's time. There was a Susan . . . a Susan Graham . . . and a Brigid Mallory . . . and I think a Margaret Mallory as well, perhaps her cousin. Brigid was a pretty young thing. I recall her mother, too—"

But the jeweler was no longer listening; he had turned his back to the speaker, and seeing that he had said more than what was wanted, the old man fell silent, letting his long bony arms hang at his side like dead branches half wrenched from their trunk. He had once been a chamberlain at Westminster. Long retired, he knew everyone at court and was gifted with a prodigious memory. He was so given to gossip that he would cheerfully have provided it to Castell for nothing, but in fact the jeweler kept him on a small retainer, which the former chamberlain took eagerly, thinking what intelligence he passed on to Castell was to be used to make lucrative business contacts.

The chamberlain was afflicted with palsy; his right hand trembled as he spoke. His eyes were azure and watery.

"No Susan Mallory," Castell murmured to himself.

"What, sir?"

"I said nothing."

He should have confirmed the letter earlier, before approaching Cecil. His error had been a fatal one. But why should he have suspected it and its tale of adultery anything but the truth? The girl's foolish mother, the plump baggage with the funny hat and the swarthy skin, had seemed genuine enough. And now to discover that she was Stock's wife, that Stock, too, was alive and aiding Cecil.

It was certain that even Castell's house and shop were under surveillance. Thank God for Beauclerk's big ears. The man had been quick enough to put what he had overheard together, quick enough to perceive there was money to be made by conveying word to Castell straightway. At least his investment in Beauclerk, a modest allowance dolled out intermittently, had paid off.

He slipped a few coins into the chamberlain's palm and told him to go. Then Castell turned his attention to Ortega.

The Spaniard had arrived an hour before in response to the jeweler's urgent message, snatched half dressed from a brothel in Cheapside. At the moment he was sitting at the window, his hat in his lap, his long legs sprawled before him as though his chief concern was the cut of his hose. But the Spaniard had been all ears since arriving, and rather than being dismayed by this unlucky turn of events he had actually seemed to take pleasure in Castell's growing awareness that he had been duped.

"I warned you against playing with Cecil," Ortega said when the chamberlain had left the chamber. "See now. He and his constable have made a fool of you."

Castell regarded Ortega coldly and forced a grim smile. The Spaniard returned his gaze very smugly, and Castell felt murderous. "Even now the constable and his wife are being conveyed to Newgate," Castell said.

"Cecil will find out. He will rescue them."

"Not in time he won't. How will he learn of it? Not from Beauclerk."

Castell stood directly before Ortega gazing down on the man. "Newgate is another name for hell. Who dies not there of the pestilence is murdered for his boots. But I've taken care of all that. You'll see, they'll not live to swear against me, by God."

"We shall see," replied Ortega languidly, as though he had suddenly lost interest in Castell's business. He rose to his feet. "By the way, what have you got on Beauclerk that he does this service?"

"Him? Nothing less than his greed. His ambition is very large. Twice, nay thrice, the size of the man."

"I advise you to quit England as soon as possible."

"No," replied Castell, making no attempt to hide his hostility now.

"You are no longer useful to us," said Ortega, smiling sardonically.

"I don't understand why this is so amusing to you, Count. It is your lord who would see his sister enthroned."

"And so he shall," replied Ortega, maintaining his smile. "But without your assistance."

"I have risked a great deal for your cause," returned Castell angrily.

"You are no longer useful to us," repeated Ortega, turning to go.

Castell made a dash for his desk, grabbed the pistol from where he had concealed it beneath some papers, and aimed it at Ortega. Ortega had seen the movement. In the same instant he had swiveled and drawn his rapier.

"Very pretty," said Ortega, looking at the weapon in the jeweler's hand. "Wheel lock, isn't it? A great improvement over the old matchlock but I still prefer a good Toledo blade. Fire it, sirrah, and you're a dead man."

"Thrust and I'll fire," Castell answered.

The two men stood there glaring at each other, killing each other with their eyes. Then Ortega said, "We seem to be at a stalemate. Perhaps we should lower our weapons and—"

Ortega never finished his sentence. The report was thunderous. Ortega's eyes widened with surprise and he fell backward, still holding his sword.

The explosion brought Starkey hurrying into the room, his own weapon drawn. He saw what had happened and knelt down beside Ortega, who was flat on his back with one long silken leg crossed over the other. There was a hole the size of a penny where his heart was.

"You placed your ball well, Mr. Castell," observed Starkey. He stood up and looked at his employer. "The man's dead."

"Good," said Castell, turning away. The pistol, a pocket dag of the latest and most clever design, still smoked. It trembled in his hand like a living thing. "Take care of Ortega, will you? And when you have done, take care of Matthew Stock and his wife. Make their deaths appear to be the work of some felon. It will be likely enough."

Starkey hesitated in answering and Castell turned to look at his servant. Starkey had risen to his feet and was regarding his employer coolly.

"What is it, Starkey?"

"What shall I have for it—for lugging off the Spaniard and killing the Stocks?"

Castell, his ears still ringing with the report, suppressed his irritation at Starkey's delay in carrying out his orders. "You may have the Spaniard here—his purse and his weapon. Will that suffice?"

Castell turned away again and presently behind him he could hear Starkey ravaging the corpse. Castell thought with disgust, The man will carry Ortega out stark naked before he's finished. Starkey had probably been listening at the door. That would have been very like him, sensitive as a hound to the prospect of his employer's failure, his imminent arrest. There would be no trusting him now. Through the diamond-shaped apertures of the lattice, Castell could see the red-tiled roofs of neighboring houses, a generous swath of azure sky, a scattering of delicate clouds moving indolently eastward to the sea. Birds sang in his garden and the leaves of his trees were splendid in the sun, but Castell took no joy in these things. The Spaniard's death had not been in the reckoning and he was sorry for it. Not for Ortega's sake but for his own, for the needless complication of disposing of him and of covering his own traces. He thought of Ortega sprawled behind him, the man's eyes still wide with surprise. He was half naked now if the obscene sounds of Starkey's pawing meant anything. Was the young Count's soul in heaven or in hell? Remembering Ortega's theology, Castell decided he was in purgatory. But Castell doubted that. No, Ortega was nothing, *nada,* a whisper in the air no sooner uttered than vanished forever, along with his pride in birth, his pride in his pure Castilian blood. Starkey was right to take the purse, the sword, the shirt. When they were gone there would be nothing.

Castell turned just in time to see the last of Ortega, limp on Starkey's shoulders. He turned back to the window, and saw the strangers standing beyond the garden wall staring up at his house. With the instinct long nurtured in such matters, he knew at once who they were. Cecil had lost no time in having the house watched.

He went to the top of the stairs and called out to Roley below and when Roley came he told him to dress himself in the dark velvet robe with the rolled sleeves that Castell often wore in the City. Accustomed to assuming disguises, Roley did not question these instructions. He donned the robe which fit him very poorly since he was slender of girth and long of arm; Castell told him the poor fit would make no difference. By the time Cecil's men realized who it was they were following the jeweler would have gone off in the opposite direction.

He told Roley to proceed to the shop, lock the door of the house behind him, and go by way of the garden, the better to draw attention to himself. When Roley was gone, Castell dressed himself in the laborer's garb he had worn during his interview with Cecil, filled his purse with all the loose silver in his desk, and withdrew from its hiding place the little book with its priceless list of names, dates, and places. For a moment he stood paging through the book, taking an almost sensuous pleasure in the feel of its leaves, in the fleeting glimpses of the names, and remembering how those names came to be there. Then he tucked the book safely within his shirt. The silver would be spent within the month, but the little book would keep him in clean linen and good wine forever.

TWELVE_____

That same afternoon Joan and Matthew were transported to New-gate by cart, along with a housebreaker, a pickpurse, and a little tailor sent up for debt. The cart jolted to a stop before Newgate stairs and the officer in charge leaped from his seat and hurried around to open the tailgate. He was a tall, lanky fellow with a face afire with boils and pustules and two little gray eyes that peered out beneath almost invisible blond brows. He was very boisterous and self-important, making much ado out of a simple job and obviously pleased with the impression his authority was making on the small crowd of persons gathered to watch the spectacle of newly arrived prisoners.

Matthew and Joan climbed down with the others. They stood around in the street, staring up at the prison.

There was a considerable amount of traffic going in and out, visitors, released felons and debtors, victuallers, various officers of the sheriff, magistrate, and courts, and a small troup of entertainers, dressed in motley. One of the entertainers led a brown bear on a chain while a little spotted dog yelped heroically at its feet.

Suddenly Matthew felt Joan take his hand and caress it. He turned his eyes from the prison and looked at her questioningly.

179

She had lost her cap and there were pieces of straw from the cart clinging to her hair. His heart almost melted at the sight of her stricken face.

"God keep you," she said, moving her lips, not making a sound at all, and looking at him with her intent, dark eyes.

Then they were put in a line and led single file up the stairs into the prison lodge where their fetters were removed and they came under the scrutiny of a half-dozen prison warders standing around conversing and smoking.

Matthew was relieved to find a different officer in charge from the surly fellow he had encountered on his previous visit. The deputy keeper was a stout, powerfully built man of about thirty-five with a very ruddy face and a large, bulbous nose that seemed to have been designed by some satirist bent on mocking the normal human visage. The deputy glanced once at the prisoners and then continued to converse with two of his men. The deputy had a commanding voice and presence, and the men were listening to him with obvious respect. Matthew looked nervously about him; his mouth was very dry and his heart racing. It was the same lodge as before and the warders and turnkeys may have been the same, but the place had a different look to him now, now that he was no casual visitor but an inmate. The clutter and filth of the lodge, the confusion, the surliness of the officers, assumed a threatening aspect. Slowly he began to realize how prosperity and civic honor in Chelmsford had misled him about life. He had taken them for granted, as his due. But *this* was life. London. Newgate. His happiness as a man, husband, father, constable, citizen, had been stripped from him in an instant, just as his mortal life had nearly been, in the river. All that remained now was his soul, that quintessential sprite of the air, but here, here in this godforsaken place, he wondered if he would be able to retain even that.

He prayed silently, feebly.

Matthew noticed the little tailor who had come to Newgate with them was weeping and had commenced to relate his story to one of the turnkeys. The turnkey paid no attention, but busily searched the tailor for weapons or valuables. When he had satisfied himself, the turnkey told the tailor to shut his mouth and stay in line. The tailor wiped his eyes with his sleeve and stood still in the center of the chamber.

An elderly man with sparse white hair and scraggly beard was bent over a square wooden table in the center of the room writing down the prisoners' names and the crimes of which they had been charged. This information was given to him by the magistrate's man, who proclaimed the names in a loud voice for the edification of the assembly.

Matthew was in line behind the cutpurse and Joan behind her husband. Matthew shuddered as he heard the word "thief" intoned after his name and felt even worse when Joan was called that, too. It seemed an eternity since morning.

"Are you the wife of this man?" inquired the recorder, peering at Joan and nodding in Matthew's direction.

Joan answered yes; the recorder appraised Matthew coolly. Matthew thought he could read the recorder's mind. There was Matthew, a middle-aged man of solid countenance and middling dress, but what of that? These days any thief could find his way into a good suit to mock the gentry withal.

"Move on," growled the recorder, inscribing something in his book. Joan joined Matthew in the corner where the tall, lanky magistrate's man picked his nose and observed the proceedings with wry amusement.

The recorder then looked up to announce that the prisoners would be assigned their wards. This seemed to occasion much discussion among the deputy, the turnkeys, and the recorder, and it was a full ten minutes before the assignments were made. During this interval the deputy and turnkeys scrutinized the prisoners and whispered among themselves. Matthew strained to overhear, although he could well guess the substance of their talk. He knew that a prisoner's assignment in Newgate rarely bore a relation to the severity of his crime; it had, rather, to do with the capacity of his purse. As a result, prison officials considered themselves businessmen, and their appointments, especially to the higher office of keeper and deputy, were much sought after.

The housebreaker and cutpurse were first assigned to their quarters, whereupon the two men immediately commenced negotiations for better ones, and after another period of haggling, they assumed satisfied expressions and began to chat familiarly with the warders and turnkeys as though they had been companions of long standing. Someone had brought a bottle from the taproom and was passing it around. Quickly the lodge took on the atmosphere of a common tavern. All that was wanted was a company of aproned drawers to mingle with the patrons. While this was going on, Matthew noticed that the magistrate's man and deputy keeper were looking at him, nodding their heads, and whispering.

Matthew and Joan exchanged glances; Matthew drifted over to where one of the turnkeys had been leaning idly against the wall since their arrival and inquired if it were possible for a married couple to be confined together. No, replied the turnkey in a tone implying that the question was a foolish one, this was not possible. The men were on one side of the prison, the women on the other. Of course visits could be arranged, he said. But there was a charge.

"Of course," responded Matthew dryly.

Presently the recorder announced that Joan Stock was to be sent to the Waterman's Hall on the second floor of the jail and Matthew to the Middle Ward on the first floor, on the common felons' side. From his previous visit, Matthew knew the general locations of these wards. He also knew that they were not the worst the prison had to offer and he withdrew his purse to pay the required sum. He had no sooner done so than the deputy approached him and informed him of the charge.

Matthew began to protest, for the amount seemed exorbitant. He might have had board and room in the best inn in Chelmsford for less.

"The charge," explained the keeper defensively, "is for your wife and for yourself. For another shilling you can have admittance to the Press Yard." The deputy enumerated additional charges, which involved lesser payments to cooks, attendants, turnkeys, and swabbers—the last being responsible for cleaning the prison of its nightsoil.

"Naturally," observed the keeper ironically, "if this sum seems high you could pay for yourself alone. There are lesser accommodations for the women. Or perhaps it would please you to save a penny by lodging in the Stone Hold, in which case you could feast on the Newgate rats for naught?"

Matthew shuddered. He knew about the Stone Hold. He remembered poor dead Ralph. The wonder was that the boy had lived as long as he had, in the darkness and the filth.

Matthew paid the sum, knowing full well that another man could have had the same accommodations for less and that the charge was padded to ensure that the keeper and his cronies got their share. But what could be done? He was only thankful that in

182

the confusion of their arrest he had remembered to bring money. During their journey from the magistrate's, he had managed to pass some to Joan as well. She had, also, her ring, and what was left of her gown, some parts of which might be sold for cloth of less expense, with the difference going to provide necessities of survival. Could he somehow get word to his friends in Chelmsford there would be money enough, enough for the master's side, where prisoners of the better quality could live quite comfortably, or so he had heard. Yet he hoped not to be interred here for that length. His chief concern at the moment was how he could notify Cecil of their misfortune.

As Matthew stared into Joan's face, her troubled eyes seemed to mirror his own confusion and disbelief. What was happening to them? They knew where they were and why, but it was as though their sense of who they were was slipping from them along with their physical freedom. He struggled to shut out this encroaching, alien world with its wrangling, leering wardens and turnkeys, the uproar from the adjoining taproom, the dismal insignia of the prison house—fetters, chains, halberds, and pistols; he took his wife in his arms and brushed her forehead with his lips, clearing away the strands of dark hair that had fallen about her face like a shredded veil. Her forehead was hot and moist to his touch; he could feel her trembling limbs. With one hand in the small of her back pressing her to his body he raised the other to caress her face, but beneath his fingers the familiar contours gave him small comfort. She of all things he was loath to lose—separation would be a little death—and even as he embraced her he could already feel her immense and growing distance.

But then, suddenly, he felt her pulled away. It was not of her own will. One of the turnkeys was rushing her off. She was looking back at him, her eyes round with fright, and as he watched Joan vanish into the maw of the prison he felt his eyes fill with hot tears of anguish and rage.

The Middle Ward of Newgate was a great cheerless hall with a few tall dirty windows and a high ceiling. There were no beds for the inmates but there was a good oak floor on which a sleeping place could be made of straw and blankets which constituted the ward's sole furnishings, except for the scattering of small personal articles the inmates managed to preserve against the depredations of thieves and the warders. Upon arriving there, Matthew was immediately surrounded by other inmates wanting to know his crime, eying his clothes enviously, and desiring to sell him some service or privilege or have news of friends or family. But this interest proved to be fleeting, for when they learned he was a stranger in the city, they left him alone, and he wandered about his new habitation aimlessly, feeling sick at heart.

Despite the dismal surroundings, the prisoners were active. They played cards, diced, or stood about conversing. They were a very mixed group: some were well dressed and others practically in rags but here, oddly, social condition was no bar to intercourse. Imprisonment made them equals; the gentlemen chatted with laborers, the merchants with cutpurses—the ward was a little Paul's Churchyard, brought indoors. Tobacco and liquor were much in evidence, and it was clear that the latter had much to do with the prevalent bonhomie.

After a while Matthew drifted down to the end of the hall where there was a wall covered with notices and proclamations. Some of these were very old—tattered and illegible. They offered rewards for information leading to the capture of malefactors. To while away the hour, Matthew read them. What a God's plenty of thieves, conycatchers, murderers, traitors, and vagabonds there were. He read their names, their descriptions, their acts. The traitors interested him the most. By right, thought Matthew, Castell's name should be blazoned there on the wall, along with that of his lieutenant, John Starkey. And so they should be when Cecil discovered the Stocks' imprisonment and released them.

He remembered John Beauclerk's false testimony before the magistrate. Why had the secretary lied? And Starkey, why had he manufactured that story about the chain? Had it been simple malice, or another devilish stratagem?

Matthew paused in this catechism to reorder his thoughts. Both Starkey and Beauclerk had lied, and as a consequence Matthew now stood in Newgate awaiting the next sessions. That would be a good month from now, time aplenty for Cecil to learn of Matthew's arrest and secure his release. So what was to be gained by bringing him here?

And then he knew what it was, as he stared at the proclamations before him. Newgate was the citadel of crime. All about him were men very much like those whose heinous deeds were described in the proclamations. Here Matthew, and Joan, too, were in the company of murderers and highwaymen. In Newgate anything could happen. It was like the pulling cascades at the London Bridge, a wild disorder of elements; he and Joan would be swept away in the flood and there would be no one held accountable.

It would happen soon. Before Cecil could save them.

At this, Matthew saw the ward anew. Suddenly the activity of his fellow prisoners took on a cast more sinister for its very appearance of normality and what had struck him first as good fellowship now seemed the flimsiest of façades. There were no true men here, no, not a one. Only evidence that money no matter how ill-gotten could make a decent suit while inside was all rottenness and treachery. He noticed that several of the inmates were looking at him. Was there something about his expression, his stance, or dress that invited their scrutiny, or did they know well enough who he was and what price the jeweler was willing to pay for Matthew's life?

Realizing he must warn Joan, he rushed over to one of the windows that gave out into the Press Yard, but escape offered the dimmest prospect there. He watched the scene with growing futility. Prisoners mingled sociably. There were a good many warders about, identified easily by their leather jerkins and caps, but it was difficult to tell whether they were keeping order or merely fraternizing with the inmates.

A tapping noise behind him caused Matthew to return his attention to the ward again. One of the warders was fixing a new notice to the wall. Matthew walked over to examine it. It announced worship service on the following morning in Newgate Chapel.

"Do they all go to service?" Matthew asked, peering over the warder's shoulder.

The warder turned, his expression one of annoyance for this disturbance of his labor. He had an immense girth, a low forehead, and a bushy orange beard that covered the lower half of his face. He replied to Matthew very curtly: "A few, a very few—those with religion and those to be executed and their friends. There's plenty of good sermons then. The condemned kneel about the coffin, you know."

Matthew had heard that story. All the world knew it. The condemned were forced to kneel about a coffin while above them in the pulpit a preacher admonished them to repent. The prisoners received the sacrament; they made absolution, readied themselves before God. Who would not, with his chin propped upon the solid box into which his mortal remains would repose until Judgment? Sometimes the prisoners made speeches denouncing their crimes and exhorting their fellows to forswear unrighteous courses. These were often very entertaining and were published as broadsides for the edification of the public. Hiram Smallwood, a merchant tailor of Chelmsford, had seen it all with his own eyes. Hiram had told Matthew of it.

"The women go as well?" Matthew asked the warder.

"The women?"

"The prisoners."

Bushy-beard smiled lasciviously and regarded Matthew with new interest. "Women come indeed," he answered. "They don't sit together. Nay, that's forbidden them—and the common side lot and the master's side lot, they're kept apart, too. Yet the odors of heaven rain upon all."

The warder rolled his eyes heavenward in an expression of mockery. It was evident that religion was something with which he had nothing to do. Then he drew close to Matthew and whispered conspiratorially, "You've got the itch, you have, and not an hour within doors?"

"The itch?" asked Matthew, thinking the warder might be referring to some infliction of vermin for which the prison was famous.

"For women," Bushy-beard replied with a worldly air of one who knew a great many of the creatures. As it turned out he knew a particular one—one of exceptional qualities, by which he meant she had a clear eye, paps like rosebuds, and a well-turned calf as smooth and white as an egg. The warder expatiated at some length, but Matthew was a poor audience for his discourse. He could think only of Joan.

"Her name's Diana," said the warder climactically, as though the name itself was one of the woman's exceptional qualities.

"Diana?"

"In the woman's second ward, very convenient, indeed, sir."

For a groat she would gladly meet Matthew in the Press Yard; for two she would converse with him where he willed. The warder wanted something for her safe conveyance. He named the price; the first point of business was her rates.

When Matthew explained that he had no interest in just any

woman, the warder acted offended and began to draw away, but Matthew detained him.

"It's my wife," he said.

"Your wife? She's here?"

Matthew wanted to know more about the church service—the time, location of the chapel, whether the inmates had opportunities to converse.

"To converse, you say?"

"To talk. I want to talk to my wife."

The warder stroked his beard, then placed his hands upon the amplitude of his stomach. It was like a natural shelf. "I suppose you can go to chapel as you please," he said. The warder was obviously not yet recovered from his disappointment at Matthew's damp amorousness, nor yet had he come to Matthew's motive for wanting to go to chapel. Religion was all very strange to him, and those who took it seriously were even stranger. The warder continued: "But you may not sit by her, that's a fact. Such is the rule here and a very good rule it is."

To appease the warder, Matthew agreed that the separation of the sexes was a very good rule, but what a piece of hypocrisy was there. Anyone who knew anything of Newgate knew that it was easy to catch the pox there as in any Bankside brothel. The wardsman's pimping made that clear enough. Matthew decided at that very moment that if circumstances allowed him within twenty feet of his wife he'd warn her of her present danger or die in the attempt. This sudden resolve emboldened him, even while he recognized its elusiveness. He was not a violent man; what did he expect to do, burst through the crowd of prisoners to his wife's side?

Seeing that the warder still had some notices tucked beneath his arm, Matthew asked: "Where are you bound with the rest of those notices?"

The warder said he was going to put them up in the other wards. That was his job. The notices always conveyed the same information, but because the prisoners defaced them they had to be replaced once a fortnight. The warder didn't blame the prisoners for their scrawling. Were he an inmate, he would do likewise. He assured Matthew he knew a word or two that he would gladly see published in that manner.

"Will you be going to Waterman's Hall?"

"Anon." Bushy-beard hesitated, looking at Matthew expectantly. Their conversation had drawn the attention of other inmates who had formed a circle about them. As inconspicuously as possible, Matthew felt for a coin within his shirt and pressed it into the hand of the warder. This action, rather than attracting attention to the conversation between Matthew and the warder, now seemed for his audience to resolve the question of its subject, and the curious inmates resumed their previous business.

"This is yours if you'll bear a message to my wife who lies in Waterman's Hall."

The warder took the coin. Of course he would convey the message. Who was his wife and what words did Matthew wish to convey?

"Joan Stock of Chelmsford. Tell her to attend service in the prison chapel tomorrow. Tell her that her husband will do likewise and that it is he who has conveyed this message to you."

The warder repeated the name. "You can trust me to convey your message, sir," he said.

Bushy-beard removed a dirty cloth from his jerkin and wiped his brow, thrust it into his jerkin again, and then tucked the mallet into his belt. Matthew watched him stride off, whistling happily as he went, and wondered if he had spent his coin worthlessly. There was no reason for him to trust the warder. That he was a prison official meant absolutely nothing, and the man didn't even have an honest face to recommend him. But what was Matthew to do? Here he had no friends; one man was as trustworthy as the next, or as faithless. Perhaps Joan would receive his message, perhaps not. Yet Matthew recalled with what profound satisfaction the warder had received the coin. Certainly it was not the message that had inspired that satisfaction. It was the employment. Perhaps, Matthew concluded, the promise of further reward would make the man honest.

The warder had no sooner disappeared from Matthew's view than he saw Abraham come into the room.

"Matthew Stock, upon my life," he cried. "What, now, come again to visit those whom God has forsaken? You did get my message about poor Ralph? He'd dead, you know, stone cold."

Matthew answered: "Yes, I heard that, worse luck. I'm one of you now, though not, I trust, godforsaken as you deem yourself. My wife and I have been falsely charged."

Abraham made a keening sound from somewhere in his throat

188

and looked up at Matthew from beneath his scraggly reddish hair with moist sympathetic eyes. He took both of Matthew's hands and held them; the little Jew's fingers were bony and cold and they trembled as he spoke. "Has it come to this, then? It will be no time at all before all good men are here and the malefactors on the outside." His eyes closed in pain. He continued: "Tell me your tale, Mr. Stock, by what misfortune have you come here?"

Briefly Matthew recounted the circumstances of their arrest, describing at the same time Starkey's attempt on his life and Matthew's fear that a second effort would be made now that both he and Joan had been imprisoned. Of Cecil and of Castell's plot he said nothing, not merely for secrecy's sake but because he thought it would only make his long narrative hopelessly complicated. To all of this, Abraham gave rapt attention. His bony hands grew warmer in Matthew's; his face was drawn into a mask of infinite pity and concern. Then Matthew told him about his plan to contact Joan at the chapel service.

Abraham nodded his head sagely. "A wise plan—a practical plan," he said. "It's true the women are separated from the men but they file in two lines with no more than a span betwixt them. You may well have time for a word or two before they sit you down. But take care the warders don't see you conversing. If they discern it's your wife you're chatting with they'll want to charge you for the privilege, take my word upon it."

Everything Matthew had seen in Newgate confirmed Abraham's opinion. At the present rate of extraction his little supply of coin would be exhausted in a few days. He thanked Abraham for his advice.

"But now you can do me another favor," said Matthew, drawing close. "I must get word of our imprisonment to certain friends, high friends. Can you do that for me?"

Abraham said that he would try. He wanted to know to whom the message was to be conveyed.

"Sir Robert Cecil, First Secretary to the Queen."

Abraham's eyes opened in amazement. "Cecil, you say." He shook his head dubiously. "It is one thing to get a message out of Newgate, but to direct it to so great a person, well . . ."

"But Cecil must know that I—we—are here. I swear I will make it worth your while."

Abraham agreed to do what he could. Matthew watched him

move off into the crowded room. It was only after he had left that it occurred to Matthew that it would be very unlikely for a message to go directly to Cecil. It would go first to the doorman, at best to one of his secretaries. Perhaps even to John Beauclerk, who would have no reason to see that his master got the message. Matthew realized letting Cecil know of his whereabouts would not be easy.

Much distressed, he went to a corner of the ward and sat down. Presently two warders struggled in bearing a huge iron pot hanging on an oak beam they bore upon their shoulders. They set the pot upon the floor and then began ladling its contents out into the wooden bowls of the men who had gathered around to receive their portion. These, Matthew observed, were the poorer inmates, the thieves, vagabonds, and sturdy beggars who depended on public charity. They held their bowls in their hands meekly while waiting for them to be filled; they stood without talking and with the vacant stares of men remembering happier times. Matthew knew he could have had better fare—fresh bread, apricots and jam, beef or lamb, and wine of good quality—if he had only been willing to pay for it. But that day he felt he had paid enough. He resented the continual supplication of the prison system, which had made him feel like a milk cow being milked dry.

Yet he would eat the stew, he thought grimly, as the strong odor of fish filled his nostrils.

He joined the line of men waiting to be fed but by the time his turn had come the pot was nearly empty. He looked into the pot. On the bottom a mackerel's head with stark, glassy eye and what looked like niggardly bits of carrot and onion floated in a thin, milky-white liquid. He declined the gruel, thankful that hard rolls were included in the supper, and wandered off into the corner to probe the stale roll for maggots. Relieved at finding none, he ate it bitterly.

"That's a most beauteous gown, sweetheart. A most beauteous gown indeed. Did a gentleman buy it for you?"

The eyes, nose, mouth, and chin of the woman all struggled to dominate the small, pale face. She was all skin and bones, and Joan could see the thin blue veins in her arms like little serpents and, beneath the ragged smock she wore, the severe outlines of her shoulders. Her manner was childlike, and this coupled with her devastated appearance made her present attention all the more

190

horrible. She reached out to touch Joan's gown, to feel the texture. Joan recoiled instinctively. The woman smiled with a mirthless grimace, with a dog's breath.

"Beth won't hurt you. Beth won't hurt the pretty lady."

Joan longed to slap the hand away, but she was afraid, afraid of the haggard creature that touched her, afraid of the other inmates who were watching her curiously. How glad she was that she had thought to conceal her ring. She had tucked it into her stocking; she could feel its comforting hardness next to her ankle.

Since her arrival in the ward, Joan had stayed to herself, studiously avoiding conversation with the other women. Of these, there were fifty or sixty crowded into the high-ceilinged, crumbling vault with its dirty walls, its stench of urine and unwashed bodies, its total absence of anything to interest the eye or delight the heart. There were windows on one side of the chamber but they were far above eye level. How she wished she could look out of them. But, then, what would she have seen? The grim parts of Newgate, sooty London. Joan felt abused and defeated; she could not restrain her tears.

"What's your name, sweetheart?"

Joan did not want to tell the woman her name. She thought of inventing a false one, but reconsidered. What difference would it make now? Her own true name meant nothing here. A false name would not rid her of her shame. She said, "Joan Stock is my name."

"Joan, Joan Stock?" The woman screeched with laughter. Other prisoners, as wretched as she, were drawing about Joan now, staring at her clothing, enjoying her discomfort.

"Let me guess," she said. "You used overmuch courtesy to some strange man, the law came upon you, and having no money about your person at the moment you could not buy your freedom from the sheriff's men. Do I say truly?"

"I shouldn't be here. I'm innocent. I and my husband," Joan said, gathering up her courage. She was now the center of attention of a dozen women, slatterns with hard, savage faces.

"Ah, your husband came with you," exclaimed another woman, drawing close to Joan. The woman's breath stank abominably of the fish broth the woman's ward had been served for supper, and Joan drew back. This gesture seemed to excite the resentment of the others. One, a girl with raw red skin and straw-colored hair hanging down over her face, reached out and pinched Joan painfully. Joan pushed the girl away.

"Stay, there!" a masculine voice commanded. Joan looked up. One of the warders was approaching them. The man had a full, red beard and beneath his arm he carried a sheaf of papers and in the other he had a mallet.

"Lord, Lord, it's handsome John—he that hides his visage in that monstrous growth of fur upon his cheek."

"A bear, a bear," several of the women cried mockingly.

The warder cast the women a threatening look and inserted himself between them.

"Are you going to take us all on with that mallet, John?" asked the hard-faced prisoner who had begun the taunting.

"If I have to, Beth, if I must. You know what happens to prisoners who fight, don't you? We drop them into the Hold. It's filthy there—"

"It's filthy enough here," interjected the girl who had pinched Joan.

"The rats are bigger there."

"And hungrier," added another woman, cackling as though the idea of the rats was a great joke.

"Back off, I said," snarled the warder, whereupon there was a hail of curses from the prisoner called Beth. This outburst seemed to satisfy the rest and they dispersed, leaving Joan and the warder alone.

The warder turned and said, "You wouldn't be Mrs. Stock, would you?"

Joan looked at the grinning man with the huge stomach. She had never seen him before. How did he know her name?

"I have a message from your husband. It's yours for tuppence."

"You gave her her husband's message?"

"I did, sir."

"And how did she reply?"

"She said I was to convey back to him that she would come."

"Good."

"Will you want more of me?"

"No. Here."

The warder stuck the new reward in his purse with great satisfaction. He was paid very little for his job and it was only by doing extra favors for prisoners and others that he was able to live.

"Thank you, then, sir. Remember me, please, when you have need. Shall I continue to watch this fellow?"

"Yes. He's a dangerous man, although he seems harmless enough on the outside. I wouldn't be surprised if he and his wife try to escape. Perhaps they meet in the chapel for that purpose."

"In faith, they shall not!" cried the warder.

"Marry, never fear," said Starkey in his lilting voice. "They shall meet, but they won't escape."

THIRTEEN⸻⸻

Joan had hardly slept. How could she, propped as she had been against the filthy wall while mice rioted on the bare tables for scraps and the snoring of her fellow inmates resounded in the ward like the plainsong of frogs in Chelmsford pond? There was a bed of sorts; all the women's wards in Newgate had beds, and she had been issued a blanket, but the straw was alive with vermin and the blanket—she shuddered as she thought of it—was torn, nay, chewed upon, and stained suspiciously with a dark brown stain she was sure was blood. She had sat against the wall all the night, thankful only that it was not winter, and as the morning began to glow through the high windows of the ward she was almost as much past feeling as past hope. Now she observed the other women as they awoke from sleep. There was not a face among them that did not seem weary and ashen, not an eye that did not seem dull. The women rose reluctantly, then sat about in a kind of stupor, staring vacantly at the walls, or at their hands. They did not look at each other; that would have been too painful. A warder brought fresh water, some of the women washed, but the others seemed too tired.

Breakfast consisted of stale bread and a thin gruel. Joan might have fared better had she been willing to pay for breakfast. A fresh egg, a cake, a bottle of good ale—these might have been hers for a few extra pennies and a smile at the mean-faced knave who had proffered them and won her enmity with his supercilious airs. Joan's pride would not permit her to part with a penny of the little store of coins Matthew had conveyed to her. She was left to breakfast on her pride and a poor unsubstantial dish it was.

When the warder returned to collect what had not been eaten by the women Joan approached him to inquire about the chapel service. The warder was a wiry little man with intense dark eyes, a grizzled beard, high flushed cheeks, and a belligerent manner. She had heard the women call him Wat, although whether this was his Christian or family name she could not tell. The women taunted him with jibes about his size and beard, and he repaid in similar coin in a high-pitched, churlish voice, moving among the beds and tables of the ward like a little animal scurrying among stumps in a forest, and seeming to enjoy the exchange of caustic wit.

"Ah, then," said Wat, looking at Joan with a clearly defined sneer, "wanting to make peace with God, are you?" His narrow eyes scrutinized her from top to toe.

"If it please me—and Him," Joan retorted, responding to the man's impudence with a frigid stare. She was satisfied to note at the same time that she and he were of the same height and that she had the advantage of weight. But her boldness had little apparent effect on Wat. The warder balanced himself on the heels of his boots, rocking to and fro as though at any moment he would hurl himself at her in his fury. On his hip he carried the wooden trencher and what remained of breakfast; his load was very light, for the women had eaten ravenously and what they had not consumed they had concealed.

"I have heard tell," she said in an icy, disciplined voice, "that the preacher here has a most commendable tongue—a golden tongue, indeed."

"Oh, have you now?" replied Wat bumptiously. "Well, so he may for all I know. I have nerve heard the man."

She asked again, "What time is the service?"

"Anon," said Wat, his little face screwed up maliciously.

"An hour, half-hour, or wain?" asked Joan, pursing her lips.

"Anon," repeated Wat.

"Anon, anon, anon," Joan mimicked, much vexed now. In disgust she stamped her foot and showed him her back. She was walking away when she heard him cry out behind her.

195

"Patience, goodwife! You're not amongst your minions or servants now. You have here no docile husband to scold. Trulls and cabbagemongers are your peers in the ward. Mend your manners or I'll show unto you neighborhoods of Newgate that will make where you stand seem a pleasure palace."

Joan swiveled around, all patience flown, her face burning. Every woman in the ward watched her, but she cared nothing for that. "You log, you salamander!" she shouted, shaking her fist at the warder.

But already Wat's back was to her. He was making for the door, laughing and flinging his taunts from side to side like a rich man casting alms to beggars, an enemy to all he passed and apparently not a whit less happy for that.

Feeling quite miserable and struggling to suppress her tears of anger and mortification, Joan went over to the pallet she had disdained to lie upon and sat down. She was no longer the object of attention and, seeing her privacy restored, she yielded to the full measure of her grief and wept like a child.

"Wat is a great fool," said a woman who, it seemed, had come to comfort her. She had round eyes and a pale white forehead. She had been pretty once but age and Newgate had done their work: her countenance was now marred with grief and hopelessness, and her tattered garments had a musty smell as though they had been laid away in a chest for years.

"My name is Adriana," said the woman. She sat down beside Joan and put her arm around her. To this maternal gesture Joan yielded; choked with tears, she couldn't speak. "Wat treats us all so," said Adriana. "He would sooner cast an insult than catch a compliment. It's his way. Pay him no mind."

Joan told Adriana that she had only wanted to know the time of the service. Chapel service was at seven, Adriana told her. She pointed to two women who were dressed in black. One of these Joan recognized from the night before, the hard-faced vixen with the mouth of filth and the termagant's temper. But the woman's fury was cooled now. Standing there, dressed for the grave, she seemed almost serene, the hard lines of her visage dissolved in the earnestness of her communication, which was obviously as intense as it was intimate. The girl with whom she spoke was very young. She was painfully plain, with a long jaw and little pig's eyes. Joan thought, what had the child done to deserve this—murdered her lover, assaulted a constable, filched a loaf of bread? The women stood apart from the others, not by choice. They were being shunned because their death was to be very soon. Their garb testified to the fact.

Then Wat returned, announcing in a high, shrill, impudent voice that chapel service was to commence presently. Those inclined to attend, he said in a tone implying that there would be very few, should form a line. He raised his thin arms in the air to indicate just the point on the floor at which the line was to form. The condemned women moved forward, a handful of others joined the line, and Joan took her place behind the others. Wat surveyed the chamber with the authority of some great lord and then, when it was apparent he had collected all that morning's faithful, with a great show of ceremony he bade them follow him.

The chapel of Newgate was a lofty chamber on the third floor of the jail, very bare of the furniture of holiness and with high barred windows and a gallery crowded with onlookers come to the prison to see the sights. At the center of the chapel, directly beneath an empty pulpit, was a rectangular enclosure in which benches were arranged around an oblong box. At first Joan thought this a table, but then she realized it was a coffin. A handful of male inmates, garbed in black, were already assembled there under the watchful eye of two of the turnkeys. Around the enclosure pews were arranged and these were already nearly full of inmates, most of whom were behaving rowdily and exchanging greetings and insults with their acquaintances or making obscene remarks to the women, who were, she was relieved to find, seated separately. Ahead of her, Joan heard two of the women comment on the size of the congregation; one of the two responded that this was typical of a service for the condemned.

Wat ushered Joan and the others into one of the pews, warned them sternly to keep silent, and then disappeared out the door from which they had entered. Joan sat down and began to search the faces in the crowd for her husband's. Faint from exhaustion, hunger, and fear, she found the faces were indistinct, but then her vision sharpened, cleared, and presently she discerned Matthew's features in a pew directly opposite hers. They saw and recognized each other in the same instant. Matthew's expression changed from anxious inquiry to joyful recognition. Then as suddenly his countenance was transformed. His brow darkened, his jaw set. He was staring intently at something—or someone—above her. What had he seen? Joan turned in the pew to look upward to the gallery.

It was John Beauclerk, Cecil's secretary and their betrayer. He was seated among the visitors, looking very prim and neat, his lips curled in a derisive smile. And next to him was Starkey.

Joan's heart sank. The two men were looking down at her and were both smiling. Then Starkey whispered something in Beauclerk's ear and the younger man laughed and fidgeted in his seat.

Joan's eyes sought her husband and found him again. The significance of his anguished countenance suggested that even in this assembly, in this sacred place, they were in great danger.

A sacristan with a tall staff was pounding on the floor of the chapel for silence, but if anything the talking and laughter increased. The warders began to patrol the pews bidding the noisier inmates to keep order but to no avail. The uproar continued. Finally, the sacristan, a round little man with a shiny bald pate, looked appealingly to the warder who seemed in charge of the rest and he leaped upon the coffin at the center of the chapel and, with his legs spread apart and his fists planted firmly in his sides, he ordered those to keep silent or he would have the chapel cleared. This threat, issued in a strident, commanding voice that rose above the clamor, took its effect. There were a few final outcries and jibes, a general stirring in the pews and in the gallery, and then quiet as the congregation waited for the preacher to appear.

Behind the pulpit was a small door, which presently opened to admit the man of God, a tall, almost emaciated figure with a long narrow face, a complexion of sickly pallor, and dark eyes that appraised the congregation with a stare of disapproval. The preacher, dressed in black, placed his hands on the pulpit and leaned forward.

In a clear, resonant voice he announced that the service would commence with a hymn. Then he began to sing, and some of the congregation joined; afterward he delivered a lengthy prayer, read several passages from Holy Writ, and then began to preach, taking as his text a verse from the New Testament that spoke of hell. As he spoke, he became animated, gestured dramatically; his forehead, high and pale, shone with sweat, and his eyes grew larger, darker, and more fiercely intense. He described hell with such vigor that one would have thought he had just returned from a tour of inspection. But no mortal had seen hell, he insisted. Man's imaginings fell short of its terrors. There, he declared, in hell's fiery reaches was the abode of murderers, the sorcerers, the liars, and thieves.

He paused. During this recital his voice had risen to a feverish pitch. A number of the women present, both in the pews and in the gallery, were weeping, while in the pit, a young girl had apparently fainted.

"Have you ever singed your finger in a fire?" asked the preacher. "Thrust your foot into boiling water? This was naught. Have you ever broken a bone, seen it protruding from your flesh, all white and glistening? That was naught. Have you ever—"

But the preacher's question was interrupted by a piercing shriek from the condemned pit. Joan looked to where the young woman had recovered from her faint and was now standing on her feet. She had thrown the caul from her head and was tearing at her hair and flesh. Her companions were trying to restrain her. The preacher glared down at the girl, extended one long, accusatory finger, and said: "Well may you weep, woman, knowing the hell fire that awaits—"

But he did not finish his sentence. He was prevented by a thunderous explosion that shook the building and brought everyone to his feet. It had come from the gallery where thick clouds of noxious yellow smoke were rolling across the ceiling of the chapel, and John Beauclerk was standing on his feet with the rest of the visitors shouting "Fire" at the top of his lungs. But the congregation hardly needed this warning. The sermon had set the scene for the panic to which the strange explosion, the cry of fire, and the billowing smoke had now given the final touch. Everywhere there was confusion as the inmates climbed over each other to escape.

For a moment Joan was too stunned to move. The other women in her pew pushed her aside in their rush for the doors, screaming. In vain she looked for her husband, but the chapel opposite her presented a chaos of bodies and indistinguishable faces. Those who were not coughing from the smoke were yelling appeals, curses, or mindlessly echoing Beauclerk's cry of fire. Some of the visitors were leaping from the gallery to avoid the flames and landing on the heads and shoulders of those below. In the high pulpit the preacher whose eloquence had incited the panic had now vanished while the warders and turnkeys had relinquished all control in order to save themselves. The doors into the chapel were much too small. Only a trickle of persons was managing to get out and the bodies of those who had stumbled in the attempt were now blocking the escape of the rest. As the inmates became increasingly desperate, they became violent, and fighting broke out in various parts of the chamber. To add to the confusion, someone had struck the prison alarm bell located outside the door and the clamor now magnified the uproar in the chapel.

In the midst of the bedlam Joan's only thought was the whereabouts of her husband. Then she saw him, struggling toward her, climbing over the railing that separated the pews from the condemned pit. The chamber was filled with smoke; she found it difficult to breathe and her eyes watered. Her husband's approaching form blurred. She cried out to him and in the next moment they were in each other's arms.

Matthew had been pushed aside as his fellow prisoners rushed for the door; now he started for the center of the chapel for a better view, motivated by a growing certainty that the explosion, the fire, the smoke were a cover for manslaughter and that they—Matthew and Joan—were to be the victims. Of course the vengeful Starkey, shamed by his failure to drown Matthew at the bridge and enraged by Joan's counterfeit letter, would want to do the deed himself. And he no sooner thought this but Matthew saw where Starkey was, making his way from the gallery to the chapel floor. And there was Joan, standing motionless, obviously stunned by the explosion and ensuing panic, unaware of her danger. Matthew knew he must reach his wife before Starkey did.

Matthew did reach Joan, shook her to her senses, and told her to follow him. He was sure Starkey had caused the explosion. He had seen him stand and move to the rear of the gallery just before the blast and he knew it would have been no great thing for Starkey, a practiced villain, to smuggle power and flint into the prison. He prayed that what Starkey had designed to conceal a murder would as well facilitate their escape. Pulling Joan after him, Matthew ran toward the front of the chapel, bounded up the handful of steps to the pulpit and door through which the preacher had made his entrance and exit. As Matthew hoped, the door was unbolted, the preacher in his haste having forgotten to bolt it, but Matthew did not make the same mistake. The door was no sooner secured than he heard Starkey's heavy tread upon the steps and an instant later the full weight of the man's body hurled violently against the door.

"I'll kill you, Stock, I'll kill you!" cried Starkey from the other side.

Matthew leaned back against the door, praying to God that it would hold against Starkey's assault.

The door held. There were more blows, more curses, and then nothing. But Matthew knew Starkey had not given up. He saw they were in a sort of attic, a long empty room. On the bare wooden floor was a heavy layer of dust except where the succession of preachers had made a path to the pulpit door. He said to Joan, "Now we must make haste."

But Joan was exhausted; she was still coughing from the smoke; her tear-stained face was pale with fear and she shuddered in his arms. "Where? How?" she asked.

"There," Matthew said, pointing to the opposite end of the chamber where the wall was partly covered by a curtain. The curtain concealed a door. Beyond were stairs, descending to the floors below.

Joan looked down uncertainly. "Would we not be safer to remain as we are?"

Matthew shook his head. "It's likely Starkey knows the prison like the freckles on his face. If we don't hurry, he'll find us here alone and will need no fire to undo us."

The door on the next landing was also unlocked and Matthew opened it cautiously. Inside was a cloakroom. On a table at its center the man of God had cast off his vestments in the course of his flight and on the walls were hooks from which hung an assortment of winter garb and several of the brown leather jerkins that served the warders as uniforms. Beyond, another door was slightly ajar and from the other side Matthew could hear angry voices and the rattle of weapons.

"The lodge," whispered Matthew. "We've come down to the lodge."

"Then escape is futile," Joan moaned.

Matthew closed the door and waited, thinking. Presently the uproar in the lodge subsided. He said to Joan, "It is likely they've all gone up to the chapel to fight the fire or control the riot. We may be able to pass through now."

But Joan hesitated. "Will they not have the gate guarded?"

Matthew thought there still might be an avenue of escape. They had very little to lose, and he felt it was better if they were caught by the guards than by Starkey. He opened the door to the cloakroom and looked about. No weapons were kept there, only

201

clothing. The weapons, he remembered, were in the keeper's office. *The clothing*. He pulled one of the leather jerkins from its hook and then another, trying them on over his shirt. "Pray God they think me one of them," he said to Joan, who had watched his activity with great puzzlement.

"Will you leave me behind, then?" she asked in a pitiful small voice. "For I can fit no jerkin."

"You may dress as you are. I will say I am a guard and you a visitor and my charge to see you safely from the prison."

"But what if the keeper's deputy or one of the warders recognizes us?"

Matthew had not thought about this complication, but he brushed it aside. There was nothing else to be done.

He led Joan through the cloakroom and into the lodge. It was not empty, as he had supposed. The elderly recorder who had admitted them was seated at his customary place, bent over his ledger, pen in hand, his head down so that all Matthew could observe was the untidy growth of his white hair. The man was strangely oblivious to the turmoil in the prison, and Matthew and Joan were well into the center of the room before he looked up at them quizzically. The recorder's vague expression showed no sign of recognition and Matthew realized that at least as far as the recorder was concerned, the warder's jerkin Matthew wore was sufficient evidence of his new identity.

"Who is the woman?" inquired the recorder absently, turning his gaze again to his book.

"One of the visitors," Matthew replied, trying to sound casual. "I was ordered to bear her to the street—for safety's sake, from the fire and riot."

"Indeed," said the recorder. "And who ordered you so to do?"

Matthew hesitated, and looked at his wife in bewilderment. What could he say? But Joan whispered, "Tell him Wat ordered you."

Matthew said, "Wat."

"Wat, was it?" replied the recorder briskly, his head still down. "We have fallen on ill luck here then if such as Wat gives orders. I haven't seen you before in the lodge."

"I am newly appointed . . ." said Matthew.

"Indeed," mumbled the old recorder. "Well then, learn your duty—which I assure you will not consist of obeying Wat. Don't stand there gawking, fellow, bear the woman out."

"Yes, sir," Matthew replied promptly. He proceeded to lead Joan from the room and had nearly gained the threshold and the prospect of freedom when his way was barred.

Starkey stood in the doorway, smiling grimly.

"You're leaving—so soon?" Starkey asked calmly.

"By your leave, you wretch," Joan said from behind Matthew.

"Well then, I'll have a word with you both before you do. The recorder here won't mind. We'll be very quiet, won't we?"

The recorder had stopped his writing and was looking up at Starkey. He was obviously irritated at this new interruption.

"You won't kill us, not with *him* here," said Joan, meaning the recorder.

Starkey nodded his head slowly, his eyes fixed on Matthew. "You're right, Mrs. Stock. What I have in mind is best done without witnesses. But please remember that you and your husband are prisoners in this place. Escaping prisoners now. And were you to compound the felony with cold-blooded murder, say, of a prison official—"

"What official?" demanded Joan hotly.

"He means the recorder," Matthew said.

The old man's mouth was agape. He sensed trouble and was glaring at Starkey. He began to splutter inarticulately as though he had very little breath left for his words, and in a quick blow Starkey sent the old man sprawling. The recorder lay on the floor, face up, his eyes closed.

"You've killed him!" exclaimed Joan, horrified.

"Prisoners desperate to escape will do anything, Mrs. Stock," replied Starkey, grinning.

Matthew began to back toward the door to the cloakroom, his eyes fixed on Starkey. He knew the man had a weapon, probably the stiletto, and indeed at that moment Starkey withdrew it and held it out in front of him, a long narrow blade.

Matthew heard Joan behind him. "Oh, Matthew," she groaned.

"You were very clever, both of you," said Starkey. "You tried to make me look the fool—put me in bad with my master—with that business about Cecil's whore. I do not forgive easily . . . that's why I came here myself. I never trust another to do my work for me. Besides, I wanted to see your faces. At the end. Do you understand?"

Matthew understood well enough. He braced himself for Starkey's attack, warning Joan to stay well behind him. He had no sooner done so than Starkey thrust out with the knife, the blade flashed, and Matthew jumped backward, pulling out a chair and holding it in front of him to ward off the slashing blade. He told Joan to run for her life and cut of the corner of his eye saw her dart to the far side of the room. Starkey lunged for the chair, wrenched it from Matthew's grasp, and hurled it against the wall.

"You must take your comeuppance, Mr. Stock," Starkey said, crouching low, ready to spring again.

Desperately Matthew looked about him for another means of defense. There *were* weapons in the keeper's office adjoining, halberds and pikes, a half-dozen swords, if he could only reach them. They were hanging upon the wall, but between him and the keeper's office was Starkey.

Joan meanwhile had moved quietly forward while Starkey and Matthew maneuvered in the center of the room. She was behind Starkey but Matthew could not tell whether the man was aware of Joan's movements or not.

"I wouldn't try to run for the stairs, Mrs. Stock," said Starkey, keeping his eyes on Matthew. "You'll never make it by yourself. The sheriff's men are in the street. I'd pray if I were you, while you still have the chance."

Starkey charged again; Matthew moved clumsily to avoid him. It was all he could do to grab the man with one arm and with the other hold the man's arm. The blade was but an inch or two from Matthew's throat. They struggled in the center of the room and then Matthew felt his legs go out from under him and they were rolling on the floor, Starkey snarling and cursing, spitting in Matthew's face and every second bringing the tip of the blade closer to Matthew's throat. Matthew cried out, "God save me!"

But it was Joan who saved him. Suddenly Matthew prevailed; Starkey's eyes became cloudy and indifferent, his strength seemed to dissolve, the stiletto loosened in his grip and clattered harmlessly to the floor.

Matthew pushed the heavy limp body from him and only then saw the point of a halberd protruding from the man's chest. The weapon had pierced him through.

Joan was standing above them, looking down uncomprehendingly as though to ask who had done this thing.

But she had done it. She had found the halberd, had run at Starkey with all her strength, and her aim had been as true as her purpose. Starkey was dead. He lay on his side, the blood draining from him into a pool on the floor, the long iron shaft of the halberd planted in his back like a flagstaff without the banner.

"He was going to kill you," she said, repeating herself, quavering.

Matthew rose and placed himself between her and the thing on the floor.

"Oh, I shall be sick," she moaned. She hid her face and went over to a corner of the room where she retched with such violence Matthew thought she would die of it. When she was done she turned slowly to face him again, averting her eyes from the floor, and said his name.

He felt an immense relief at that. She came then into his arms, whispering, "Thanks be to God for this help. I did think the villain was going to kill you."

"You were right to think so," said Matthew. "You were but an inch from a widow's lot."

But their words of comfort were interrupted by a stirring and coughing. The recorder was not dead after all. He had only been knocked unconscious by the blow and was struggling to his feet and looking about him in bewilderment. At the same time a great commotion could be heard from the adjacent ward.

"The warders are returning," said Matthew. "Come, if we are to escape Newgate we must go."

"What of him?" asked Joan, pointing to the recorder, who had now seen Starkey's body and was looking from it to the Stocks in great perplexity.

"Let him be," replied Matthew. "His friends will see to him. Come."

They rushed from the room, down the passage to the stairs. The main gate of the prison had been secured during the riot but there was a smaller portal to the left of it guarded by a single warder. To him, Matthew gave the same story he had given to the recorder, and the warder, a great dullard, believing the lie, unlocked the portal, and Matthew and Joan passed through.

In the street outside the prison a huge crowd had gathered, drawn by the din of the prison alarm and the pleasing prospect of a violent spectacle. Between the crowd and the foot of the stairs was a ragged line of sheriff's men. Unsure as to whether their primary duty was to prevent escape of the inmates or the invasion of curious citizenry, the sheriff's men were facing in all directions, talking excitedly among themselves. As Matthew and Joan emerged from the shadow of the lodge door a thunderous cheer broke from the throng, the officers turned, and the hulk of a fellow who was their chief left the ranks of his companions to come up the stairs to meet Matthew and Joan.

The leader bore an unsheathed sword and a fierce expression and, viewing both, Matthew braced himself to defend Joan and explain their exit, but there was no need. Had a multitude armed to the teeth emerged from the prison the hardy officer would have tried to prevent their escape had he nothing more than a wooden spoon in his pocket, but he was not prepared for a man and a woman coming leisurely down the stairs arm in arm, the woman well dressed though somewhat disheveled. Besides, the man wore a warder's uniform and had a plain honest face. The officer exploded with questions before Matthew had half a chance to open his mouth. Had he seen the smoke, heard the alarm? What had transpired within?

Matthew briefly explained about the fire in the chapel. It has since been put out, he said, but now every man was needed to quell the riot. He had been sent by his superiors within to seek aid of the sheriff's men.

"God's death!" exclaimed the officer upon hearing this. "We shall quell it fast enough." Flourishing his sword above him, he commanded his men to follow and Matthew and Joan stood aside as they charged up the stairs toward the lodge. There was momentary confusion as the men attempting to enter confronted a group of warders attempting to leave and the leaders of both parties endeavored to communicate above the uproar. But then Matthew saw a familiar face among the warders. It was John Beauclerk. So he, too, had escaped the fire.

Their eyes met in the same instant of mutual recognition. Then Matthew saw Beauclerk say something to the men with him and point to where Matthew was, hemmed in by the onlookers. What Beauclerk said was lost in another great cheer from the crowd, now prepared to greet each emerging party in this fashion, but Matthew guessed its purport. Starkey's body had been found and the old recorder would have identified them as the murderers. Grasping Joan by the hand, Matthew fled into the throng.

FOURTEEN _____

It was noon before Matthew and Joan reached Cecil's house, bedraggled and exhausted from their flight, only half believing in the reality of their escape and reluctant to identify themselves at the door for fear of being hauled back to Newgate again. However, no sooner had Matthew informed the doorkeeper of his name than the man's stern, businesslike air was transformed into a strange excitement. He said that the master had been awaiting their arrival this half-day and that he looked to have a reward for the good luck of being at his post when the Stocks had finally come.

They were ushered directly to Cecil's apartment, where they found the knight delighted to see them. "You twain have come in good time! I thought to set the hue and cry after you. In God's name, where have you been?"

"We were imprisoned," Joan declared when the doorkeeper had left them.

"In Newgate," Matthew added. They were almost too weary to speak of all they had experienced since their last interview, but Matthew proceeded with the tale, with only occasional interruptions from Joan. Cecil listened. He had already had report of the fire and riot at Newgate but of the Stocks' imprisonment he had known nothing.

"Starkey is dead, too," Joan blurted out, when she saw her husband had concluded his account without reference to its bloody climax.

"Starkey? Oh, yes, he's the one who tried to drown your husband in the Thames."

"I killed him," Joan confessed in a flat, thin voice that sounded coldly matter-of-fact even to her ears.

"It was to save my life she did it," Matthew hastened to explain, glancing nervously at his wife and then back at Cecil again.

"He was killed at Newgate?" asked Cecil.

"At the keeper's lodge," Matthew said. "He would have killed us both had Joan not struck from behind. As God is my witness, it was as honest a blow as was ever struck against one head over his heels in iniquity."

Cecil looked reassuringly at Matthew. "I don't doubt it. Never fear, the stroke will save the state the cost of a hanging. But look you now, I have my own news which I pray you find cheering after your ordeal. Castell—"

Before the knight could complete his sentence there was a vigorous knocking at the door, Cecil said, "Come," and the same doorman who had led the Stocks into the house thrust his head into the chamber to announce that John Beauclerk had returned and requested an immediate audience with his employer on a matter of great urgency.

"Tell Beauclerk to wait," said Cecil. Frowning, he turned to Matthew and Joan and in a lower voice said, "It seems my faithful secretary has found his way home again, like a truant hound. We shall presently hear what manner of story he concocts to candy over his treachery. Both of you, go quickly to the next room. Leave the door ajar. Return when I bid you, and in the meantime listen carefully."

Matthew and Joan did as they were told, and they had no sooner concealed themselves than they heard Beauclerk come into the chamber and begin speaking in an excited, high-pitched voice, giving first a garbled account of the Stocks' arrest and imprisonment and then an account of their murder of Starkey and escape from Newgate. Cecil allowed the man to run on without interruption.

When Beauclerk finished, they heard Cecil say: "The Stocks were arrested yesterday and yet you wait until this hour to tell me?"

There was a long silence at this, and Joan yielded to the temptation to peer through the half-opened door. She could see only Beauclerk's back. The young man had changed clothes since that morning, a fact that obviously accounted for their ability to reach Cecil's house before him.

"I did not think . . ."

"You did not think I would care? Tell me, how did you know of the arrest?"

"I was at the magistrate's hall when they were brought forth— or rather I came there just after they were carried off."

"Well," demanded Cecil, "which was it? Were you there or were you not, to witness in their behalf?"

"I was not," replied Beauclerk in a quavering voice.

"But of course you would have certified to their honesty had you had the opportunity," Cecil said with heavy irony.

"Of course, sir."

"And then this morning you were at Newgate?"

"Oh, no, sir, I have been in my rooms all morning."

"Indeed you have. How is it, then, I smell smoke about you?"

"Smoke, sir?"

"Yes, smoke. You know what that is, don't you?"

"Most certainly."

"Well, I smell it upon you. Pray tell me who ordered you to dog the Stocks fron one end of London to another?"

"He is a liar who says so," protested the secretary hotly.

"I say so," replied Cecil, fixing the young man in a withering stare. "You were at the magistrate's and at the prison for the same reason—to make trouble for the Stocks and for me."

There was another awkward pause.

"I did have business there," the young man asserted without conviction.

"What manner of buiness?"

"My purse . . . it was stolen . . . in Paul's. Not a week since."

"Your purse? You lost a great sum?"

"Not a great sum, sir."

"A small sum, then, a minuscule trifling sum, hardly worth the notice? Such a sum as a man of modest means would stuff the poor box with?"

Beauclerk's reply was low and cautious. "Well, it was two angels, sir—and some odd pieces."

"So then you were there to accuse the thief?"

"Yes."

"Who was the wretch you say stole your purse?"

"A scurvy serving man, sir. One Stephen Wright, man to Lord Havering."

"Oh, indeed," retorted Cecil, obviously not impressed with Beauclerk's powers of invention. "Then you just happened to be at the magistrate's when the Stocks were dragged in, accused of theft themselves. Whereupon you came forward to identify them?"

"No, sir, I mean yes, sir."

Beauclerk fell silent in confusion.

Cecil said, "I think you were at the magistrate's indeed. There to aid and abet the slander against those honest people. There to fill your purse rather than protest its theft. There to do treason along with one Starkey in whose fate you may now see a mirror of your own."

Joan held her breath, pitying Beauclerk despite herself. Then she saw him fall upon his knees before Cecil, whimpering, pleading. But Cecil was firm. He told Beauclerk to stand and to be silent, which the young man did, shaking before his outraged master. Cecil called out to Matthew and Joan to come forth.

At the sound of the movement behind him Beauclerk turned abruptly and his eyes, glistening with tears, widened with amazement.

"You!"

"Yes, no thanks to you or your fellow Starkey," said Matthew.

Forcing a smile, Beauclerk turned to appeal to his master, pausing only long enough to control his voice. "But see, sir, how I was deceived by false report. Here is a matter of good cheer!"

"You denied knowing us," said Joan accusingly. She remembered the scene all too well, the fear and the humiliation, the leering faces of the crowd happy to be entertained by their arrest. Now she felt little pity for this quaking wretch, a false friend who had betrayed them.

"Yes, yes," protested Beauclerk, grinning ridiculously, his face pale and tear-stained. "That's true, but only because I thought my silence would further our cause."

"Shame upon you, sir," Joan declared scornfully. "Just how should our imprisonment have furthered any cause but Gervase Castell's?"

210

"We had all been commanded by Sir Robert to keep privy what had passed between us."

"So then," said Cecil, the irony in his voice even more devastating, "it was excess of zeal to comply with my instructions that stopped your mouth. Where was this zeal I would know when you carried our counterplot to Gervase Castell? How much was the traitor to pay you for the information?"

"I will kill the man who has accused me of *that*," cried Beauclerk, glaring menacingly at Matthew.

"You are looking at the wrong witness against you," said Cecil, continuing in his tone of cold interrogation. "I have ample witness of your treachery, chiefly the man to whom you conveyed it, the jeweler himself." Cecil turned to address Matthew. "It was what I was about to say when this rogue's entrance prevented it. Castell is lodged in the Tower. My men found him this morning not three miles beyond the Spitalfields. He was dressed as a common laborer, but I knew that particular disguise, having been myself its victim. Since his arrest he has told a good deal about his activities in the City and will doubtless tell us more when properly persuaded. You will find his discourse fascinating. We shall all go there presently. You, too, John. Indeed you, my man, shall go before us."

Cecil rang a little bell on his desk and had hardly done so but the appointments secretary appeared with two armed servants behind him. It had all been planned. The men went at once to seize Beauclerk by the arms.

"Go, now, sirrah. These men will provide you with a jolly escort to the Tower where I trust you will find accommodations according to your deserts."

Beauclerk was led out, weeping openly. As the door closed behind him, Cecil said: "If it is one thing I cannot stomach, it's a traitor. High treason they call it in the law. They would with more reason call it low treason, for a man must stoop low—indeed, must crawl upon his belly like a serpent—to practice it."

"What will happen to him?" asked Joan.

"Beauclerk?" Cecil smiled grimly. "He will be tried and then hanged and quartered. It's a hideous punishment that a Christian nation would be well to abjure were it not for the example it sets to others."

Joan shuddered at the very thought of the appalling, ghastly death. She did not so much hate Beauclerk now, despite his

211

treachery. But she knew her pity would be to no avail. The young man had condemned himself. Avarice or ambition or whatever it was that had wormed its way into his heart had brought about his tragedy.

"Now," said Cecil with obvious satisfaction, "we shall all follow to the Tower—and to the jeweler, who awaits our coming."

But Matthew looked at his little wife uncertainly. She seemed overcome with fatigue. He said, "Joan is weary, sir. Could she not return to our lodgings?"

"Why, of course," the knight announced expansively. "Beshrew me for not seeing it myself, Mrs. Stock. I will have some of my servants see you back to the Bell straightway. In the meantime your husband will be my companion. Come, Mr. Stock. You will see and hear things that will sober you, sir. Trust me."

In the late afternoon huge leaden clouds moved over the city and seemed to rest on the very rooftops. In the distance there was the persistent rumble of thunder and flashes of lightning. It began to rain; pedestrians scattered, merchants shut up their shops, while the braver sort of ragamuffin and idler stood about in the street gawking at the sky. Then the rain, which fell lightly at first, came down harder; soon the streets were awash with mud and debris, all traffic stopped; horses bound still to their wagons and carts shrieked in alarm as the wind rose and the rain slashed sideways at the houses. The violence of the sudden storm was awesome.

Then, as suddenly as the torrent had commenced, it ended. There was a great stillness, and only the leaden clouds remained, swollen and threatening, covering London like a cowl. In the houses on the streets lamps had been lighted; people came outdoors and stared up at the glowering heavens and inquired among themselves what this savage storm meant.

With the storm's end Cecil's coach resumed its course toward the Tower. From its windows, Matthew could see, as they neared, the walls, battlements, and bastions with their frenzy of embrasures and turrets and the central keep of grim limestone like a little city unto itself. His heart began to beat with anticipation. The coach rumbled to a stop and from within the walls of the structure he heard the clamor of voices. The coach door opened, Cecil made a remark about the weather, looked up at the sky dubiously, and beckoned Matthew to follow.

The portals of the Tower were heavily guarded but no one stood forth to check their progress, to require identification, or to seek to know their business. They passed beneath the portcullis, and thereafter doors opened before them with a marvelous efficiency; heads bowed mechanically; halberds dipped in salute with their little pennants limp; husky voices used to silence cried aloud, "God save you, Sir Robert," "Good day, Sir Robert." Cecil strode forward energetically, eyes front, occasionally acknowledging a greeting with a murmur, a name, or a little wave of the hand as though he could hardly contain his impatience to come to where the jeweler was. Matthew followed him, looking about him curiously with heavy-lidded eyes weary of flight and danger and ready simply to absorb the strange new scene.

That the Tower was a palace, the seat of kings, Matthew knew, but there was little in this grim pile which suggested a regal presence. It was, rather, a fortress and a prison—like Newgate, although sparsely populated, discriminating as to its inmates, and endowed with a portentous seriousness that was never so apparent as in the demeanor of the guards and warders, well-outfitted men, resolute in their duties, no idlers and vagabonds such as those who had found employment in the city prisons. In some remote apartment, Matthew recalled, the illustrious Ralegh had languished for the love of a lady; in another, and recently too, the young Earl of Essex had suffered for ambition and love of glory. Now Matthew Stock, clothier and constable of Chelmsford, trod upon these same ancient stones, caught up in the wake of the most powerful man in the realm.

Soon they came to where Gervase Castell was lodged, a square, low-ceilinged room, dimly lighted and clammy, as though the torrential rain had managed to find access through the thick stone. The jeweler was sitting in a chair in the center of the chamber, his hands and feet bound. He was dressed still in the garb in which he had been apprehended, a dirty shirt open at the collar to show the white flesh beneath, plain workman's breeches fitted with leather patches upon the knees and snug-fitting in the thighs, and an old pair of boots.

At the jeweler's side standing stiffly at attention was a heavy muscular yeoman of the guard in gold and scarlet. The man had a square, handsome face, thick, black brows, and a small mouth. Upon recognizing Cecil, he saluted and then stared straight ahead of him as though he and his prisoner were once again alone. Warily, Matthew took in the rest of the chamber. The chair in which Castell sat was the room's sole piece of furniture. Two windows in the far end of the chamber admitted a feeble light, and the room smelled of sweat and urine, as though it had been a barracks, recently vacated. Cecil approached the guard, whispered something Matthew could not hear, and the guard left the chamber. Matthew heard the door bolted behind him.

He looked at the jeweler. Castell's face was pale and drawn. There were no signs that he had suffered more than the humiliation of having been arrested and bound, but his eyes, which had been raised to note Matthew's and Cecil's entrance, remained now fixed defensively upon some invisible object above them all.

"Look you now," said Cecil, turning from the prisoner to address Matthew. "Here is your Eye of the Basilisk. Much good he will do his master now, now that his eye has lost its luster. Isn't that right, jeweler?"

Castell made no response. It was as if he remained alone in the room, amused by the singularity of his own thoughts.

"The man mimics the stoical disregard for his personal fate," remarked Cecil with disgust. "He will show no sign of pain, no interest in life, no regret, no fear for the life to come, although he and his Spanish friends would have damned us all to a wicked Queen and a false religion."

Through this, Castell remained silent. Cecil paused, scrutinizing the jeweler. Matthew did not know whether to respond to Cecil's comments or remain silent himself. He was not sure why the knight had asked him to come. Was he to swear an oath here, with only Castell and Cecil present? Or did Cecil merely want an audience for his interrogation?

Cecil began to walk around the bound man, holding his hands behind him, his head tipped forward as though in deep meditation. He continued his orbit around the chair for some time. Matthew thought of heavenly bodies. Cecil was the sun in its glory, resplendent and influential. Castell was the earth, the fixed center and yet dross, inferior, earthy. Matthew stood by awkwardly, watching this cosmic dance, waiting for Cecil's next move, while the jeweler's gaze remained fixed and his expression inscrutable.

Then Cecil said: "We see here where greed comes at last. From assorted treacheries of a misspent, idle youth, the sort of crimes children perpetrate upon their playfellows—a stolen ball, ring, toy, or what have you—then these grow from misdemeanors to felonies to enormities in an inevitable progress and come at last to the greatest crime of all, treason."

"I have told you it was not money," said Castell in a dry whisper, without looking up at his accuser.

"So you did. A man may tell many things to another, but where is the truth?"

Castell's lips moved as though he were about to smile. Cecil turned to Matthew. "It seems our jeweler doesn't wish to speak. I am loath to use the torturer's tools, but I swear before God I will use what tools I must to come to the bottom of this conspiracy." Cecil looked about the chamber as though he were seeking such a tool. There was another long silence; Castell's face hardened again into an insolent indifference. His lips were pressed tightly together; his knuckles were white.

Then all of a sudden Castell seemed to relax, as though he had reconciled himself to his fate. He looked up at Cecil and said: "You can forget your instruments, your tools, Sir Robert. I grant that I would find any one of them too painful to endure. I am not much for pain. See, I confess it openly. I begin with a plain truth: I am a coward."

"So, you will speak—and the truth?"

"I have commenced to do so," replied Castell. He was smiling now, but it was a hard smile as though the expression required great determination and discipline. "Since the plot is finished there is no point in further concealment. Besides, it will satisfy a certain pride in me to relate it to you. It has a beauty about it."

"A beauty?"

"The plot. I think you will understand, Sir Robert, although I doubt our friend the constable will, being the plain simple soul he is."

Matthew dismissed the slur, never one to take offense easily. Besides, the interrogation was Cecil's business. Matthew resolved to keep quiet whatever the jeweler said, as long as he spoke no slander against Joan. That Matthew could not bear, no, not if the Queen herself were present.

"It is a long story," said Castell. "But I will not be tedious about it, for I doubt not but that it is a story you have heard before, Sir Robert. I am not a greedy man, as you seem to think. Money means little to me, but early in life I observed how important it was to other men. The world, sir, is in the shape of a coin, and in faith, in this emblem we see its very soul, hard, brittle, and treacherous—like coins of the realm that buy and sell—goods, cattle, men, indiscriminately."

"And jewels," said Cecil.

"And jewels. Yes, jewels, too."

Castell paused, as though to catch his breath, then he began to speak in the calm, measured phrases of one who has another man's story to tell. "My mother was a servant in the court of King Henry. She was of good family, fallen into hardship; she was no drudge to carry out chamberpots and sweep rushes, but a personal servant to one of the ladies-in-waiting to the King's last wife. She was my mother, and for that I honor her, but she was yet a woman, and she fell from grace—got herself with child—and came at last to marry when she was as large and round with me as a ripe pear. I would have landed upon my head on the chapel floor had she not married within a week of my appearance. This man was an old scholar of Latin. An old, besotted fool. Why did he marry? Pity it was, I think. Perhaps it was love. I have never known either impulse so how could I tell? So I had a father at the eleventh hour to smile upon my christening, but throughout my youth I was known as the bastard and treated scurvily by my fellows, the pages of the court who were my superiors in place but not in strength or cunning."

"You have a very high opinion of yourself," said Cecil.

"Had I not such opinion I would have thrown myself into the sea, for my childhood was one of such wretchedness that you would think it a tissue of lies were I to tell it."

"Come, be quick, man. Tell us about Spain."

"Spain? It's a country in Europe, I think, full of fops and savages, another England."

Cecil's face flushed and he made a threatening gesture.

Castell said: "Strike me, Sir Robert, it will ease your anger and put you in a good mind for supper. I am most uncomfortable here, sir, bound as you see me. May I not have the leisure to tell my tale at its own pace? I assure you all is relevant to its ending."

"Speak, then," Cecil replied impatiently. "We will hear you out, but be sure you come to your end anon, for then you must see the headsman. He's most concise, I assure you, in his work."

Castell smiled, looked quickly at Matthew, then back to the

216

private sector of stale air in the middle of the chamber from which he seemed to be fetching these recollections. "My mother died within a year. I have no memory of her at all. I have been told that she was fair, and that in her beauty lay her fault, for she was taken advantage of by someone—I'll not say by whom—not now at least. As for my presumptive father, he was old when he married. An old bachelor. As rotten as his books. He bequeathed to me only his name, which I englished soon enough, for he was a Florentine by birth and the English can hardly bear an Italian in their own country."

"So on to your wretched childhood. It could not have been that wretched. Even the lowest of servants eats well in a king's court."

"Well enough do they eat, but how do they live? Man doth not live—you know the rest, an old saw, much belied by experience, I think. But it was true of me. I fed well enough, became stout as you see me still. But I knew not a man or woman of the court but I hated him—or her—for what they thought of me. They called me bastard, you know. The shy stepson of a sniveling scholar, a cuckold. They had many such names for me, and every one of them burned upon my heart. Could I open my breast you would see them still."

"You are full of a womanish self-pity. Don't tell us that their ill use of you led you to treason."

"And why not?" cried Castell, straining at his bonds, his eyes fiery now with anger and purpose. "Money is a drab, obvious motive—as common as a flea although I grant it is more wholesome. I was wronged. I was wronged." Castell's voice became shrill. "I was no son of a scholar with ink in his veins and a privy member as useless as a broken spar to hoist a sail upon. Look at my face, Mr. Secretary, my nose, mouth, eyes, brow, you who have spent your days in the palaces and great houses of the land. Have you seen anything like it? Does it not resemble another face—one that you are too young to remember but one your father, the great Lord Burghley knew, a face for which he would have laid down his life. Look at my face, for if ever a face bore the imprint of the father mine does."

For a moment Cecil studied the prisoner's face. "Royal Henry?" said Cecil.

"Well may you say royal Henry," said Castell, a tear glistening in his eyes like a little pearl.

"What proof have you?"

217

"Proof? Wherefore proof? You see the face, the eyes are Henry's, the nose, the mouth. Yes, look at the mouth, small and delicate though the face be round and fleshy."

"Well, jeweler, I grant there is a likeness, but that hardly proves a thing. The King had an English face. Your mother was English. He who begot you may well have been English, too, but that hardly proves royal blood courses through your veins."

"There was a ring."

"A ring."

"My mother had it. The King gave it to her as a pledge."

"When?"

"Not six months before he died and I came into the world to be called bastard. How great his lust was need not be told. It's a matter for chronicles. His appetite was unsatiable."

"Unsatiable, yes. What has happened to the ring?"

"It was lost."

"How convenient," said Cecil cynically. "So now you alone remain to testify to your paternity—as though you were present at your bastardizing."

"You may mock me if you will," replied Castell sullenly. "What I have said is the truth. As God is my witness."

"God will not witness for you, Mr. Castell. Since you have denied him, he will deny you. But what's all this to the purpose? Even if you were great Harry's bastard you must share the honor with a hundred or more, those not since hanged, that is. Elizabeth would be no less a Queen, nor you more noble a subject. Your illegitimacy would have barred you no less than your priority among Henry's offspring."

"I cared nothing about *that*. I mean about being King."

"Nor about the money. Well, what was it, then? Tell us, man, we've not all day to stand about conversing here with you."

"You want to know about the Spaniards?"

"Of course."

The jeweler closed his eyes as though to bring the memory into focus; he took a deep breath; he shrugged. "Why not? It makes no difference now. Save that were I not to tell, you might never know and that would be a great pity."

"For whom?"

"For me, most of all. I want you to know, Sir Robert. Oh, yes, I want you to know. Would that all England might know."

"Pray, no more enigmas. Speak."

"I lived at court until I was fourteen or fifteen. I served in the scullery, and stank thereby in the nostrils of my fellows. I sought employment elsewhere, but because I had no family, no friends, there was nothing for me. I had my choice at last of turning thief or soldier, two occupations between which there is very little difference, I assure you. I chose the former and found myself among a merry crew of conycatchers and pimps, great professors of their art. They kept a hard school but I was most diligent as a pupil and soon struck out on my own. No trick of the trade did I lack. In those days I had a cheerful countenance, a sinewy leg and a stomach as flat as a wall. My face was honest, though the brain was full of mischief, and there were few who penetrated my stratagems. I plied my trade in London for five years, until I fell afoul of the law and was brought before the magistrate for my crimes, an old bearded gentleman near seventy with bleeding gums and great watery eyes that never blinked. This reverend gentleman prided himself upon his stern punishment and wanted to have me hanged forthwith. So he sentenced me, but I escaped by greasing the palm of my jailer and since my face and fame had by that time been bruited about the city I resolved to quit the country. By good chance I found myself in the retinue of a wealthy young man of good family about to take the tour. I puffed my little French up until it became a mastery and was soon employed as a tutor. Thereupon we traveled to France where my young master finished his education in the Parisian brothels. I say finished by design, for finish he did, graduating quick-pace magna cum pox."

"Then?"

"Shortly I was out on my ear again. In Paris, without a shilling to my name, one sword, two suits of livery, and some little experience as my inheritance. I would have resumed my former profession but I knew not the tongue sufficiently. I drifted south, came to Spain. There I encountered certain clergymen, Jesuits, hardy fellows with agile brains, clever tongues, and stomachs of unexplored dimensions. Out of guile or goodness—God knows—they took me in and fed me. They worked mightily to convert me to their religion and I let them think they had succeeded, for I soon saw it was to my advantage. I taught them English that did not already know it, and in due time made the acquaintance of some of the gentry and at last the nobility of the region, telling them that I was the younger son of an English earl. They never disputed my story. There I lived for many years."

"When did you become a Spanish agent?"

"I do not recollect the year. I had come to know a certain duke—"

"His name?"

"No matter. He was a fellow of little consequence."

Cecil was listening intently now.

Castell continued, "At that time he was an old man and he harbored a bitter hatred of the English. It was something to do with treasure ships sunk by that devil Hawkins, or perhaps it was Ralegh. I do not recall. This duke had been in his youth a hellion, but in his dotage, pious. His house, I recall, was floor to ceiling in popish images of this saint or that, of the Virgin Mother in a thousand languorous poses. One day I sat at his table conversing with him while he told me as he had done often of English perfidy, seeming to forget that England was my country—or perhaps remembering very well and delighting in the slander. In any case, the old man broke off suddenly, thrust his head at me, drooling from the nether lip, and asked if I would do him some small, inconsequential service for which he would pay a great sum. By God, I will, said I, though it be to my peril. This I said jokingly, you understand, thinking that the old devil wanted naught more than to appoint me as secretary or tutor to one of his family. But no, that was not his intent. He wanted me to return to England bearing certain instructions to personages of his acquaintance."

"Spaniards or Englishmen?"

"Some Spaniards, some Englishmen. By this time it had been nearly twenty years since I had stepped upon my native soil and I admit to having a certain curiosity as to how things had changed in my absence. Besides, I knew there would be no danger now. The magistrate who had sentenced me was long moldering in his grave, and time, so much scorned by us all, had invested me with the best of disguises. Shortly thereafter I set sail, journeyed straightway to London, delivered the messages, and returned within the month, thinking all the while how I might spend the wealth the duke had promised me. To shorten my tale, I came to the duke's house and he had not finished counting out the gold into my hand but he asked me if I would be so kind as to continue in his service."

"As a courier?" asked Cecil.

"Yes," replied Castell. "It seemed simple enough stuff. I

thought it likely these letters contained more than accounts of Spanish weather and the price of sherry, but what was that to me? I had no love for England, less for Spain. I was of the mind to take any man's coin offered me. But I was a curious fellow, though no longer young, and I took to opening the packets and perusing the letters at my leisure. The most seemed innocent enough—what one would have expected. Full of trivia—the news of court, weather, well-wishing, a deal of Roman moralizing stolen from Tully or one of his apes, or unctuous counsel to console some Christian fool. Save one or two of these, which were so garbled in their sense I knew at once they must be ciphers. This they proved to be, I deciphered them, and they spoke to me as clearly as you cold sober would command your servant to fetch your supper."

"What did the letters contain?"

"Those that traveled to England put certain questions. Some of these regarded ship movements, men, and munitions, inquired about court intrigues, the whereabouts of certain Jesuit priests and so forth; those that traveled to Spain answered back again."

"How long did you do this?"

Castell frowned thoughtfully and said, "A year, perhaps two."

"Then what happened?"

"One day when I had come fresh from my travels the duke drew me to him. He said he had become quite fond of me. He told me he knew I had myself become familiar with the letters I bore and complimented me on my wisdom. A man who will carry an unopened letter for another—knowing not whether it may do him ill or good—is a fool, he said. Now, said he, you know which way the wind blows?"

"What did he mean by that?" Matthew asked, and then regretted it, for he remembered that this was Cecil's business and that it was his duty to keep silent. But Cecil did not seem to mind the interruption. The knight said nothing, his face intent still on the man in the chair.

"Why, the plot. He meant I knew the plot. The Spanish were gathering intelligence. Of all kinds. Specifically about English ships, about fortifications, especially along the coast. This was in the year of eighty-seven."

"The year before the great Armada," said Cecil.

"Indeed. That was the plot. The Spanish were preparing the way for the invasion."

"But the invasion failed. The Armada was scattered and destroyed."

"Indeed, it was, but the failure was not due to a want of knowledge of English affairs."

"So, then, your plotting came to nothing," murmured Cecil, looking at the jeweler with great contempt.

"For the moment. The duke died—of disappointment, I think, because of the defeat. I was out of employment again. I traveled with the money I had put by to Italy and then to Greece, but soon grew weary of that and came at last to Spain again where I lived in quiet retirement for the next few years. Then, about ninety-four or -five I was approached again by the Spanish. My services had not been forgotten. The old Spanish King, though infirm, had retained his ambitions to conquer England. He wanted to try again."

"Another Armada?"

"Yes."

"Philip took you into his service?"

"His agents did. I never had the pleasure of conversing with His Highness. I suppose *that* would have been beneath him." Castell said this bitterly. "During my years in Spain I had amassed a fine collection of gems and jewels. I became knowledgeable in the trade. Philip's agents gave me a considerable sum to come to London and begin a business. That, said he, would put me in the very middle of English affairs. I had retained my old contacts, of course, It was not a month before I was conveying intelligence to Spain again."

"You had no qualms about betraying your country? You are not even a Catholic," said Cecil.

"I have neither country nor religion. The one was taken from me as a child, the other—well, that was so much nonsense to my mind."

"What did you hope to obtain in blackmailing me?" asked Cecil.

Castell laughed. "Oh, you're puzzled by that? Well, the Spanish were often puzzled as well. I mean about my . . . clients. The Spaniards were concerned about military intelligence—information about ships, troops, alliances abroad, plots and counterplots at home. I pleased them in that. In time, however, any information would do for me, so long as it was some unsavory stuff the revelation of which would torment the man. I cared not a groat about statecraft. What was that to me? I found me men such as yourself—wellborn, smug, contemptuous—"

"Cur, you go too far," Cecil snapped, his eyes ablaze with anger. He struck the jeweler on the side of the face. Castell flinched but quickly resumed his expression of stoical fortitude.

"I beg your pardon, Sir Robert," Castell said, "but a man speaking the truth should be allowed some tolerance. All men are sinners. You want the truth of my history, do you not?"

"Continue."

"Well then, I enjoyed their squirming, delighted in seeing them beg. No man ever left the back room of my shop quite as tall as he entered. I whittled them all down until their pride was lost amidst the shavings. Killing them would not have given me so much pleasure."

"You wanted to humiliate me, then?" asked Cecil, very coldly.

Castell laughed a low, humorless laugh. "My employers were often mystified as well, but they were too satisfied with the intelligence I conveyed to complain. They were fools with their dreams of conquest, as though stealing a country gives one-tenth of the satisfaction of stealing a man's pride, puncturing the great swollen bladder of his vanity."

"So you made the Spanish King *your* fool."

"Yes, yes. For them my spying was a means to their end, to me it became the *end*. I cared nothing for their Armadas, their religion. It meant not a damn thing to me."

"But what of this new Armada? That old Philip persisted in his dream of conquest I can well believe, but his son has, since his reign commenced, been more temperate."

"Indeed he has, but he has those about him who wish he were made of sterner stuff."

"When was the invasion to take place?"

"They wait for the Queen's death. The confusion to follow coupled by my long undermining of certain key persons was to give them the advantage. Fewer ships were to be used. We are speaking of no great fleet, but of a smaller force, directed at London, slipping between the folds of England's mourning garment before she knows who has struck or why. The Infanta was to be proclaimed Queen."

"Well, varlet, it won't happen now," cried Cecil with determination.

Castell looked upward; his face was hard, full of bitterness and scorn. "Do you think I care? I have had what I wanted. I have had it for years. For each of my torments I have tormented. I have caused them all to suffer exquisitely. Take from me my head, divide my parts. Do what you will but you shall not take from me my satisfaction."

"Impious villain," shouted Cecil, raising his arm to strike again. The arm hung in the air. Castell was smiling, chuckling beneath his breath. Cecil dropped his arm to his side in a gesture of futility.

"I have others who will do this work," he said.

"I will say no more," said Castell. The jeweler stared straight ahead. A glazed expression fell upon his countenance and he sat there as one contemplating a theme of infinite complexity. To Matthew it was clear that the interrogation had concluded. Castell *would* say no more.

Cecil turned to Matthew. He spoke in a high, taut voice as though it was all he could do to confine his rage. "Come, Mr. Stock. Our time here has not been pleasant, but it has been well spent. We will leave this person to enjoy the last hours of his satisfaction as he calls it. He will straightway be carried to another place for trial where your word and the word of others will convict him of treason and sentence him to death."

Matthew followed Cecil to the door. Cecil called to the guard to let him out, and while they waited, Matthew turned to look at the solitary figure in the center of the room. He was sitting as fixed as a statue but he was no longer staring into space in bold defiance of his fate. He had shut his eyes and seemed as one asleep, as though his own tormented spirit had forsaken the body so soon to be hideously abused by the executioner. Matthew shuddered. With relief, he heard the guard's footsteps outside the door and the key turning in the lock. Then the door opened, he cast a final look at the jeweler, and stepped out into the passage. As the door shut behind them and was locked again he heard the cry, hardly human, beginning deep and low like a growl and then rising and swelling until it became a shriek of blind terror.

It had come from the chamber they had just left. It was Castell; it could have been no other. But Matthew could not associate this horrible sound with the smooth and calculating traitor and blackmailer who must still be seated alone there. It was horrible to think of.

Cecil walked ahead as though he had heard nothing. The

guards accompanying them seemed unperturbed as well. Was it Matthew's imagination? He could hear nothing now, only the dripping of water on stone somewhere ahead of them, the tattoo of boots, the rustle of leather harnesses. Full of nameless dread, Matthew hurried to catch up with the others.

"We have the jeweler's book," remarked Cecil casually as the knight's coach rumbled to a stop before them.

Matthew wanted to know what book Sir Robert meant. He was still shaken by the unearthly scream. The horses stamped impatiently on the wet pavement. It had begun to rain again, a cheerless drizzle that made the coach look freshly varnished.

"The book in which he wrote the names, dates, and facts. It is a compendium of espionage. I have never seen anything like it. I doubt that Walsingham had, and he knew more of spies and spying than any man in Europe."

Matthew glanced at the book which the knight held in his hand. It was small and had a worn leather cover. He had often seen the like on the booksellers' stalls.

"What shall become of it?" he asked, more out of politeness than curiosity now.

"It will be used as evidence at the trial, then destroyed. Castell's was an evil work and this an evil book. Yes, we will destroy the book . . . when proper use has been made of it."

Cecil smiled absently as the last phrase fell from his lips and tucked the book beneath his belt. They climbed into the coach and the coach sped away. The window drapes were pulled. Matthew could no longer see the Tower and he was glad. He didn't want to see it again. He had had his fill of prisons, of London and its treachery, its complicated motives and web of deceit. He wanted to return to Chelmsford and his shop, to his wife and daughter and her child, his first grandchild, and the sooner the better.

"Was the jeweler really the king's son?" Matthew asked.

Cecil laughed heartily. "Most unlikely. Though Henry might have wished it so, it would have taken a greater miracle than that worked upon Abraham and Sarah to quicken the old king's loins. He was unable, syphilitic. The jeweler dreams, Mr. Stock, he only dreams."

FIFTEEN⎯⎯⎯⎯⎯⎯⎯⎯⎯⎯⎯

It was early evening in the week following and they were all gathered at the table in Elizabeth's spacious kitchen; supper was nearly done. Through the windows that William had newly glazed the motes of dust floated in a flood of waning sunlight like little ships upon a stream.

"This is all very pleasant, our being here together again," Joan said.

"Marry, that's God's truth!" cried Matthew between mouthfuls, for only he continued to eat. He had picked at the bones of the fowl until they were white and glistening. Grinning, he leaned forward, planting his forearms on the table between the wooden cups and pewter plates and said: "I'll have just a bit more of that bird, if it please you, Elizabeth."

Plump and happy in the fading light, Elizabeth rose from the table to carve for her father, glancing at the same time to the corner where on a woollen coverlet her newborn son slept peacefully, undisturbed by the talk and clanking of pots and plates and the moving about of stools. Opposite Matthew and Joan, the brothers William and Thomas Ingram conversed about the farm.

Presently Matthew announced that he had had his fill of the

goose and made a great comical show of pushing back from the table. Everyone laughed, for Matthew's appetite was ever the subject of their jibes, which he never failed to take in good humor. The baby woke and began to cry, and Elizabeth wiped her hands upon her apron and hurried to pick up her vociferous charge, cuddling him to her bosom, kissing him upon the face and crooning to him in a soft, musical voice. "He is hungry, too, poor babe. That's what he complains of."

"And his grandfather here has left precious little to gnaw upon," observed Joan good-naturedly.

"Elizabeth will find something," Matthew said with feigned defensiveness. "After all, I am not the only one here who is well fed this day. Look at William there, his nether lip is still besmirched with fat—and Thomas, Thomas Ingram, what devil possessed you to gluttonize at table? I am a witness against you, Come then, wife, kiss me as you must, for naught else will remedy the wrong your accusations have wrought."

"I, wrong you?" Joan cried, after yielding to her husband's embrace and kissing him long and hard upon the mouth. "How so? Have I slandered that monstrous stomach of yours which even now presides over the ruin of Elizabeth's goose? You are bold to blame your son-in-law and young Thomas for gluttony. Fie upon such hypocrisy! Why, look you now at those bones. You have left not a smidgen. And the plate before you, what Lenten fare is here! Now a churchmouse could not fetch a mouthful from your plate."

But their pleasant raillery had alarmed the child. He waved his little arms frantically, his face was red, and Elizabeth, ever the careful mother, scolded them all for their light-mindedness.

"Lightheartedness, rather," said Joan, growing serious now and not quite ready to take correction from her own child, even if she was a woman grown, an inch taller than she, and in her own house. "A light heart makes for a winsome countenance," she reminded them all.

"Mother, you are ever ready with your proverbs," Elizabeth chided. "But forbear this merriment. My child is all in terror now that his grandfather has consumed the last bite on earth. Come then, child. Your mother will show you how well she has provided."

Outside the door was a well-tended kitchen garden, and beyond that a little copse. On a fair day Elizabeth resorted there, and sat beneath the trees in the soft grass, and looked out across the fields and woods beyond. It was to this place that she invited her company now, and they followed willingly, for the kitchen had grown overly warm and there was general agreement that the open air, a great stirrer of the appetite, was likewise a great aid in digestion once the feasting was done.

They found places beneath the trees and watched while the sun contracted into a little fringe of gold on the horizon. Elizabeth nursed her child, and they talked of their lives, of the years to come, and of the years that had passed. They begged Matthew to sing and he did, one song of his own composing, and when he had finished Thomas said, "How I shall miss this place when I am gone."

Joan turned toward his voice, for Thomas Ingram was but a shadow now. Was he leaving, then? She had not heard that. What of him she could discern was faced out over the land, the dark fields, the indistinct hedgerows. His jaw was set and she could not see the scar on his forehead, but she knew that it would never disappear, that Thomas would bear the mark of Starkey's treachery to the grave.

"Thomas has decided to leave us," Elizabeth explained. "He has been a great help here, but we will not keep him if it is in his mind to seek his fortune elsewhere."

"You won't go again to London, Thomas?" Joan asked, concerned.

She heard him chuckle. He said, "Nay, I've had as much of London as the constable here has had of Elizabeth's goose. This is William's farm; there's not enough room for the two of us." William protested, but Thomas continued: "No, not enough room. Besides, I'm no farmer. I thought I'd go to Colchester. There, they say, are opportunities aplenty for strong young men. I am still of an age to apprentice myself, and William has agreed to pay my bond."

"As long as you don't apprentice yourself to a jeweler," said William, and everyone laughed, for they had all heard by this time of the Stocks' adventures in London.

When the laughter subsided Thomas said, "So my former employer is dead."

"I have seen his remains," replied Matthew solemnly. "Stuck atop the bridge in London, like an apple upon a spear, ready for roasting. Now he looks down upon the very city he despised and would have betrayed."

"Had you not prevented him," said William.

"Had *we* not prevented him," replied Matthew, meaning to include Joan.

"Sir Robert Cecil deserves the greater credit for that," Joan ventured modestly. "It was he who apprehended the man while Matthew and I were still in Newgate looking to be rescued from our false imprisonment. Sir Robert brought him to judgment posthaste, and saw to his execution."

"But," said Thomas, "Sir Robert would hardly have done so much had you not alerted him to Castell's treachery."

"Well now," said Joan, "you, Thomas, alerted us. So why then might we not give you thanks for your part, for had you not gone off to London to serve as his apprentice, the jeweler's plot may well have succeeded."

"Well," said William, "whoever deserves the credit, the jeweler has gone to his reward, and let the Devil have him for all I care, for he wished this land and people ill enough."

They all agreed that Castell was a wicked man and then fell silent. There was not a breath of wind; they could smell the earth beneath them and overhead the stars were venturing forth more confidently. In the middle distance, the vague shadow of birds, slow to give up their diurnal courses, soared in the dusky air.

"But why," asked Thomas, "why did he do it?"

"Castell?" said Matthew.

"You said he was no Papist, no seeker of gain, no striver for a crown."

They all turned to where Matthew sat beneath the tree. They heard his voice as though it were the tree speaking. "I heard the man's confession. He told us a long tale of his youth. Yes, it was quite a tale he told. He said he was a bastard, but then so are many men whose lives turn out quite differently. He laid claim to having been the son of King Henry and perhaps he was, for I am told that King had many bastards. But to me that explained nothing, for not poverty, nor ambition, nor religion made him the man he became. Yet what makes a man but these?"

Matthew ceased to speak. He had not answered Thomas's question, which now seemed more a riddle than ever. But presently Joan answered, for in the weeks since the escape from Newgate she had often pondered the question of Castell's motives.

"Gervase Castell grew up in a royal court, which was a great misfortune for him, for his mother was but a maidservant who had been got with child by some lord or knight, the King, he said. Early, then, he observed the way of the court—its wealth, power, and intrigue, its honor and grandeur—but in these things he could have no part, though he believed he deserved them because of his parentage. How it must have vexed him, well made and comely as he surely was then, to see lesser than he secure all manner of honor, while he was put down as a maid's bastard, for though his mother married a schoolmaster, yet it was known abroad that she came to his bed already a mother, her womb round and growing even as her vows were said."

"But how could he know . . . that he was the King's son?" William asked skeptically, his eyes on the distant figure of Elizabeth, nursing their young son at her breast. "Did his body bear some mark? Was there some witness to swear it so?"

"I don't know," replied Joan. "If there was mark Castell never said. Isn't that right, Matthew?"

Matthew shook his head and agreed. It had taken the jeweler a good hour to tell his tale, but how little the man had revealed, as though he wanted to tantalize them all with his great mystery.

"He was a strange man, in faith," remarked Joan. "Perhaps treason was his way of settling the old debt."

"What debt?" asked Matthew, turning to his wife. He could hardly see her now, half hidden as she was in the dark leaves.

"Why, his debt with the others, with the young boys who were his playfellows and tormentors. As he grew older they would have gone beyond his grasp, to other cities and lands, to death even. He could not revenge himself then for their laughter, for their ridicule and scorn. But there was England, vulnerable and, in his mind, guilty. England that had denied him his right of birth, the honor due him. He must have concluded that the whole country should pay for what he had suffered, for his wretched youth, more wretched for its very proximity to wealth and honor."

"Yes," Matthew said, himself in a philosophical mood, "it's better to be born a simple man with a modest number of desires, all within the compass of an average reach. But you make the jeweler's vengeance sound like the pursuit of justice."

"Well so it may have been," Joan returned quickly. "I imagine every vengeful soul aspires to his own conceit of justice, though it be twisted beyond recognition in the eyes of God."

"So Castell never wanted to be King," said Thomas.

Joan answered again, "He was no fool. He knew that even if his birth were proved it might mean nothing more in the end than his undoing, for many men and women of high birth have learned to their sorrow what dangers their birth brings to them. No, he did not think to be the Queen's successor himself. What he did want was . . . was . . ." She rummaged among her store of words for the word. At last she said, "Reverence."

"Reverence," echoed her husband. "Well, he failed of getting that, except what reverence he earned in his trade. At that I understand he did very well."

"But he got his revenge, too," continued Joan thoughtfully. "I doubt the Spaniards understood that, since their mind was all on the great fleet, on the invasion and the succession. But look you now, every gentleman, knight, or lord he managed to lure into his web gave him a kind of pleasure. He sought to remedy his pain by humiliating his enemies and all of the highborn were his enemies for they had denied him. Knowing he was not of their faith, the Spaniards must have wondered at the jeweler's dedication, his industry. His secret was that he cared nothing for Spain; he only wanted to mortify England. In the end he must have realized the futility of it all."

They ceased to speak, enjoying now the fellowship of silence, of common understanding. In the gathering darkness they could hear the infant suckling. Matthew rose and said, "Come, Joan, let us walk together in the fields."

He helped her to her feet, she brushed the grass from her gown, and then she took his hand and they began to walk. The evening air was mild and sweet with summer flowers, and Joan's heart swelled with a profound satisfaction, a beneficent glimmering with no other content than a sudden, inexplicable joy. It was all a cause of wonder to her, this world she lived in, this heart that beat within her own breast. How beautiful it all was, but also sad, for she considered the danger she and Matthew had faced, from Gervase Castell and from Starkey, whose bloody demise now seemed no more substantial to her than a bad dream. Her country had been threatened, too, from within as well as without, but now all was secure again. The old Queen continued to live and rule, her faded majesty casting its splendor still on their doughty island kingdom.

Even as she thought this a small voice seemed to whisper in her ear that these things could not last. Nothing in God's creation lived forever. The Queen would die, and soon.

But to this voice Joan paid no heed. The glimmering prevailed, and she felt passionately the joy of the moment, drawing in greedily all these generous tokens of God's goodness: the tranquil eve, the mild air, her husband's hand in hers. She felt the hand, Matthew's rough, strong hand, and squeezed it affectionately. She looked at Matthew. He was walking with confident stride, his head forward and slightly raised. He was humming to himself and even in the darkness she could discern the smile upon his lips.

ABOUT THE AUTHOR

Leonard Tourney is an associate professor of English at the University of Tulsa, Oklahoma; he has a wife and two daughters and is a long-distance runner.